Kiss It Better

Between her legs, he worked her, rocking the tiny, sensitive crest of flesh without let up or mercy. Half-crazed already, it took barely seconds for Sandy to achieve his objective. She arched against him, limbs jerking, her pussy melting.

But even as she came, she grabbed and scrabbled at him, wanting more, wanting connection as if her life depended on it. With his hand still squashed between them, she rubbed her pelvis against his, inviting and imploring him to fuck her.

'Please,' she gasped, 'please, please fuck me.'

There was a moment of still, silent shock. Had she really said that? She'd never really talked dirty in bed, always been quiet, taken her cues from her man, responsive but not proactive. But now, with this man, she could do or say anything.

By the same author:

Gemini Heat
The Tutor
The Devil Inside
Gothic Blue
The Stranger
Hotbed
Shadowplay
Continuum
Entertaining Mr Stone
Suite Seventeen
Gothic Heat
In Too Deep
Ill Met by Moonlight (in the Black Lace novella collection
    Magic and Desire)
Buddies Don't Bite (in the Black Lace novella collection
    Lust Bites)

Kiss It Better
Portia Da Costa

This book is a work of fiction.
In real life, make sure you practise safe, sane and
consensual sex.

First Published by Black Lace 2009
2 4 6 8 10 9 7 5 3 1

Copyright © Portia Da Costa 2009

Portia Da Costa has asserted her right under the Copyright, Designs
and Patents Act 1988 to be identified as the author of this work

First published in Great Britain in 2009 by
Black Lace
Virgin Books
Random House, 20 Vauxhall Bridge Road,
London SW1V 2SA

www.blacklace.co.uk
www.virginbooks.com
www.rbooks.co.uk

Addresses for companies within The Random House Group Limited can be found at:
www.randomhouse.co.uk/offices.htm

The Random House Group Limited Reg. No. 954009

A CIP catalogue record for this book is available from the British Library

ISBN 9780352345219

The Random House Group Limited supports The Forest Stewardship Council [FSC],
the leading international forest certification organisation. All our titles that are
printed on Greenpeace-approved FSC-certified paper carry the FSC logo.
Our paper procurement policy can be found at www.rbooks.co.uk/environment

Typeset by Palimpsest Book Production Ltd, Grangemouth, Stirlingshire

Printed and bound in Great Britain by CPI Bookmarque, Croydon CR0 4TD

This one's for Queen Bella Michelle Buonfiglio, with many, many thanks for her friendship, her kindness and her enthusiastic support of my writing.

1

'Fuck! Fuck! Fuck!'

Throwing himself on the bed, Jay gritted his teeth and rode the pain.

When the hell was this going to get easier? It had been over a year now. Well over a year of feeling as if someone was driving red-hot spikes into his joints and bones whenever he overdid it. Months and months of fighting the fight against taking weapons-grade painkillers. Surely one of these days he'd be able to run again without ending up feeling as if he'd been put through an industrial grinder?

Pulling his 'worst' leg up to his chest, he tensed and released, tensed and released, longing for the almost supernatural ministrations of his masseur, yet knowing such luxuries were off the menu for the time being.

One of the many prices to be paid for mixing business with the irrational pursuit of an adolescent dream.

Heaving himself upright again, he glanced around. It was an old-fashioned room, a little too fussy and chintzy for his taste, but immaculate. The Waverley Grange was a deeply weird hotel, but it was in the area and he'd wanted to stay here and find out what all the fuss was about. He'd never seen his father quite as pissed off as he'd been last year over this place.

The old man had had the Waverley in his sights, only to be denied by an unexpected management buyout. At one time, this would have pleased Jay mightily. He'd been at odds with his father for so long. But in recent years, they'd come to an accommodation, and begun to work together at last. And now, the Waverley was ideally situated for Jay's current mission of fact-finding and general reconnoitring of the area. Not to mention the fact that the cable porn on offer was first class, the hottest and most explicit he'd ever seen. He'd never expected such a degree of sophisticated cosmopolitan perversion in a provincial country house hotel, but it seemed to be a speciality of the Waverley.

No wonder the old man had been niggled at losing out.

The thought of porn, sex and women made Jay frown. Back to that bloody conundrum again. He shuddered as if someone had stamped snow on his grave.

I am so screwed up. I haven't a fucking clue what I want. Or with whom.

And yet here he was. Chasing a fantasy. Probably a figment of his imagination. But one that made sex, and his dick, come alive again, despite its confused and fragmentary nature.

He reached for his wallet. There was a secret treasure in it, something only he knew about, a little clipping from a magazine, with a photo. The tiny scrap of paper was a bridge between the present and the past. And an unlikely fantasy that unscrewed his screwed-up libido.

You stupid prick! Mooning over her like a moronic teenager! Is this what getting mangled in an Aston Martin has reduced you to? Weaving sick masturbation fantasies over an idealised memory, but struggling to get it up with a real live sexy woman?

Recent memories of humiliation and disappointment surged up in his throat like bile, but with a supreme effort he banished them, and returned to the panacea of dreams where he was in control, where his body was unfaltering and always obeyed him.

With reverence, he unfolded the clipping. He'd found it by chance in a local magazine, amongst his father's background materials, and the thought that he might just as easily never have flipped those pages made his blood run cold. Now, he traced his fingertip lightly over the gentle heart-shaped features and the mass of wild red hair of the smiling woman in the picture. She looked just the same as she'd looked fifteen years ago, if you didn't count the scrapes and bruises and the terrified, thunderstruck and numbed expression she'd had then.

You were a very very sick young puppy, man.

But he could still remember the slight weight of her body as he'd carried her, the scent of her fresh girlish perfume, and the sweetly yielding softness of her lips, in that one brief kiss.

Kiss it better.

He'd meant it as a comfort while they'd been waiting for the ambulance, but shame washed through him even now, remembering how horny he'd felt, even while he was doing his saintly, rescuing knight act. He'd felt as bad, if not worse than he would have done if he'd been the bastard who'd knocked her to the ground.

He lay back on the bed again, holding up the little magazine clipping like a religious icon as his dick hardened spontaneously in his sweaty jogging pants.

LOCAL CAFE OWNER GETS FRESH FOOD AWARD.

'Alexandra ... Alexandra ...' he rasped, savouring the printed name on his tongue, his damaged voice rougher than ever because he was tired.

His bitter laugh rent the air. She'd probably tell him to take a running jump. She had every reason to. The twists and tangles of life's ironies were unlikely sometimes, but this juxtaposition of circumstances beggared belief.

'You'll probably never fuck me in a million years now,

3

Alexandra, and yet you're the only woman I seem to be able to get it up for now. How about watching me toss myself off instead?' He shook his head. Fatigue and pain were making him demented. He was convinced the face in the picture had winked and smiled at him.

'OK then, a wank it is.'

He pressed a kiss on her image, and placed it carefully on the bedside table. Then, not without a groan and a profanity, he hitched his aching body around until he was sitting propped up against the pillows, with a perfect view of her smile, her amazing hair and those sweet curvaceous breasts in a pure white T-shirt.

He drew in a deep breath and then let it out as a sigh. He slid his hand into his joggers and took a hold of his penis. Fingers tightening around himself, he sank into a familiar fantasy.

Princess.

That was what he called her in these secret private moments. Because she did look like a perfect fairytale princess with her long red curls and her huge green eyes. And her hands that handled his cock as if she loved it.

Slowly, slowly she worked him, her imaginary hand cool and light, moving the skin of his organ seductively over the hard core within. She teased and she twisted ever so lightly, almost threateningly. Mm, just the way he liked a woman to touch him. Her fingertips rode him delicately, cajoling and coaxing one moment, ruthlessly pumping and pulling him the next.

Oh, God, yes! Princess!

But no, not Princess any more. Now she had a name and it was time to get used to it.

'Alexandra.'

Closing his eyes, he slid down on the bed. He didn't need the little picture any more, because now his mind showed him the product of fifteen years of visualisation, speculation and obsession.

In his fantasy, Alexandra Jackson peeled her pristine white T-shirt off over her head to reveal her adorable breasts beneath. His imagination dressed her in a lace bra, just the sort he liked to see on a woman. It was white and sheer, showing nipples like sweet dark berries through the mesh. As she wiggled out of what he speculated were a pair of skinny jeans, she revealed a tiny matching G-string beneath, a scrap which only enhanced the view of her pussy rather than impeding it.

No ballet dancer, no athlete could have been more graceful than Alexandra as she climbed astride him and, using her slender skilled fingers, guided him into her, pushing the fragment of lace aside. In his rational mind, he knew it was still his own hand that pleasured him, but since when had his rational mind had anything to do with *this* relationship? He'd had fifteen years to develop its verisimilitude.

Oh Lord, but you're tight! And so hot. So embracing.

In his mind, her expression was everything seductive. Her lips were sweet and soft and full, curving into a slow, greedy and deliciously lascivious smile. She was pure sex but at the same time fresh and tender.

Yet despite his lurid imagination, while fucking him she remained an enigma. And it was that sense of mystery, and the tight caress of her sweet, hot and totally illusory pussy that tipped him over.

White-hot pleasure poured down his spine, up from his balls and jetted from his penis. Dimly registering that he'd have a cleaning-up job to do when he was finished, he surrendered himself to bliss and blind sensation. He was a victim of his orgasm, a willing slave to it.

It took him a while to come down. He lingered in a floating hinterland between consciousness and sleep, not quite aroused, but skirting it, his mind awash with vague scenarios. Fairytale princess fucking. Perverse scenes from the Waverley's high-class porn channel. Fond memories of kinky experimentation, and the sexual adventures he'd indulged in prior to the day he'd woken up in traction and with his entire head swathed in bandages.

Finally he sat up, clearing his mind of fantasy in order to focus on reality.

It was time to take a shower, trim his beard, make himself as presentable as was possible nowadays. This afternoon he was heading for the Little Teapot Café.

2

The back of her neck was prickling again.

Sandy Jackson spun around on her heel, and sure enough there he was, the man from the Teapot. The scarred husky-voiced stranger with militaristic shaven head and the roguish little goatee beard. The one who'd been scrutinising her so unremittingly that afternoon over his tea and scones. She wasn't sure what he was doing here tonight, but he was definitely the same one who'd never taken his eyes off her once. Even when her back was turned, according to Kat.

He wasn't watching her now. Or at least, if he was, his reflexes were like lightning. Right now, he was chatting to a handsome middle-aged woman, his stern expression mellowed by an attentive sexy smile, his dark eyes twinkling and flatteringly focused on his companion.

Git! I thought you were my *stalker.*

Irrationally jealous, Sandy turned her back on the aggravating man and inched away towards the edge of the room. She felt like a fish out of water at this Chamber of Commerce soirée. She'd only come in the hopes of picking up some news about the supposed development of the old Bradbury's supermarket site. If the surprisingly reliable rumour mill was to be believed, and Forbes Enterprises was going to make it over into a new open-all-day food pub, it might well mean the end of the Little Teapot Café.

Forbes Enterprises. More gits!

Plastering on a smile, she fabricated a few bits of semi-auto small talk with one or two fellow guests. Blah, blah, blah, wasn't it hot? Blah, blah, wasn't this place splendid? Blah-diddy-blah, did you know it has a rather risqué reputation?

A waiter appeared at her elbow with a tray of hors d'oeuvres and, still on automatic, she took one.

Mm, not bad. Something tomato-flavoured, a bit like a large cheese straw. Before the lad could get away, she grabbed a second one, a miniature tartlet filled with what tasted like minced prawn in herb mayonnaise. Again, not bad at all. She hoped that Kat, her cook, was taking notice of all this stuff. It was always nice to try out a few new flavours and more imaginative goodies in the Teapot now and again, instead of concentrating on basic confectionery and then simple grills and fries at lunchtime. If they could grow their reputation for irresistibly moreish snacks, it might help them survive the onslaught of that bloody fun pub.

Her neck did the prickle thing again and, before she could stop herself, she looked round again, searching for Mr Hard-Case Stalker with the sexy goatee beard.

And there he was of course, but this time he didn't bother to hide the fact he was looking at her. In fact, he nodded slightly, tipped his glass, and favoured her with an enigmatic half-smile.

Sandy flashed him a vague semi-smile of her own in return, although she tried not to make it too encouraging. For some reason – she couldn't work out why exactly – she wasn't all that sure she *wanted* to talk to him. He looked like a brutally attractive serial killer, and there was something about him that scared her and made her nerves twang. He was probably perfectly nice when you actually got to know him, but looking at him now was like having him walk straight through her soul.

Not my type. Not at all. Too battered. Too macho. Probably far too complicated.

The wine in her glass was indifferent, but she sipped at it anyway. It wasn't strong enough to act as an anaesthetic, but she had to do something to take her mind off 'The Man'.

And her feet. Why in God's name had she let Kat persuade her into wearing these stupid heels? They looked fabulous and did wonders for her legs. But they were seriously killing her and it demanded an Oscar-winning performance just trying not to show it. Sweat popped out at her hairline as she smiled brightly at one of the Teapot's patrons. If she needed to make a quick getaway, she certainly couldn't run for it tonight.

A psychic sideswipe made her almost spill her dreary wine.

Getaway?

A powerful fist seemed to clutch her innards.

What, after all this time? Why think of such ancient history all of a sudden?

A memory both sharp and fuzzy zipped through her mind, bringing with it cold fear and the warm fleeting image of a face. A smooth young male face, almost angelically handsome. Long, thick, rather shaggy dark hair. A soft voice and soft lips on hers, her saviour whispering, 'Kiss it better.'

But as soon as the impression appeared, it began to fade again, leaving her shaking her head and, back in the present, glancing around.

Shrugging off the last of her disorientation, she focused on her surroundings.

This was the first time she'd ever been to the Waverley Grange Hotel and, probably like most people here, she was curious about its rumoured reputation. The place was supposed to be a den of rampant sexual iniquity beneath its sleek veneer of luxury and old-world charm, and some of the prints on the wall of the Lawns Bar certainly seemed to confirm the provocative whisperings.

Sandy fanned herself with her fingers. God, it was hot tonight. And that was even before you got near the saucy artwork.

In front of her was a stylised photograph of a naked couple tangled up in a complex mandala of limbs, sweat and sensuality. Sandy sincerely hoped the rather prim Mayor's wife didn't catch sight of it, because its blazing frankness made her own blood stir and pulse. The man's hand was between the woman's legs and, even though the resolution was indistinct, she could almost feel those ghostly fingers touching her. They seemed to move in the cleft of her pussy, stroking and paddling and playing. She almost whirled around again, imagining the man from the café just behind her. Or maybe someone else, someone impossible, from a dream.

The sensation made her giddy, and the claustrophobic crush of real bodies around her made her heart trip. Excusing herself, she slid away between two other art connoisseurs who'd been attracted to the photograph. Someone wasn't using quite a strong enough deodorant, and she wrinkled her nose as she moved on in search of fresh air.

Next to an open window, she found another art photograph on the wall. It showed a handsome man with long dark hair also standing beside a window, in dramatic shadows. He was gazing out into the middle distance with a pensive expression on his face and, like the couple in the previous shot, he was stark naked.

Not my type either. But you do look familiar.

Narrowing her eyes, Sandy leaned close, and then chuckled, recognising the rather sexy owner/manager of the hotel, to whom she'd been introduced a short while earlier.

'So, is he your type?'

Sandy rocked – literally – on her silly heels. She knew exactly who was standing beside her, and the deep and strangely raw voice really seemed to fit him. She'd only heard it briefly in the Teapot because Kat had served him, but it was unmistakeable, never to be forgotten.

Schooling herself to stay calm, she turned slowly towards the hard man with the beard, who'd been watching her and who was now only a couple of feet away.

'Not really.' She dared to look up at him. His eyes were sharp and intelligent, dark grey and glinting with a strange disquieting light. Shaken, she returned her attention to the man in the photo – the rather glamorous Signor Guidetti. 'But I do believe that's our esteemed host, the hotel manager.'

'Indeed it is.'

For several seconds, they stared at the image in silence, then, as one, they scanned the room, looking for the hotel's suave, slightly flashy Italian proprietor.

'So, why isn't he your type?'

Put on the spot, Sandy frowned. What business was it of his? Yet still the ghost from her past resurfaced.

'He's too groomed. Too slick. Too perfect.'

Unlike you.

She suppressed a flinch. Up close, her tough-looking man was tougher than ever. Tall, he towered above her, his shoulders broad and his lean yet muscular limbs strong looking beneath a rather beautiful lightweight suit in midnight grey. His buzz-cut hair was dark and looked velvety against his fine nobly shaped skull. He had the look of a Roman Emperor, civilised yet savage.

But it was his face most of all that made her swallow. She was both intrigued by it and also faintly frightened. His features were even, sculpted and masculine, and just as imperial as his cropped hair. But the network of fine white and pink scars that traced the planes of his high cheekbones, his mouth and jawline, framed by his crisp dark beard, spoke eloquently of pain and suffering.

'Unlike me.'

The fierce damaged face softened in a smile as he echoed her thoughts, and Sandy almost gasped. Once again, a fleeting sense of memory almost rocked her.

'There's nothing wrong with looking as if you've lived a bit,' she countered, regaining her wits. For all his scars, the tall man had charisma. And his strong body was affecting her, making hers quicken irrationally. Was he scarred all over? Were the clean hard lines of his limbs marked and battered? It suddenly seemed important to find out.

'Well, that's good to know.' His low laugh was as rough as his speaking voice, but Sandy felt it reach out and touch her like a phantom hand. Hormonal reactions fired throughout her body and she experienced a tingling all over her skin, as if the fine sheen of sweat on it was creating a subtle field. She'd been hot before, but now she was burning up.

'Care for another drink?'

Her companion nodded at her glass, which Sandy suddenly saw was empty. She couldn't remember drinking the wine, but obviously she'd been nervously swigging away without realising it. Another drink would slip down well, and soothe her parched throat, even if it was a tepid and uninspiring vintage.

'Yeah, great! I'd love one, thanks.'

She held out the empty and, as the tall mysterious man took it from her, their fingers briefly touched. Electricity seemed to arc between them, ramping up the tingling sensation. She suppressed a gasp as his dark eyes widened. He'd felt it too.

'Be right back. Don't go away.'

The urge to defy him, and run like the wind, welled up in

her, and if her shoes hadn't been so bloody ridiculous she might have succumbed to it. Something about his broad dark-clad back as he walked away from her was deeply unsettling. Threatening. Everything about him made her senses leap and prickle and, if she was going to cope with that, she needed some air first. If he was sufficiently interested, he'd follow her outside, wouldn't he?

It was a while since she'd experienced spontaneous desire like this, and to feel it for a scarred and troubling stranger was just as unsettling as he was. But she couldn't ignore it or shut it off, hey presto. It was there, palpable nagging lust, low in her groin like a heavy and not entirely uncomfortable weight.

I should go. I should really get out of here.

Where was Kat? They'd shared a taxi here. She'd have to tell her friend she was leaving.

She's probably getting it on somewhere with Greg.

A sudden, sharp image of herself getting it on only heightened the spiralling sexual mayhem. She swayed as images rushed in again, but not the usual fairly soft-focus ones of her mysterious rescuing prince from years ago, or the occasional movie star or actor. No, this time the scarred and bearded stranger who'd just left her was centrestage. And he was touching her in a way that no imagined or remembered lover ever had. Doing things her cook had described getting up to with her sexually adventurous boyfriend, who worked here at the Waverley part-time.

Swiftly, she moved away from the photo of Signor Guidetti and walked purposefully in the direction of the exit to the hotel's reception area. Her feet screamed blue murder but she ignored the gathering pain.

'Leaving so soon?' enquired a voice in her ear as she attempted to sidestep a chattering knot of guests that barred her way.

Her mystery man of scars was holding out a glass to her. The wine in it was effervescing, and an exquisite pale gold. She had a feeling it wasn't from the general vat of industrial Chardonnay that everyone else was slurping. It looked as if the stranger had brought her a glass of Champagne.

'Thanks.' She took it from him, careful to avoid touching his fingers this time. She didn't want to spill a fine vintage all over him. 'And no, I wasn't leaving. I just thought I'd slide outside and get some air.'

Grey eyes like brushed steel narrowed infinitesimally, as if he didn't believe her story, and their controlling expression compelled her to turn back towards the centre of the room. 'And you were confident I'd follow and find you then?' He clinked his glass to hers, and then took a sip of his wine. 'Mm ... that's better. Drink up!'

Sandy sipped, and then sighed spontaneously. Oh, what a pleasure! The Champagne was superb, dry and crisp yet almost buttery, the very essence of French glamour in a glass.

'Thanks,' she said again, with much more fervour, 'this is delicious. Thank you very much.'

'You can thank me properly by telling me your name.'

The steely eyes challenged her. Sandy felt her stomach flip. If names were exchanged, the game was on in earnest. She couldn't just walk away. It wasn't a casual but disquieting 'moment' any more.

'I'm Alexandra Jackson. It's a pleasure to meet you.' She shuffled the strap of her bag on her shoulder, swapped hands with her glass, and then held out her right one to him. He swapped his glass to his other hand far more smoothly than she'd managed to, then offered a large tanned right hand that seemed to dwarf her slender paler one. There were even crooked white scars across the backs of his knuckles.

'I'm Jay Bentley. And the pleasure is all mine.' There was a wealth of meaning in the low gravelly words, and Sandy stifled a gasp as, between her legs, her sex fluttered.

'Er ... is that a capital "J" or like the bird?' she burbled, saying the first thing that came into her head to cover her confusion.

'Jay' laughed, his sharp eyes narrowing. 'Either. Or both. I've never thought about it. You choose.'

Surely you know your own name?

'Like the bird then.'

'"Jay" it is then, Alexandra.' Reaching forward, he finally took her hand.

His skin was warm and smooth and dry, and Sandy was instantly aware that her own palm was sticky with nervous perspiration. She tried to snatch it back, but Jay held on, staring directly into her eyes as if engaging her in a contest.

'It's "Sandy" ... my friends call me "Sandy".'

'So I'm your friend then, am I, Sandy?' He tilted his closely cropped head on one side, still holding her hand, still pouring a stream of electricity into her body that found its way unerringly to her groin. 'I had a feeling that you didn't really like me all that much.'

Blood burned in Sandy's face. He was right in a way. She'd found him intimidating, worrying. She still did. And much more so now.

'I ... Well, I don't really know you yet.' She almost threw the glorious Champagne down her throat, insulting its magnificent quality.

'And yet you want me as a friend?'

Again that raw sexy laugh that seemed to play across tender sensitive areas. The man was starting to goad her, provoke her. Did she like him? She still wasn't sure. Especially as there was the possibility he was stalking her.

But you want him, Sandy, don't you? Boy, how you want him.

'You know what I mean. Don't be perverse!'

His grin looked almost boyish all of a sudden, and lights danced in those North Sea-grey eyes.

'Me, perverse?' He took a long swallow of wine, his strong throat undulating against the open collar of his dark shirt, then paused, licking a droplet off his lips. 'Well, not in that way.' He finished his drink in another deep swallow. 'I'm a plain and simple man, Sandy. I just see what I want and go after it.'

'Like me?'

What on earth was she thinking? What had she said? It could be pure coincidence he was here. But then again, what was a perfect stranger who she'd first set eyes on this afternoon doing at a Kissley Chamber of Commerce cocktail party? She'd lay odds on the fact that he'd gate-crashed and, if he had, was it specifically to meet *her*?

His laugh pealed out, a rough sexy sound that drew the attention of folk nearby, mostly the women. The way they looked at him suggested that his scars and his fierce appearance didn't reduce his attractiveness one bit. In fact, their hungry glances told Sandy that the way he looked made him infinitely more desirable, rather like a glamorous pirate or some other ruthless sexy scoundrel.

'You're very direct. But then, so am I. As a rule.' Long, dark and splendidly thick eyelashes flickered down for an instant. 'I'm staying here at the hotel for a few days. Would you like to come up and see my room, Sandy Jackson?'

'No.' *Yes!* 'Of course not.'

She cursed a blue streak inside, feeling her face colour with a furious revealing blush. Hell, she didn't know this man from Adam but suddenly she *did* want to go up to his room with him. It was insane, it was dangerous and it was downright sluttish, but there was something about his strange, scarred but still handsome face, and his large powerful body that spoke directly to her own body, making it want him.

'Why not?'

'Because I don't know you. I'm not sure I even like you. And I certainly don't sleep with perfect strangers just minutes after I've met them.'

Jay shifted his weight between his feet, his eyes on her. She didn't know how he was doing it but she couldn't seem to move a muscle.

Her eyes moved though. She couldn't stop skittering all up and down him, noting his white taunting smile, his uncompromising haircut and the long muscular lines of his limbs beneath his good suit.

She also noted, with a thud of her heart, that he was starting to get the makings of an erection.

Looking up again, her face crimson, she found his eyes upon her. Dropping her gaze again, she focused on her glass, twirling its pointless emptiness in her fingers.

'More Champagne?'

He was laughing at her, the beast, laughing his arrogant sex maniac's head off.

'No ... no thank you. I think I'll get some air now. It's been nice meeting you, Jay. I'll see you around. Presumably ...'

Still clutching her glass, she spun and darted for the door, cursing the stupid shoes that meant she couldn't walk as fast as she wanted to. A second later, Jay was at her side. 'Good idea. It's too hot in here. I'll join you.' Reaching out confidently, he plucked the empty Champagne glass out of her fingers, and deposited it and his own on a passing waiter's tray. 'Let's go that way.' With his hand beneath her elbow, he began to guide her towards a set of open patio doors that led out to the Waverley's gardens.

Disorientated, and fighting both Jay and her shoes, Sandy stumbled, only to be caught around the waist and held upright, almost off her feet, as if she weighed nothing. A piercing sense of déjà vu swept through her, and she teetered dangerously. Not pausing to give her time to protest, Jay gathered her up in his arms and began to carry her towards the open doors to the garden.

'Get off! Let me down! It's just my shoes!' she hissed in his ear, but his grip only tightened and his smile became infuriatingly arch and he-man.

'All the more reason for me to carry you. Don't make a fuss, woman.'

Sandy's brain sent messages to her hands and arms to beat at Jay and to her body to wriggle in order to get loose. Her little evening bag swung on its chain from her shoulder as he walked and she felt like catching hold of it and using it to batter him around the head with. Yet somehow the nerve impulses got sidetracked, swept away by the raw power not only of him but of a deep persistent memory.

Transported across time, she relaxed, became pliant and curled her arms around his neck. She was suddenly living in the world of fifteen years ago, being rescued and carried to safety by her perfect knight. A beautiful Prince Charming figure, barely out of his teens, a scruffy backpacker, large and wonderful in his strength and kindness, with the face of an angel and long dark hair that tumbled to his shoulders. She even seemed to smell again his distinctive odour of male sweat and some musky incense-like cologne.

The expressions of astonishment and interest all around her seemed to come through a thick filter. The cocktail party was a million miles away. All that existed was the warm haven of protective arms, keeping her safe and comforting her after trauma.

The cooler night air of the Waverley's formal gardens rudely awakened her though, reminding her that she was a grown woman. She hadn't just been mugged, and this was most definitely *not* the romantic Bohemian prince of her dreams whose large hand was curved evocatively around her thigh. Instead, it was a rude and overconfident man who might well have an unhealthy fixation on her. And one who'd just seen fit to make a complete exhibition of her in front of many of Kissley's worthies and quite a few of her friends and acquaintances!

'What the hell do you think you're doing?'

Wriggling like fury achieved nothing, and she was about to escalate to thumping and punching when Jay stopped in front of a bench in a deep, hedged alcove, and set her gently down on it. Sinking to his knees on the turf, he pulled off first one of her offending shoes, then the other.

'Your feet were hurting and I carried you,' he said, giving her a look as if she were an airhead. 'God knows why you women wear these stupid things.' He tossed the borrowed slingbacks away with obvious male disdain.

'If you must know, they're not mine and I was persuaded to wear them because they look good with this dress.' It should have come out assertively, but the sweet relief of being out of the horrible shoes was warping her mind. All she could do was lean back on the bench, wiggling her liberated toes and trying to get her bearings.

'Hobnail boots would look good with that dress as long as you're wearing it.'

Sandy's eyes had closed in bliss because her toes were hurting less, but now they snapped open.

Perfect knight-type compliments too?

She opened her mouth, but couldn't think of a single appropriately gracious remark. Jay's eyes were glinting with a strange, vaguely confused intensity. He wanted her, that was obvious, but there was more than desire there. Something indefinable and enigmatic and possibly not even connected to sex at all.

'Let me give you a foot massage.'

His rough voice was soft and low and, before she could answer, he took her right foot in both his hands, cradling it as if it were fashioned out of porcelain. Then he began to massage, delicately and yet with assertion, and what had been bliss became sublime, almost breathtaking pleasure. The sensation of his cool hands on her hot skin was like having an orgasm right there in her foot, and unable to stop herself she made a noise that told him so.

'Good?'

'Oh God, yes.'

What the hell am I doing?

She tried to wrest her toes from his grip, but he held on firmly. The pressure of his hands was unyielding without hurting her abused foot.

'Hush ... hush ... Why are you struggling? You like this, don't you?'

His fingers began to move again, pressing, circling, releasing tension and unwinding knots.

What is this? Reflexology?

Never one for alternative therapies, Sandy suddenly found herself an instant convert. His sensitive kneading of her metatarsals was having effects in most unexpected places.

Her sex. It was as if he was touching her sex. Stroking. Pressing. Fondling. Exploring. The impending orgasm was no longer confined to her foot.

'No,' she murmured, closing her eyes again, her face flaming. She tried to struggle again, but it was half-hearted, merely token.

'Yes,' he asserted, fingers still moving and circling.

Sandy slid down in the seat, her thighs parting. It was like being hypnotised by touch, mesmerised by sensation. All her negative reactions to him were dissipating like mist in the heat of the delicious night, leaving only a woman's yearning for his strength and his mystery.

He was intent on her foot, studying it closely as he worked. Sandy felt drugged and dreamy, her body loose now, and fluid. Her sex was soft, open and ready, and she could feel silky arousal drench the crotch of her panties.

It's a fantasy... just a fantasy... It's not real.

And it seemed that way as she shifted her hips on the bench, bunching her dress beneath her as Jay continued to caress her foot. Drenched in euphoria, she stared down at him, loving the dark fuzz of his hair as it clung to his scalp, and the focused expression on his austere face. There seemed to be nothing sexual in his expression, but in her gut she knew he knew precisely what he was doing. The foot massage was a deliberate assault, a careful strategy for seduction.

And God, was it ever working. Her pussy felt wide and pouched. Surely he could smell her arousal? He was close to it, and her dress was thin and silky, and her knickers even less substantial.

As if he'd heard her thoughts, he looked up at her, and with one last squeeze of her toes he abandoned her foot and ran his long fingers deliberately up her calf, to her knee. He cupped his hand around the back of it, the very tips of his fingers on the underside of her thigh, then he gripped harder, shifting her leg a little to the side on the bench, making space. Edging forward a little, he grew closer, ever closer to the heart of the matter.

Seemingly satisfied with his position, he slid his hands down flat, one on each of her thighs, and began to edge the silk hem of her dress up her freshly waxed legs. The dress was dark green, slightly iridescent with flashes of emerald, and it seemed to fluoresce in the twilight as if reacting to a magnetic field, or just the presence of Jay.

Looking directly into her eyes, he slid the edge of the silk up to her crotch, right up to the level of her panties. His expression was more complex than ever. Hot and hungry, but with drifting shadows in the dark-grey depths of his eyes. He seemed to want her, but not like a normal man. There was a strange reverence in his face, as if he too couldn't quite believe what was happening.

Then, with a gasp, he pushed her silk skirt further, in a bunch, exposing her knickers.

Sandy felt weak, yet somehow also strong. Suddenly it was as if she were some kind of erotic goddess, exhibiting herself for his pleasure, and she sagged against the hard back of the seat, her body loose and boneless. Wanton.

Let whatever might happen now happen. She no longer cared about propriety or what was sensible. She no longer cared that she barely knew this unusual scarred man. All that mattered was the way he looked at her, and the way that made her feel.

And *she* could smell herself now. A gust of warm, musky arousal seemed to float up from her crotch, from the saturated gusset of her fine panties. They were thin and lacy, not her usual style at all, and tiny curlicues of red pubic hair escaped the confines of the elastic at the edges. She supposed she should have trimmed or waxed there too, but there just hadn't been time. Life running a small café on the edge of viability was always busy, and she was a practical girl, not a finicky fashion victim.

Two long, square yet tapered fingertips settled against the lace, flexing, pressing ever so lightly. The touch barely registered, yet at the same time it was the most profound sexual contact she'd ever experienced.

He'd been watching, watching what he was doing, and suddenly he looked up again, a raw question in his eyes.

Do you want this? he seemed to say. *Only say stop, and I will.*

Not needing to think once, let alone twice, she nodded.

His grey eyes widened. His entire face almost seemed to glow. Suddenly he looked divinely beautiful to her, beard and scars and all, and whatever was going to happen was right. Was good.

His flexible fingers hooked into the waistband of her knickers, and he raised his other hand to the job, tweaking the silk and lace down with both hands. Deftly, he teased the garment down over her thighs, and instinctively she lifted her bottom to help him take them off her.

As he tossed aside her pants, he let out a hiss of air, as if he'd been poleaxed, sideswiped simply by the sight of her fragrant ruddy-haired pussy. Before she could analyse his reaction, and this unexpected expression of awe, he dipped forward and pressed a kiss to her pubic floss.

It seemed perfectly natural to cradle his skull in her hands, and she gasped with delight at the sensation of touching his scalp. It was like suede, heated suede, as if he was running a temperature.

He kissed the surface of her pubic hair, nothing more, lightly nuzzling her and uttering rough male purrs of wonder and delight. She opened her legs wider to him, loving the strong shape of his head beneath her fingertips, and as he pressed deeper she felt him murmur something against her, a word, low and fervent.

What had he said? She could barely tell... but it sounded like 'Princess'.

3

Paradise. He was in paradise. Within the capsule of this moment, she was everything he'd dreamed she'd be. And more.

Inhaling her scent, tasting the essence of sex on the soft hair of her pussy, Jay felt giddy. His knees were screaming from kneeling on damp turf, but the pain felt as if it were in another universe. The only thing that touched him was her fragrance, her heat, her total femininity, all available to him.

He pressed his lips more closely against her, nuzzling, and drawing in more of her intoxicating bouquet.

How had it come to this, so soon? He could barely credit it. They hadn't even kissed on the mouth yet. But he couldn't argue. He couldn't stop. He could only feel.

And hear. She was gasping, and breathing heavily, as excited by the moment as he was. She moved uneasily, but she wasn't struggling to get away from him any more, she was rising to him, opening her thighs, welcoming him to the heart of her mystery.

Maybe I died in the Aston and this is heaven?

Still kissing her pubis, he flattened his hands on her bare belly and began to part her soft red hair with his thumbs. It was thick and lush and flossy, but with care he exposed her, baring the gleaming rosy geography of her sex – the plump lips, the gloss of her juice, silky and abundant, and her clit, proud and exposed, peeping from its hood.

Fighting for control, shaking with emotion, he extended his tongue in a furled point and delicately licked her.

'Oh. Oh God.'

Her voice was reedy and shocked, and he lifted his head in alarm.

Shit, fuck, damn. What was wrong with him? He'd only really spoken to her for the first time less than half an hour ago and now he had his face between her legs. He started to back away, but her small hands closed around his scalp, her fingers shockingly strong.

'No ... please ... don't stop.'

Her eyes were brilliant when he looked up into them, vivid green, yet dark, slightly spaced.

Your wish is my command, Princess, he told her silently, and began to lick gently, savouring her sumptuous foxy flavour. The taste of her told him she wanted him, even if she didn't know him.

This was easy. This was wonderful. There was no stress, no angst about this. He went to work, giving, giving, giving, revelling in pleasuring her. The cries she uttered thrilled him. Little gasps, mutters, grunts. Exciting, but somehow unexpected. Not the pliant helpless sounds of surrender that had coloured his 'rescuing' dreams and fantasies. No, these were the noises made by a grown woman who knew what she wanted and was pleased to be getting it.

Almost angrily, he increased the pace of his tongue, went in harder. At the same time, he slid his hands under her spread thighs, lifting her, opening her further, making a ripe fruit of her for his delectation, and to feast on. Gripping the globes of her bottom, he slid his fingertips into the hot groove there, playing wickedly, touching and taunting, opening her in other ways.

Her heels kicked against him but he didn't feel it. He could only taste, inhale and relish her. When she growled something indistinct and gouged her nails into his shoulders through the cloth of his jacket, he thought his heart would burst with pride and possession, sweet emotions both. As her pussy pulsed against his face, his cock throbbed too.

He could do it now, he thought as she subsided, still holding onto his jacket. Right now, he could rip open his trousers, free himself and plunge into her. With her, at this supreme instant, all would be well.

But it was too soon, too much of a shock for her. He couldn't just fuck her like that, because he wanted to and because she was probably the only woman right now who it would be so simple and easy with. He needed to romance her, woo her, gift her with all the niceties and foreplay she deserved. You didn't fantasise about a woman for fifteen years and then shag her senseless without so much as a by-your-leave.

After dropping a last kiss on her perfect pussy, he drew away. He knew it was better to wait, but there was a nag of regret, of unease. He'd just passed up a chance to prove to himself once and for all that there was nothing whatsoever wrong with his potency, and that his previous problems had simply been part of the healing process. To prove to himself that he was still, and had always been, a man.

I'm such a screw-up, Princess. If I told you only a fraction of what's going on with me, you'd tell me to fuck off and never touch you ever again.

But, rising to his feet, and grimly suppressing the pain in his still recovering bones, he knew he couldn't tell her anything just yet. He wanted a little window of time to get to know her. To uncover the truth of *her*.

Was she the woman of his dreams, or another woman entirely? And if she *was* that other unknown undiscovered woman, what pleasures and sexual explorations might they still share?

Sandy struggled to sit up. To wake up. It was like she'd been in a dream for the last fifteen minutes or so, but now she was back in the real world with a vengeance. Sitting on a bench with her pussy hanging out in front of what amounted to a total stranger.

What the hell was I thinking?

To give him his due, Jay looked as if he'd been in some kind of dreamland too. His dark eyes were slightly hazed, as if he'd been taking something. God, what if he was a junkie as well as some kind of sex maniac? But she didn't think so, he looked too hard, too fierce, too self-disciplined to succumb to pharmaceutical entertainment.

'Where are my knickers? I'm feeling a draught here. Can you see them?'

Hardly the most romantic thing to say after a guy had given you pleasure and apparently taken none for himself, but the weird expression on his face was spooking her. Seriously so. Flipping down her skirt, she patted it into place repeatedly, as if it might fly up of its own accord if she didn't hold it down, or be lifted by some kind of mind control on Jay's part.

As she watched him, he blinked, and seemed to come back to earth alongside her. His scarred brow crimped into a slight frown, and the sudden hard set of his mouth seemed to suggest that her less than grateful utterance had annoyed him, perhaps as much as she was annoyed with herself for blurting it out.

Swooping down, he caught up her knickers from where he'd cast them on the turf but, instead of handing them to her, he bunched them in his hand, then lifted them to his face and inhaled, very pointedly. His dark brows lifted and, what with the scars and the piratical beard, he looked like the very devil himself. Sandy blushed, knowing how strongly her little panties would be scented. And not just with Miss Dior either.

'I thought I might keep them.' He took another deep sniff. 'A souvenir. Or perhaps a reward, for services rendered.'

Confusion engulfed her. Embarrassment made it difficult to think. Suddenly getting back to normal social cocktail-party interaction seemed infinitely desirable. Risky sex games with a peculiar stranger just weren't her usual scene and, right now, they scared her. She grabbed wildly for her knickers and he let her take them, eyeing her with another frown as she struggled to wiggle them back on. At first she resisted the arm he put out to support her as she stepped from one foot to the other. But when she allowed herself to succumb, his hard-hewn muscle felt like a hunk of solid granite.

'I have to go. I need to get back. I came with someone.'

As she reluctantly freed his magnificent bicep, the antipathy in his eyes was unmistakeable.

'And no, it isn't a man. It's Kat, my cook. You know, she served you in the café ... I came here with her and she'll be wondering where I am.'

Why do I need to explain myself to him? He's just a man I temporarily lost my mind with. With luck I won't see him again after tonight.

'Good. I'm glad it's not a man.'

What was it to him? Did one orgasm make him think he owned her? Anger and other mad emotions set adrenaline pumping in her blood. She had to get away, think, cool down. Being around him, even though things were getting prickly, was messing with her senses and her judgement. Her mind might be processing antagonism, but her body was still responding to his brutal beauty like a filly in season flaunting her availability to a stallion.

She grabbed her bag, turned on her heel, and started to walk. Or tried to. Her upper arm was suddenly in a vice. A gentle vice, but one that wouldn't yield.

'Let me go!'

The vice opened. She was free.

So why didn't she dart away from him, run and never look back?

Because, even without physical force, he still seemed to be holding her. Those dark eyes constrained her just as securely. They were softer now, and mellower, but still as compelling.

She stared at him for a long moment, unable to look away from his grey gaze. Why did he suddenly seem so familiar? Not the face, but the eyes. They looked like ... no ... that was impossible. It was just a trick. There was no real similarity at all between the kindly shaggy almost angelic boy of fifteen years ago and the battered militaristic man of now.

'I'm sorry,' he said, his voice raw, 'I didn't mean to frighten you ...' He paused, and she noticed again how beautifully long his eyelashes were as they flickered, completely at odds with every bit of the rest of him. 'But you'll need your shoes before you go anywhere, won't you?'

Her feet looked pale and vulnerable against the grass, but the sight of them sent a frisson of sensation speeding through her, an echo of his fingers caressing her instep. And other places. And not just his fingers.

As she grappled for self-control, Jay retrieved her shoes, and a second later they were doing the 'take my arm while you dress yourself' dance again. Stubborn independence whispered to her to flop down on the seat again and put the hated shoes back on unaided, but it was just easier not to fight, and accept his help.

'I'm sorry that I took advantage of you.'

The words took Sandy by surprise, and for a moment she

wondered what he was talking about. Then she remembered in a flash of heat as Jay made an eloquent gesture with his strong, tapered fingers and his mouth quirked slightly in a way that could have been accidental but which was probably deliberate. 'It's just a strange night ... sort of like magic ... And hot.' A smile appeared, and that was definitely deliberate. 'In more ways than one.'

Sandy's heart thudded slowly, thumpety-thump. He was arrogant, and he seemed dangerous, and he did frighten her. But she couldn't turn away, couldn't flee. There was an aura of excitement about him, like a net, a thrilling bondage. She hadn't had this sense of connection with a man in a long time. Perhaps never. Maybe now was the time to reach out and make the most of it?

'I'm sorry too.' It came out on a total impulse, but it was true. He hadn't hurt her, had he? In fact he'd given her pleasure, unselfishly, taking nothing for himself. 'Wh-what you did for me ... It was lovely. More than lovely. I feel as if I owe you. In fact I do owe you something in return.' Trying to be surreptitious, she glanced down at his crotch, to see if he was still erect. But his loose fluid jacket was in the way, creating shadows. She looked up again, and found him tracking her every tiny movement, like the Terminator.

'Don't worry about me.' His voice was shockingly brusque after the gentleness of his apology, but he immediately modified it. 'We'll get to that. Let's have a drink for starters, eh? A real one. I've got whisky in my room, if you'd like some?'

Disquiet flared again. His room? It was too risky, too much his domain. She needed to keep at least a semblance of control over the situation. And herself.

'Er ... no ... but why don't you come to my place? To the café? We could have a cup of tea, and there are some of Kat's apple turnovers left, still nice and fresh.'

What? He almost certainly wants to fuck me and I'm offering him tea and a bun?

The amusement in Jay's face almost banished his scars altogether, and his grin was white and wicked in the frame of his dark immaculate beard.

'Well, that's different. But why not?' He laughed softly, then nodded in the direction of the Lawns Bar. 'Aren't you supposed to be socialising though?'

'I was ... but I only really came here to find out if there was any fresh gossip about a new development in the town centre, on the site of the old Bradbury's supermarket. But it seems nobody's talking.'

Dreary reality took the edge off the night's magic. She didn't want to think about the fun-café-pub or whatever it was squeezing the life out of the Teapot's business.

'Perhaps no decision has yet been made?'

There was an odd note in Jay's voice, and his expression was strangely shuttered again.

'Oh, I'll bet it has. Forbes Enterprises will build one of their super-mega open-all-day fun coffee pubs and that probably means the end of the Little Teapot.'

The vehemence in her own voice shocked her. Why was she sounding off to a stranger? Well, obviously, he wasn't *entirely* one now, seeing as he'd kissed her pussy and made her come. But he was about sex, not the grim reality of losing her livelihood and the business she'd inherited from her beloved grandmother. The two things were in two different universes. They couldn't mix.

'But your café is a niche business, and has a loyal clientele, I would imagine. Hopefully it will still thrive,' observed Jay as by unspoken agreement they fell into step along the path. His light touch on Sandy's back made her quiver almost as much as his tongue had done. Dark thoughts about the Teapot's future seemed to recede, drop behind a barrier, obscured by the here and now of the distinct glow of heat emanating from Jay's fingertips.

'I suppose so. But can we not talk about that now?'

'What shall we talk about then?'

'I don't know, but I'm sure you'll think of something.' Glancing over her shoulder, she found him watching her intently, speculatively. But starting to smile again. 'But first I've got to find Kat and tell her to make her own way home. She probably would anyway ... She and her boyfriend Greg can't keep their hands off each other.'

'Really?' Jay's eyes widened.

'Yeah ... I could tell you some tales about what they get up to, believe me.'

Could she? Could she really? Tell this stranger about the kinky things Kat had so enjoyed describing ... Wouldn't that just be asking for trouble? Or something.

'I'll look forward to it. You can tell me all about it over tea.'

Yeah, right ...

Back at the Lawns Bar, Sandy began a rapid circuit of the room, searching for her cook, while Jay left to get his car, saying he'd meet her out front in ten minutes.

But Kat was nowhere to be seen. Where the hell was she? Holed up somewhere with Greg, doing something horny and experimental no doubt.

The rather plush ladies' cloakroom revealed no Kat either, but Sandy took the time to prod a few wayward strands of curly red hair back up into her loosely assembled knot.

Oh shit! Did I really let him do that?

The enormity of what she'd done made her hand shake and nearly jag her lip gloss across her cheek. She didn't know the man, and yet his breath, his lips, the stroke of his tongue against her sex had all felt right. Wonderful. Unbelievable. Exquisite. Her body quaked and shimmered as if he were licking her again, and deep in her loins heat gathered, tightened, condensed.

She needed to come again. A woman who barely even masturbated, or thought about sex these days. But now a pair of steely dark eyes and a scarred bearded face seemed to challenge her and, as if it were looking up at her from between her own thighs again, the shade of Jay winked at her.

Heart and sex pounding, she plunged into the cubicle and locked the door.

4

Safe behind the door though, things did not come so easy. Time, all of a sudden, weighed heavy. Jay was waiting. And yet it wasn't her strange new friend who seemed to steal her orgasm. It was the man from her past, Prince Charming, pretty much Jay's antithesis.

It didn't make sense, she was hornier than she'd ever been in her life, and she had an exciting man waiting for her, but a fragmentary dream from her past was messing with her head and standing in the way of what she needed.

Closing her eyes and subsiding onto the closed toilet seat cover, she leaned back against the cistern, trying to recover the moment.

Images danced before her eyes. The vague snapshots of what Prince Charming might have looked like flicked and phased, becoming Jay and totally confusing her.

Past. Present. Past. Present.

When she touched herself, though, her fingertip stirred echoes of Jay's nimble daring tongue. Lust flared again, and her sex clenched as elusive orgasm floated back within her reach.

Rubbing quick and hard, she focused on her strange new knight, so dark and troubling, so flawed and threatening, yet so desirable. Displayed on the screen of her imagination, she was in a room with him, spread on a bed, open and available. But this time, he didn't hold back, he took his pleasure.

With no idea what his body was like beneath his expensive

clothes – beyond the feel of his hard, developed musculature – she imagined him big. In all ways. With a cock as perfect as his face and hands were scarred. And he'd fit her perfectly as he pushed in, filling her and stretching her.

Rocking on the seat, she worked herself two-handed, fingers inside, fingers on her clit. There was no finesse, but she didn't need that. She had to come.

As her dream of Jay cried out hoarsely, her body convulsed, the pleasure as savage as the imagined expression on his face.

As Sandy rushed through the foyer, she barely noticed the twinges from Kat's ridiculous slingbacks. She felt as if she were skimming over the carpet, buoyed up on a raft of confused and lingering pleasure.

A glance at her watch told her that her ten minutes was now more like twenty-five. What if Jay had got tired of waiting for his casual conquest and decided to look elsewhere? He might be sharing that whisky in his room with another, more biddable partner.

The idea of that particular scenario made her grind her teeth, but she forgot it in an instant when she stepped out onto the Waverley's elegant forecourt.

'Oh my God.'

A car out of anyone's dreams stood on the gravel, with the man who was half-dream, half-nightmare leaning casually against it. His dark brows lifted in amusement when he caught sight of her gaping at his fabulous chariot.

Sandy wasn't a petrol-head, but she was enough of a fan of television motoring shows to know an Aston Martin when she saw one. And enough a fan of James Bond movies to recognise 007's latest vehicle of choice.

Jay straightened up, and shrugged. Then strolled around to the passenger-side door without saying anything.

'It's an Aston Martin,' observed Sandy, aware she sounded mildly inane. Jay was perfectly aware of the famous *marque* of his beautiful car. As she touched the gleaming steel-grey coachwork she acknowledged vaguely that it was just a few shades lighter than her companion's eyes. Eyes that were now darkened with an odd, almost resentful expression as he opened the door for her, that seemed, curiously, to be directed at the car.

'This is a beautiful car,' she said as he slid into the racing seat beside her, and did a little shimmy as if it was hard to get comfortable. For her own part, it was like being cradled and caressed by the leather upholstery, and the whole experience was like gently sinking into an aristocratic dream of luxury and high performance.

A new thought popped into her head.

What on earth was he doing in Kissley? It's not exactly where a jet-setting single man with an Aston Martin would choose to holiday. That is, if he was single. He wore no ring, but that didn't mean anything. Some guys simply didn't wear them.

Jay still didn't speak, and Sandy realised he was glowering at the steering wheel, that peculiar sense of resentment writ large on his damaged features.

'What's the matter? Don't you like your own car?' As she watched, he squared his shoulders and reached for the Aston's distinctive rectangular ignition unit, already sitting in its slot. Pressing it filled the air with a silky, almost erotic roar of engine music. 'It's amazing. Most guys I know would give their eyeteeth for a Bond car.'

After a long pause, and in a low weary voice, he said, 'It *is* a beautiful car, and I wouldn't drive anything else.' His long fingertip stroked the fine leather encasing the steering wheel. 'It's just that Astons and I... well, you might say we have issues.'

In a moment of revelation, the scars explained themselves.

Jay had been in a car smash. A bad one. In an Aston Martin. The accident had nearly killed him, judging by the visible damage he'd incurred.

As he revved the engine self-indulgently, her blood ran cold. If he'd crashed once, he could crash again.

Still feathering the accelerator, he glanced at her as if he'd read her qualms on her face. His eyes narrowed. Yes, he *knew* what she was thinking. 'You're right.' His raw voice was very low. 'I totalled my last Aston. I admit it.'

He turned off the ignition and the silence seemed louder than the engine noise.

'I'm sorry to hear that ... What happened?'

Long fingers tapped the leather-covered wheel again. 'I swerved to avoid a fox, hit a pot hole and, hey presto, me and the car are doing a triple somersault ... with pike.'

Images of twisted metal and carnage assaulted her eyes. Jay's body twisted and broken. His face ... his face ... She couldn't see it, no matter how she tried to picture him based on his appearance now. It was like one of those strange surrealist paintings where the subject's features were blank. She simply couldn't imagine the original Jay at all.

'Were you badly hurt?'

He nodded, not looking at her. 'Yep, fairly mangled. Broke more bones than I can name, and said goodbye to my pretty, boyish face.'

He turned and looked at her, the angles of his mouth and jaw hard. He *wasn't* pretty, that was true. But still, she found him compelling in a way that went far beyond classic ideals of good looks.

'You don't look so bad.'

'Yeah, right ...' But he laughed, and shrugged, and seemed to accept her cautious compliment. 'So, knowing what you know now, do you still feel safe to ride with me?'

'Yes, of course.'

A part of her didn't feel safe at all. A part of her felt in deep peril, a danger that was nothing to do with his driving capabilities. She feared herself, as much as him, in his presence. Even as she slid down deeper into the comfortable form-fitting seat, the urge to slide her skirt hem towards her crotch bubbled up inside her.

'OK then.' He flashed her another grin, and she almost wished he hadn't. These smiles of his were dynamite, and they stoked her insane urges even higher. 'And if it's any comfort to you, when I got back behind the wheel again, I took a course in "conservative driving techniques" at the Institute of Advanced Motorists. So you're perfectly safe with me.' He waggled his dark brows. 'In the car, that is ...'

'Oh, that's *very* reassuring,' she shot back, her voice tarter than she'd intended, his sudden playfulness rocking her.

Jay just laughed, jabbed on the ignition again, and gunned the car. Then with no further ado they were gliding down the gravelled drive, oozing along with a stealthy panache that James Bond would have been proud of.

Where are we heading? she mused as Jay smoothly exited the Waverley's drive and pointed the car in the direction of Kissley.

The question was nothing to do with the drive home.

The presence of a beautiful woman in the car with him should have created tension. In fact, he should have been all over the place.

For one thing, Alexandra Jackson was *not* his Princess. Yes, she was the girl he'd taken care of briefly, all those years ago. But she certainly wasn't the gentle sweet paragon he'd always fantasised about. No way. She was combative, stubborn, strong-willed. It was a bloody miracle he'd got her into the car at all.

Only where sex was concerned did she seem to be pliant and responsive. Hell, he'd never met a woman like her, and his wayward cock was kicking even now, thinking about the sweet taste of her delicious body and those awesome, rough, out-of-control sounds she'd made as he'd pleasured her.

And that was the other thing. Tonight had gone completely off the rails. He'd never planned to move so far, so fast. But he'd run out of control himself at the slightest hint of her pussy. Just like the randy teenager he'd been when he first met her.

Weirdest of all though, despite everything about tonight and the woman at his side being completely out of kilter, she still had a weirdly Zen-like, almost soothing effect on him. He couldn't explain it. Sandy might not be Princess but, for the moment, he didn't mind.

He kept his eyes on the road, a keen awareness of her body and her familiar face distracting him from the fine jagged thread of fear that always plagued him when he drove. When he glanced in the rear-view mirror he was astonished to catch himself smiling. He couldn't even bring himself to feel guilty for the fact he was lying to her.

Would she ever forgive him for not telling her immediately that he was the handsome lad who'd once helped her? Would she still want to sleep with him if she knew he was the son of the man who was probably currently her worst enemy in the whole wide world? Probably not, but he'd face those bitter truths – and their ramifications – when the time came.

As surreptitiously as she could, Sandy snuck a glance at Jay.

A slight smile was playing around his mouth, giving his bearded face a devilish saturnine cast. Combined with the scars and the generally hard look of him, it made her heart feel as if it was rolling over in her chest. Especially bearing in mind that, driving course or no driving course, he could still well be a reckless testosterone-addled driver whose next supercar smash could be his last. That line about the Institute of Advanced Motorists was probably utter bullshit. Once a boy racer, always a boy racer.

Even so, despite more speed than she was used to, his driving style was silky smooth and perfectly controlled. Contrary to all logic, she actually felt safe with him. Well, in the car at least, as he'd so rightly teased her. Otherwise, he was totally outrageous.

And yet she'd still invited him back to her place. Now it was her turn to smirk.

She wanted more of what he'd given her. More of the same, and a lot of different stuff too. Kat wasn't the only person who was interested in sensual experimentation. With Jay Bentley, so mysterious and daring, Sandy sensed that her chance to sample the new and the hot was here.

'What are you thinking about?'

It was the classic girlie question, but Jay seemed man enough to ask it.

'Oh, just my friend Kat. I couldn't find her at the party. I've no idea where she is, but she probably found Greg and they're shagging like bunnies somewhere … or doing something extremely kinky.'

Jay laughed. 'Ah yes, you were going to tell me some tales.' He licked his lips, his tongue flicking out quickly, darting in a way that reminded her of his prowess in the garden. She felt an intense urge to wriggle in her seat.

'Well, Kat's always been one for the blokes. She's got a heart of gold and she's a dear, dear friend, but she likes to have fun. She's always the one who suggests a Chippendales night out, or a sex-toy party. That sort of thing.'

'She sounds like an entertaining person to know.'

'Not half. She's got no shame when it comes to talking about her sex life and, since she started seeing Greg, she's been completely outrageous.'

'Do go on.' Jay changed gear with perfect equanimity, but she could tell from his husky voice he was interested. More than interested.

'Greg's into a bit of the pervy stuff. I think it's because he works at the Waverley. He and Kat play sex games. Bondage, spanking, little power trips, you know the sort of thing.'

Jay laughed again, accelerated, that naughty smile playing around his stern mouth.

'Indeed I do, Sandy. Indeed I do.'

She couldn't speak. She couldn't breathe. That sense of being caught in an electrical field increased in voltage, and she got the impression she didn't even have to speak. He could taste her excitement like a killer snake sampling the air. As if he'd read her mind, his tongue flicked across his lower lip again.

'So ... bondage, spanking, power games? Have you tried any of those?'

'No.' Her voice shook on the word. Her throat felt dry.

'Would you like to?'

'I ... I don't know. Maybe.'

'Oh, I think you do. I think you've already started.' The car rounded a sweeping bend, hitting the perfect apex of the curve. 'Allowing a man you don't know to give you head in a hotel garden seems plenty kinky to me. Daring, at least.'

Sweat trickled between her breasts, and the place where his tongue had roved shimmered with excitement.

'I didn't intend to let that happen. It just did.'

The tips of her fingers tingled. She wanted to do something. Touch something.

'Indeed. But what about doing something intentionally? Something for me.'

Blood began to surge faster through her body. She could

feel it, and almost see it in her mind's eye, pelting along her veins and vessels. Her head nodded, completely of its own volition and, even though Jay's eyes were on the road ahead, she knew he'd seen it.

'Touch your breast.'

A sensation like vertigo gripped her. It was if she were on a merry-go-round, floating and rising in a wild unreal whirl. Her hand seemed disconnected from her arm but, as if by magic, it lifted, moved, came to her breast, across her body, and cupped the slight weight of it. Her fingertips were hypersensitised and she could feel the texture of her flesh and skin, the pattern of the lace that covered it, and the slipperiness of the delicate silk of her dress. She daren't press hard because just the faintest contact sent a tingle of excitement to her pussy.

'That's good,' observed Jay blandly, still apparently totally focused on his driving. 'But give me more. Caress yourself. Squeeze. Be a little rough. Play with your nipple.'

I can't! I can't! It's too much!

But it wasn't nearly enough, and she could do it. Because he'd told her to.

She gasped out loud as she squeezed herself, caught unawares by the heavy lurch of arousal in the pit of her belly. Her nipple was so sensitive it was almost painful when she thumbed it, and the simple action brought a drench of silky fluid into her panties. Wetness. Nature's welcome for the rampant potent male of the species. Jay Bentley.

'More. Pinch yourself. Twist your nipple ... Try a little pain with your pleasure, see if you like it.'

Obeying him, she yelped out loud. But he was right. She *did* like it. At least her body did. Her pussy rippled deliciously, and the crotch of her knickers grew even more sopping.

'Good?'

'I don't know! I don't know!' It came out as a wail, even as she shuffled in the deluxe seat of his Aston Martin, suddenly and completely his object, his slave.

How had she come to this? She'd always tried not to be a sexual doormat, to do her own thing. But tonight she'd met a man who was a thousand times her match, and seemed to be able to use just a few words to render her his puppet.

'Are you aroused? Do you want to come?'

Sandy bit down on her lip, trying to resist him. Between her legs she was hot, and wet like a river. Of course she fucking well wanted to come! But somehow she also wanted to defy the soft raw words that could well lead to all kinds of downfall.

'Don't fight it, Sandy. I can tell you're turned on. Your face is pink and your eyes are like stars. You look exquisite. Tell me how you feel.'

'A bit turned on.' She squeezed out the words, even as she squeezed down hard on her teat again to punish herself for being so easy, so lascivious and so weak in the face of his barely exerted strength.

'No, no, no. Tell me how you *really* feel. The sensations.... Give them to me in words.'

I can't, I can't, she cried inside again, even as she licked her lips, preparing to speak. Trying to stop herself, she twisted her nipple, harder this time, and let out a broken groan as her sex-flesh lurched in some kind of minor convulsion, a mini orgasm, sharp yet not quite satisfying.

'Did you come then?'

Sandy blinked, tried to focus. Had she blacked out or something? Time seemed to be passing strangely here in Jay's dream machine.

She wanted to shake her head, say 'no', but instead she admitted, 'Yes, a bit ... I think so.'

'Surely you know, Sandy. I usually know when I've come.'

Anger cut through the haze, bringing clarity, and her will again. 'Well, of course a man knows when he's come! There's – there's stuff, isn't there? It's either out or it's in, and, if it's out, you've come!'

'Stuff?' Jay chuckled, a strangely young, light sound, almost boyish. 'Now there's a poetic turn of phrase if I ever heard one.'

'Well, what the hell do you call it?'

Astonishingly, Sandy realised she was still cupping her breast. It was as if she couldn't stop until he gave her leave to. Surreptitiously, she moved her thumb across her nipple again, trying to breathe normally when desire welled again.

'Do you know, I've never really thought about it,' Jay observed almost conversationally. They glided to a halt at traffic lights on the way into the town and, when he glanced across at her, his eyes flickered from her hand at her breast to her blushing face and her reddened bitten lips. 'Semen, I suppose. Or spunk.' That wicked tongue of his swept around his lips again and, as he turned his attention back to the lights, he asked, 'Why, do you like the taste of it?'

'I . . .'

Did she? She wasn't sure. She wasn't sure it had a great deal of taste. But the thought of its texture on her tongue was so vivid, suddenly, that it made her sex rouse and glow even more. She imagined the texture, and the fugitive taste of Jay's semen on her tongue. She wanted to taste him, sample him, take him in and imbibe his essence. Which was weird, she'd never particularly been one for giving head. She didn't object to it. She just didn't do it of her own volition.

Except in her silly romantic fantasies where she happily knelt down and sucked the cock of her long-lost Prince Charming in a show of gratitude.

'So?' her companion prompted, about as far from her fantasy

rescuer as it was possible to be. The lights changed, they glided onwards, cocooned in their strange edgy world of sexual jousting.

'Er, yes, I suppose I don't mind it, really.'

I want to taste yours.

As if he'd heard her, Jay smiled wolfishly. 'Excellent. You like sucking cock. That's good to know.'

'But that doesn't necessarily mean I want to suck yours!'

It was a lie. She knew it. And she knew he knew it.

'We'll see ... we'll see ...' His voice was infuriatingly smug, but just when Sandy was about to fling back some retort at him, she knew not what, he continued, in a completely un-smug voice, 'I think we're nearly there, aren't we?'

It was true. The traffic lights they'd stopped at were the last set before the centre of town, and now they were cruising into Kissley proper. Sandy snatched her hand away from the front of her dress. There were people around, and the urban lighting was well maintained. Any of the couples and groups of either sex traversing between the pubs, the video store and the pedestrian precinct might glance into the interior of a beautiful car to see who was lucky enough to be riding in it. The glass was tinted, but far from opaque.

Still, she was disappointed that they were suddenly all business as she directed him to the small parking area in the little yard behind the Teapot. There was a small Datsun parked there and, after a moment's pondering as to whose it might be, it dawned on her that she'd seen Kat's Greg driving one like it sometimes.

'Problem?'

Sandy realised she'd been frowning, and of course eagle-eyes beside her had noticed.

'No, it just seems that Kat and her paramour have returned to the Teapot ahead of us. No guesses as to what they'll be getting up to.'

With the lights turned off, Jay's eyes were almost silvery in the shadows.

'Ah, the kinky couple. Do you think we'll disturb them?'

'I doubt if category eight on the Richter scale will disturb them when they get going. And even if we did disturb them they'd carry on shagging anyway. Exhibitionism is one of their kinks.'

'Do you like to watch? Does it turn you on?'

She gave him an old-fashioned stare, knowing he could read her in the darkness.

'Well then, shall we go in and watch the show?' said Jay softly, reaching for the door handle.

5

Leading the way, Sandy started up the steps at the rear of the building that led to the kitchen, walking as lightly as she could. Jay followed behind and, when they reached the top of the flight, she felt his breath on the back of her neck.

When his hand fell on her shoulder, compelling her to look at him, he didn't say anything, but his eyes were still gleaming, full of roguish anticipation, making him look younger, almost naughty, like a horny boy.

For a split second, Sandy imagined Prince Charming here on the stairs with her. Would he like to watch too? Had he grown up into a sexy sophisticated man of the world? A man much as she imagined Jay to be, based on the evidence so far.

Quashing the notion, Sandy bit her lip, then gave the real man behind her a nod to keep quiet. Then, making a surreptitious signal to move forward, she reached down, slipped off her clattering high heels and led the way. Light on his feet, Jay followed behind her, silent as the proverbial cat.

The back door to the café was open.

Setting down her bag and shoes, Sandy ground her teeth. Kat was a brilliant cook and an even better friend, but she could be a bit casual about security issues sometimes, especially when she had sex on her mind. Which she so obviously did now, judging by the giggles and moans and other earthy unmistakeable noises that were emanating from the kitchen at the end of the short landing.

The door was open, a good-sized crack, but the landing was

unlit. In deep shadow, there was perfect cover and an unrestricted view of anything happening in the kitchen.

And there was happening aplenty. Sandy's jaw dropped. She would have let out a gasp but, before she could, a large warm hand settled lightly but firmly over her mouth. At the same time a strong arm snaked around her waist, supporting her. Without it, her knees might have wobbled and let her down.

Kat, her dear friend and cheerfully unashamed sex maniac, was standing in the middle of the room stark naked from the waist down. The skin-tight shiny black leggings she'd been wearing were flung across the ladder-back of one of the old kitchen chairs, and her lover, the innocent-faced but lecherously delightful Gregory, was standing behind her, kissing her neck and squeezing her crotch in rude and lazy rhythm.

'Oh God... oh yes... mm... oh yeah.' Kat gurgled in her throat as her head tipped back to rest on Greg's shoulder, her black hair fanning out across his shirt.

Greg's fingers tensed. He was working her slow and hard. And she was loving it.

Driven by a heady mix of hormones and instincts, Sandy pressed back against her own sexy man. Jay tightened his iron-muscled arm around her, drawing her close so she could feel his groin against her bottom. He was getting hard, the warm knot of his erection prodding at her tender anal groove, pressing the fabric of her dress against the little vent there.

The contact was slight and subtle – Jay wasn't grinding the way Greg was against Kat – but its effects fizzed in her bloodstream like the Champagne she'd drunk earlier. *She* wanted to grind, but something in the way Jay held her kept her still. He was containing her in ways other than physical, and she couldn't remember experiencing a greater excitement, not in the Aston, nor in the Waverley garden before it. The scent of his spicy cologne made her dizzy.

And all the while the enthusiastic couple in the kitchen seemed intent on putting on a command performance, almost as if they knew they had an audience.

Maybe they *did*?

The Aston Martin wasn't exactly the quietest of cars and, even though they'd been careful, she and Jay might well have been audible on the stairs.

'Yes, baby, yes,' encouraged Greg as he squeezed and lifted Kat on the fulcrum of his hand, making her moan and whimper louder and wriggle like a she-cat on heat. Tossing her head, she grabbed at Greg's hand, urging him on, while with her other hand she cupped her own breast and pinched her teat through her thin silky top.

'You like it, don't you, you naughty girl?' Greg grinned, a slow, wicked, joyous little smirk as his fingers moved between Kat's legs. There was something so happy about the young man's expression. He seemed Machiavellian, but benign, and this, coupled with his fresh good looks and his wiry body, meant it wasn't hard to understand why Kat was so besotted with him.

Sandy craned forward, aching for a better view, and as she did so Jay slid his hand from her waist, across her belly, to cup her mound. When she drew breath, the other hand, across her mouth, tightened its hold.

Her eyes starting out of her head, she watched an echo of what she was feeling.

'You're very bad, luring me here and just leaving your friend at the party,' Greg went on, his mouth next to Kat's ear as he rummaged about between her legs. 'That was a terrible thing to do, and you should be punished for such misbehaviour, really you should.' As he spoke it became plain that Greg was pushing fingers – one, two or even more – into Kat's sex. Straining to see, Sandy stiffened, rising on her toes, as Jay pressed against

49

her entrance with *his* fingers, pushing the soft fabric of her skirt into her sticky cleft. He didn't even bother to raise her skirt, he just squeezed at her, grasping, searching, probing.

This is the second time tonight. How am I letting this happen? I barely know the man, but he knows my pussy already.

Strong fingertips pressed her skirt and her dainty underwear into the groove of her sex, parting her pubic floss and quickly reaching the heart of the matter. With a deft twist of his wrist, he curved his fingers, rocking and rubbing at her clit, saturating the fabric and using the cloth itself for friction.

Sandy writhed, feeling as if the top of her head might pop off from the pressure building and building inside her. But when she tried to twist towards Jay, pleading with her eyes for something, anything, everything, he merely nodded towards the tableau playing out in the kitchen.

Almost in mirror image, the younger couple were rocking and writhing and jerking against each other, only Kat was free to moan and whimper and curse and encourage. She rode her lover's hand like a wild pony, bearing down on him, demanding more and more and more.

'Right, that's it, you horny little bitch. I'll teach you a lesson,' Greg growled with the sort of sexual gravitas that Sandy might have expected from a rather older man, a veteran of erotic sophistication. Someone like Jay perhaps? Although he wasn't exactly ancient himself. Thirties, perhaps, thought Sandy, finding it difficult to concentrate, although with the plastic surgery it was hard to know for certain. Shying away from thoughts of surgery, she wondered who exactly Kat's frisky boyfriend might be emulating? Probably the patrons of the Waverley, the kinky ones everybody murmured about but nobody actually seemed to know.

Immolated on the hand of her own sexual sophisticate, she watched in astonishment as Greg manhandled Kat to the kitchen table and laid her face down on the chequered cloth, amongst the condiments and a few plates and cups that had been left out.

What the hell was he going to do? Punish her or fuck her? And as an aside, how desperately unhygienic was it to have a half-naked woman's crotch pressed like that against a food-preparation surface?

'So, what's it to be? Your choice.'

The young man leaned over his willing victim and whispered something in her ear. Kat squeaked in protest, but her eyes popped with excitement and she began grinding herself against the tablecloth. She muttered an answer, but it was inaudible to Sandy.

But Greg, arched over Kat's back and bare bottom, heard, and laughed. 'You are *so* dirty, but I really think I love you, Miss Pussy Kat. You really know what I like, don't you?'

What is it? What is it?

And though he was silent as a ninja behind her, Sandy almost imagined she heard Jay echoing her sentiments.

'Mm, you have such a sumptuous arse, sweetheart,' commented Greg, his hands settling on Kat's rounded cheeks and pulling them this way and that. 'And I can't wait to get my dick inside it.'

Sandy's pussy throbbed spontaneously, and without thought or conscious volition she bore down on Jay's fingers, grinding against him. She could hardly believe what she'd just heard, but anticipating the show ahead made her sex ache and saturate the cloth pressed against it anew.

The young man moved quickly, making his preparations. Pausing only to fondle his lover's bottom and crotch now and again, he unzipped his jeans, exposed his penis and then fished in his back pocket and brought out a packet of condoms.

Greg had a nice cock. A very nice one indeed, and for a moment Sandy wondered what it would be like to sleep with him. She couldn't deny he had all the goodies a girl could want.

But then, behind her were other goodies. Better goodies. A man bigger, more dangerous and far more mysterious than the basically fun-loving – and apparently bottom-loving – Greg. As if to restate her allegiances, she rubbed her own bottom against the rock-hard erection behind her, and was rewarded by a slow hard rub at her clit, and a quick kiss on her neck.

'Right, we need something to oil you up, baby,' announced Greg cheerfully, fondling his rubber-clad penis with one hand and Kat's nether regions with the other. 'Any suggestions?'

'There's some olive oil in the cupboard,' suggested Kat, squirming.

Oh no, not the Extra Virgin! Please use the cheaper stuff!

But Gregg was glancing around the room, and a second later he lit upon the contents of the table and his wicked grin widened. 'Ah ha! Just the thing! If it's good enough for Marlon Brando, it's good enough for me.'

As if her own pleasure, and her own experience, were compartmentalised somehow, Sandy watching in horrified hilarious astonishment as Greg, the outrageous devil, reached for the butter dish. She wanted to get herself off on Jay's hand, drag him somewhere and beg him to fuck her. She wanted to grab hold of him and shake him and make him tell her his secrets. But she simply couldn't stop watching the show unfolding before her.

To a chorus of giggles and groans from Kat, and his own laughter, Greg lavished the Lurpak Spreadable in his lover's anal groove, packing the stuff in and making her jerk and grind against him.

'OK, baby, brace yourself!' he cried cheerfully, positioning himself.

Kat began to growl like a she-wolf as he slowly pressed inside her.

It was the hottest thing Sandy had ever seen, the rawest. More outrageous than anything she could even imagine, there was still a sudden beauty in the rude coupling.

Greg cared. He went steadily. Carefully. Stroking and coaxing Kat and listening to her every moan and breath. He was only doing exactly what she wanted. But after a few circumspect minutes, things got crazy. It was clearly not the first time the couple had done this. They seemed to be old hands. Jammed against the table top, reaching back and grabbing at her paramour's hips and thighs, Kat's eyes suddenly popped, widening and starting as she cried, 'Oh fuck!' She was coming, and Greg wasn't far behind her.

Beneath the hubbub of Kat's groans and shouts and Greg's whoop of triumph, Sandy heard the words, 'Do you want to come?' She shook her head, but it was more in confusion than negation, and in answer Jay flexed his fingers firmly against her, wickedly playing and taunting her, his grip warm against her clit as he bore down on it through her clothing.

Tension. Pressure. Heat. All were almost intolerable, impossible to manage, and still keep quiet. But Sandy contained herself. Just. She wanted to kick, scream, ride Jay's hand just as Kat had ridden Greg's not so long ago. She wanted to come, howling and wailing and flailing her legs.

Yet she didn't. She simply watched. Her body boiling, her bottom pressed hard against Jay's cock, she clutched at his sleeve and the folds of her dress, her fingers gouging and crimping, her knuckles white.

Greg and Kat were chuckling, having the time of their lives. Sandy knew Kat adored her frisky lover, and he adored her right back. There was trust between them, and more, so much more.

Suddenly, an icicle dropped into the cauldron of her own lust.

Could *she* trust Jay? *Should* she trust him?

But the shard of doubt only increased her excitement. Jay was unknown, dangerous and complicated. Intrinsically dark with his wounds and a history she sensed was troubled even beyond the monolithic trauma of being smashed near to death in a high-speed car crash.

He could kill me. He could smash me up in much worse ways than an Aston Martin ever could. He could take control of me. Make me want him. And then just leave.

Still a squirming slave to pleasure, she felt her mind and memory still working feverishly in a small corner of her consciousness. And for the first time in a long time or perhaps ever, a tiny kernel of resentment against Prince Charming began to fester. He'd left her too. Sowed a dream in her mind that had made every relationship since him come up short. Those few moments they'd spent together had meant nothing to him, but to Sandy they'd been the bedrock of all her girlish and later womanish romantic dreams. And her erotic dreams, oh yes. A thousand fantasy moments in which her prince returned and took her lovingly to bed. A dream that would never happen. But now she had a darker prince, casting a long spell, touching her sex.

Releasing the past, she embraced a present full of grit and edge and sweat and danger.

'Jay,' she breathed against his hand, and suddenly, in a silent fury, she arched and came.

6

Jay's cock lurched, stiffening and stiffening again. He'd never felt this hard, and been this sure of it, not even in his life before the crash. It was as if his fears and injuries were a dark dream rapidly dissipating, a poisonous miasma flushed out by the light and warmth of Sandy.

As the woman in his arms arched against him in a spasm of orgasm, he almost staggered, overwhelmed by the sensations pouring through him, and by the clash of past and present, of dream and reality.

The couple jerking and shouting in the kitchen were like a puppet show, a diversion. It was the woman in his arms who kept his cock hard, sure and unfailing. And it was time to act, to seize the moment, and celebrate the miracle of his sudden unstoppable potency.

Snatching her up in a haphazard lift, he hauled her away from the door, and together they stumbled along the landing and up to the next floor with no thought of concealing their presence. Who cared if the other couple heard them? They were too far gone in their own games to investigate anyway.

There was a door on the left, and Jay kicked it open. The thump of his foot rang out and the door panel flew back on its hinges, banging against the wall beyond.

He didn't give a damn.

Luckily he'd discovered a bedroom. His eyes momentarily registered gross untidiness, and almost subconsciously he felt a stab of distaste. In his dreams, Princess had always been dainty, fastidious and immaculate, and even though he knew Sandy was *Sandy*, not a figment of his imagination, the sight of clothes flung across chairs, draped over the end of the bed and on the floor, and a Jackson Pollock scatter of cosmetics, used tissues, empty coffee cups and sweet wrappers covering every surface was a shock.

The bed was unmade too, frowsty and not quite clean.

The old Jay, used to luxury and the finest of everything, would have suggested a move to a cleaner, more sanitary room – if there was one – but the new unstoppable Jay didn't care about anything but fucking, whether it be the woman of his dreams or otherwise.

He set her down hurriedly, almost throwing her onto the far from salubrious bed, and followed her down, shrugging off his jacket and kicking off his shoes as he went. Then, looming over her, almost afraid that the whole crazy incident wasn't real, he kissed her on the mouth for the very first time since their brief encounter fifteen years ago.

Her lips were soft, and tasted faintly of wine as they parted, admitting him. Accepting her invitation, he rolled further across her, thrusting with his tongue as his hands devoured the feel of her just as hungrily, touching and travelling.

Her body felt perfect, a physical match for his fantasies at least. Beneath her thin clothing, Sandy was slender and pliant, yet full of shape. Her breasts were rounded, nipples springing to attention as he fingered them through her dress and what-ever soft underthings she wore beneath it. A gasp of pleasure puffed around his tongue as she responded to the roll of his fingertips around her nipples. First one, then the other. Her hips rolled too, as if she couldn't contain the desire his touch evoked in her.

He moved further across her, throwing a thigh over hers and circling his hips and his aching crotch against hers. His cock leaped when her small hands roved over his back and his thighs, as bold and demanding as his own.

The touch of her fingers, so often fantasised about, was electric. Delicious jolts of sensation sped through his nerves, his blood, his senses, every sublime burst of it surging instantaneously to his groin.

Miraculous, increased hardness. Like stone. Safe. Unfailing. He sent up a prayer of thanks to whatever deity was looking out for him. Thanks for the twist of fate that had brought him here to this woman.

And he had to get into her. Immediately. Now. Not because he feared he might lose his erection, but because he simply couldn't wait to fuck, to savour the sweet slide of her flesh against his, 'Princess' or otherwise.

His cock leaped again when her fingers found his belt, and started to fumble.

It seemed she wanted him just as desperately as he wanted her. It wasn't the 'first fuck' scenario he'd anticipated, but who the hell cared about idealised dream-women in luxurious hotels with immaculate linen and bowers of roses when a real woman on an unmade bed felt so good?

Sandy couldn't breathe. She wanted Jay so much she could barely think.

His weight, his size, the taste of his hard mouth and the heavy thrust of his cock, they all overwhelmed her. Between her legs she felt molten, a silent scream of lust that only he could calm.

Tugging at his belt, she marvelled at her own shamelessness. What he'd done to her in the garden at the Waverley had changed her. She was voracious now, demanding, absolutely sure of her actions and her right to satisfy her needs. She'd never felt sexual confidence like this before. If only this mighty epiphany didn't have to happen on Kat's pit of a bed though!

But desire was unstoppable, and needs must when the devil drove. Expelling all thoughts of what might have happened on these sheets, or worse still, been smeared on them, she wrenched at the elaborately crafted buckle of Jay's belt, grinding herself against him like a randy she-devil as she struggled with it.

'Here, let me,' he growled, his mouth still mashed against hers. The feel of his neat elegant beard was strangely soft against her face, and his big hands dashed her small ones away as quickly and deftly he unfastened himself.

A beautiful big cock sprang into her grasp. Hot, hard flesh, coated in velvety skin, sticky at the tip with oozing pre-come. Her fingers coiled around it as if they'd been created solely for the purpose of caressing him. Restraining her urge to grab and to pump, she slid her grip lightly up and down, up and down.

'Oh yeah ...' His husky damaged voice was rougher than ever, barely focused, almost not forming words at all. His hips seemed to move almost of their own volition, pushing the might of his rampant erection through her fingers.

But it wasn't enough to touch. It wasn't enough to hold. Even as she stroked him, she started pulling at her skirt, and then her knickers, with her other hand.

Dear God, please, please, please let Kat have condoms in her drawer!

Hands joined hers in the rush to get her panties off. Jay pulled as she pulled and, all in a jumble of tugging and touching and hot, hot flesh, they finally divested her of her underwear. Miraculously, she was still holding his cock as her flimsy knickers went sailing away across her friend's bedroom.

'Sandy! Are you OK? What's going on in there?'

The fact that Kat was bursting with laughter as she called out through the door told Sandy in no uncertain terms that her friend knew exactly what was going on. The butter incident was obviously over as quickly as it had begun, and the younger girl, and possibly her paramour, had come to see what the *other* commotion elsewhere in the flat was about. She was also clearly puzzled as to why Sandy wasn't using her own bedroom, but Kat was never one to stand on ceremony where sex was concerned.

'Wh-what do you think's going on? Go away, Kat. Use my room, whatever ...'

Jay's hand, staking a claim to her naked crotch, made her stutter over her words.

More laughter rang out, male and female this time, accompanied by muffled comments and encouragements.

'Okey-dokey! There's a couple of boxes of condoms in the drawer. Dig in, but just leave a few for us, eh?'

'Thanks!'

It came out as a squeak because Jay's thumb was on her clit, pressing hard.

As he began to circle it, it became impossible to concentrate, or coordinate, or even see straight. His cock slipped from her fingers and she grabbed wildly at his body instead, clawing at his back and buttocks, pulling him closer with every ounce of her energy.

He's going to make me come again. He's going to do it. Please God let him fuck me afterwards though.

Between her legs, he worked her, rocking the tiny sensitive crest of flesh without let up or mercy. Half-crazed already, it took barely seconds for Sandy to achieve his objective. She arched against him, limbs jerking, her pussy melting.

But even as she came, she grabbed and scrabbled at him,

wanting more, wanting connection as if her life depended on it. With his hand still squashed between them, she rubbed her pelvis against his, inviting and imploring him to fuck her.

'Please,' she gasped, 'please, please fuck me.'

There was a moment of still, silent shock. Had she really said that? She'd never really talked dirty in bed, always been quiet, taken her cues from her man, responsive but not proactive. But now, with this man, she could do or say anything.

Or was it too much?

As if confirming her fears, Jay eased back a little and looked down at her.

His eyes were an enigma, but she sensed questions, and also surprise. Was he angry? Disappointed? Repulsed by the very hunger he'd aroused? How could she displease him? This was what *he'd* goaded her into, wasn't it?

Well, fuck you, mister! You asked for it, you're getting it. And if it doesn't suit you, I'll find somebody else to get the benefit of the new me!

But when she tried to pull away, he grabbed her shoulder, and plunged down on her for another kiss, hard and savage.

He was asserting himself, she realised, dominating her, imprinting his will on her. The power of his mouth made her lips smart and her jaw ache, but she loved it. Desire peaked again, at higher tide. She felt a wild, silvery, weakening sensation flood through her veins. Not like compliance, not like her easy acceptance of a man leading the way in bed. No, it wasn't that at all. This was more total, a submission to the thrill of him, and the way he could bend her any way he wanted her. It was so easy. And it made sex easy, but also strange and new.

She melted again, coasting towards new pleasure merely on the power of his kiss and the push of his tongue against hers. When he slid his hand down her thigh and pressed, her knees fell apart, surrendering and opening herself to him.

And she just lay like that – a boneless, displayed, available thing – while he roughly wrenched open the drawer and grabbed a condom.

'Cover me,' he commanded in a tight raw voice, hefting his cock in his fingers as if compelling her to worship it.

Sandy needed no encouragement. Suddenly it seemed as if his cock was designed solely for her to adore and service. With swift care, she ripped open the wrapper, teased out the rubber contraceptive and slipped it over his tip.

Jay's eyes closed, and his head twisted to the side. For a moment, she thought she'd been too heavy-handed and hurt him, but then his hips bucked and he pushed forward, urging her to continue.

As she rolled and rolled and rolled, it dawned on her he was the biggest man she'd ever been with, and her pussy trembled as if with glee. Her ex-husband and her few carefully selected boyfriends had all been average, or puny, compared to Jay.

Suddenly, she wanted to see more of him, not just his stupendous cock. She began to pull and tug at his shirt, revealing the white vest he wore beneath it. She tried to push that up, out of the way, so she could see his abs and his chest, but he stopped her with an iron hand and a harshly growled 'No!'

His eyes were furious, dark as rain-laden thunderclouds.

Why was he so reluctant to let her see his body? Then it dawned on her.

Scars.

He had them on his face, but somewhere along the line she'd stopped noticing them, and now saw only his tough male beauty. But maybe they were worse, and more extensive, on his body?

Once again, she felt her will subsiding in the face of his. It was still there, perhaps stronger than ever, but his was greater, it overpowered her. If Jay said 'no', he meant 'no'. She had to concede. It was what he wanted. No arguments.

To her surprise, she experienced no sense of pity for him, and his healed wounds, just the overpowering urge to bow down and kiss his feet and acknowledge his supremacy. Panting, gasping with a new voraciousness she didn't quite understand, she subsided against the mattress and let her legs fall open even wider.

Take it. Push yourself in. It's yours by right.

Their eyes met as he moved over her. Silent messages passed between them that were unquantifiable in words. But she understood ... something ... and wanted more of it.

As Jay's latex-clad cock pressed against her sex, his hard lips curved into the faintest of small wry smiles. For a second, she struggled to divine it, then gave up the fight to do anything other than enjoy the all-consuming sensation of being filled and stretched and fucked.

Again she clung to him, compelled by an inchoate longing to climb inside him even as he pushed inside her. She grabbed onto his shirt and the back of his trousers, using them as leverage to push and push and push herself against him. Her feet hooked around the back of his calves, her body flexing to increase the contact and get as much of him inside her as was humanly possible.

Every sense was as sharp as a pin, yet the moment was dreamlike. She could feel every hard millimetre of his cock inside her, imposing its length and girth on the soft yielding walls of her sex. His weight bore down on her. His scent intoxicated her. The sharp rhythm of his breathing seemed to blend with the beat of her own heart as he thrust into her. And when she opened her eyes again, not quite remembering when she'd closed them, she saw a fugue state on his face that matched her own.

His expression was intense, but also contemplative, and he seemed far away, detached from her, apart. His eyes were closed, his incongruously long black eyelashes resting like arcs of silk against his cheekbones. Even his network of scars had acquired a strange and magical glamour.

The small thinking area of her mind wondered what *he* was thinking. Because she knew that he *was* thinking. Jay Bentley wasn't a man who turned his mind off during sex. Jay Bentley was a man who used his faculties, all the time.

Despite the pleasure, the ever-growing, ever-swelling pleasure as he pounded into her, despite the thumping of their bodies against Kat's less than immaculate mattress, Sandy felt a new plume of antagonism.

I'm here! It's me! Fuck me, *not some fantasy in your head!*

Scrabbling at the back of his trousers, she pushed her hands inside them, and beneath the waistband of his half-pushed-down trunks. Her fingers flexing fiercely, she grabbed at the hard, tensing muscles of his buttocks.

His eyes flew open, flaring with light, as she dug in her nails and flung up her hips in time to the concerted, rhythmic pressure. Laughing, he ploughed her harder.

'Witch!' he hissed.

'Bastard,' she shot back, hysterical laughter of her own bubbling up.

They threw themselves at each other, scrabbling, jerking, battering each other with their bodies. Jay, bigger of course, got the better of it, imposing his strength and his hard-won athleticism upon her. He'd clawed his way back from terrible injuries, that was obvious, but now he was supreme and powerful. More so, she sensed, than he'd ever been. And she was the lucky woman reaping the benefits!

Each long hard lunge of his hips knocked their bodies together. Each knock pressed and tugged on her clit, relentlessly ramping up the pleasure. Still laughing, she growled with lust, yapping like an animal revelling, without conscious thought, in pure sensation.

When the orgasm came she shouted, her loins melting and her heart soaring with a transcendent exhilaration. Dimly aware that her cries would be clearly heard in the rest of the house, if not the next street, she only whooped louder and dug her nails hard into Jay's backside.

Jay let out an oath, blue and profane, his own fingers flexing cruelly and digging into her as his body convulsed too. His pelvis jerked like a hammer and, in the midst of her own chaos, she felt the distinct lurch of his cock, and the heavy pulse of his semen pumping within her. He seemed to thrust on and on as if he'd not come for years.

Afterwards, it was like emerging from the bunker after a twister had passed over. In a moment of pure panic, Sandy thought she'd lost the ability to breathe, until she realised that it was simply Jay's weight lying on her that was hampering her chest and lungs. Bereft of strength, she pushed at him, shoving vaguely, like a Victorian consumptive on the edge of expiring. Luckily he got the message and, heaving himself off her, he rolled over onto his back, at her side.

'Jesus.' He huffed out his breath. 'Jesus,' he repeated, as if his entire vocabulary had been erased in the conflagration.

Typical man ... He's all shagged out and he's almost forgotten there was anyone else involved.

Wallowing in entirely irrational disappointment, Sandy's eyes filled with moisture, but she bit her lip, quashing the autonomic post-coital weepiness. How could she expect anything more of a man she'd only really spoken to for the first time tonight, and fallen into bed with like the easiest of trollops? She was worse than Kat. By a long chalk. Even her friend usually tried to get to know her boyfriends a bit before she dragged them into bed.

I've only got what I deserve.

Continuing to gnaw her lip, she prepared to sit up, but just then a warm hand patted and probed the bed at her side. When it found her hand, it clasped it, held on hard, then lifted their linked fingers.

The tears did come when Jay pressed a sweet and very soft kiss against her knuckles.

'Thank you, Sandy. Thank you.'

Surreptitiously she wiped her face with her other hand, and stole a glance at him. Something in the fractured quality of his rough voice suggested that he might have been crying too. But his face looked composed. In fact, he was smiling. A broad smile, without guile or artifice.

'Er ... my pleasure,' she answered, then found herself laughing again.

It certainly *had* been her pleasure. In fact more of it than she'd probably ever had before in her life, with any man. It hadn't lasted all that long but, boy, had it been *intense*!

Jay kissed the back of her hand again, and flashed her a wink.

'Would you think that I'm a crass, horrible, insensitive philistine of a typical man if I said I was hungry now?' He turned on his side and, giving her fingertips one last kiss, he released her hand. 'That was amazing but, somehow, I'm starving.'

Sandy glanced away, suddenly embarrassed, as he plucked at the condom that still enrobed his wilted cock. But she couldn't help noticing out of the corner of her eye that he was still sizeable when flaccid and, deep in the quick of her, she felt the echo of response.

'No, I'm a bit hungry myself,' she admitted, wondering if he could read the ambiguity, the half-baked double entendre.

But it seemed not, because he was already disposing of the evidence, and fastening his trousers, then his shirt. 'I just hope we can get into the kitchen now. Kat and Greg might have gone back there.' She tweaked down her skirt, wondering exactly where her knickers had got to this time. 'We are in her room, after all.'

Jay was on his feet now, tall, even in his stockinged feet. 'Yeah, I'm sorry about that,' he said conversationally as he cast about for his shoes, then, finding them, slipped them on. 'But . . . well . . .' He turned to her, smiling again, strangely shyly. 'It was important to . . . to get together as soon as we could, you know?' His muscular shoulders lifted in a shrug.

She did sort of know, but somehow she sensed there was more to it. A more compelling drive than lust, pure and simple. There were shadows about Jay, things he hadn't yet told her. Things he might never tell her.

It just depended how long this relationship, or whatever it was they had, lasted.

7

'I'm sorry.'

Sandy's head whipped round, and the spoonful of mayonnaise she was dolloping onto the salad sandwich plopped onto the kitchen counter. She wasn't yet ready to prepare any kind of food on the table, even though she'd gone over it several times with sanitiser spray, and the tablecloth – and the butter dish – were now in the waste bin.

She wasn't used to men apologising, especially when they didn't actually have anything to apologise for.

Had he steamrollered her into sex? Well, no, not really. She'd been with him all the way. Doing things she wanted to.

Had he made her do what *he* wanted? Surrender, submit or whatever? She supposed she could accuse him of that, but what difference did it make if she'd ended up wanting it too? God, she felt too confused and too tired to psychoanalyse that right now.

Mopping up the mess on autopilot, as she did a dozen times a day in the café, she stared at him. He was sitting at the kitchen table, his expression oblique and thoughtful. One of his long hands was resting on the bare scrubbed wood, and with the fingertips of the other he was absent-mindedly tracking the line of one of the scars across the back of it.

He'd been deep in thought since they'd cautiously left Kat's bedroom a little while back, but then, most men fell asleep after sex anyway, so consciousness at least was a plus in Sandy's book.

Creeping to the kitchen, they'd heard a lot of giggling and a suspiciously rhythmic bumping from the direction of the sitting room, and just now, a moment or two later, there'd been more laughing and the sound of stumbling and tussling on the stairs. It seemed that Kat and Greg had reclaimed her bedroom, and Sandy didn't want to think about the younger couple fucking in the sexual miasma of hers and Jay's recent coupling. Too weird, and very icky. But obviously Kat didn't mind, and neither did her seemingly inexhaustible boyfriend.

'What have you got to be sorry about?'

She brought the plate of sandwiches to the table, and then pressed the plunger on the coffee pot. The aromatic smell of the roasted beans revived her, and straight, clear thinking returned to her at last, emerging from the mad events of the night.

God, she was tired though. And it probably showed.

Jay gave her a searching look, and held out his mug for coffee. 'I think I was rougher than I should have been. When we had sex.' He paused and took a sip of the hot brew, making Sandy wonder if the inside of his mouth was fireproof. 'I'm usually a good deal more sophisticated than that.'

Sandy slid into the chair across from him and took a cautious sip from her own coffee. Ah, heaven. Not too hot after all, but strong as rocket fuel. 'I'm OK. Nothing to forgive. I liked it. I would have stopped you if I hadn't.'

Do you think you could have stopped me? Jay's eyes seemed to say.

Could she have done? He was big and strong. But yes, she knew instinctively that he wasn't the kind of man to force himself on a woman. Why would he have to? Even with his scars, he was sexually attractive. Big time.

Jay smiled. A wide warm uncomplicated smile. Suddenly he

looked inordinately pleased with himself, she could tell, despite the apology. He had the air of a conquering hero, triumphant. Almost jubilant. Had fucking her really been that big a deal for him?

'What exactly do you mean by sophisticated?' She took a bite of her sandwich, then another. God, she was hungry! Despite her weariness, her appetite was like a bricklayer's. That was what being fucked senseless in your best friend's bed did for you, she supposed.

'Oh, I like to build up slowly, experiment. Ease into the main meal of sex first, then gradually sample the more exotic delicacies.'

'You mean the type of thing Kat and Greg were doing?'

Sandy shuddered. Staring at the wooden surface in front of her, she was momentarily distracted by the practicalities of being a food provider. God, would she ever feel quite the same way about this table again? Maybe she ought to have it resurfaced? Watching Kat and her naughty boyfriend had been a cataclysmic turn-on, but it was still messing with her scrupulous sense of culinary hygiene.

Jay lifted the top slice of bread on what was left of his sandwich, perused its underside, and waggled his dark eyebrows wickedly. 'Well, I wouldn't say there was much delicacy about that, but I've no doubt it was pleasurable.' His long fingers glided across the bare surface of the table, and he lifted them, studying the tips as if he'd been searching for evidence of buggery.

'I threw the tablecloth away! And the butter dish too! And I've given the entire table about four coats of Dettox!'

'Just teasing.'

Unable to be cross, she smiled back at him, astonished by the way his impish grin seemed to blur his scars and make him look younger and gentler.

Who are you?

The thought sprang into her mind. It had occurred to her before, but not in a serious, concerted way. Now she really wondered. He'd just appeared out of nowhere, a polished cosmopolitan man in a small-town café, and then popped up again at a stodgy municipal cocktail bash where he really had no business at all. Then he'd kissed her sex without offering anything more than the very moment of pleasure.

Why are you here?

The question got stuck in her throat. She *couldn't* ask it, even though she knew she should. There might never be another chance to have wild sex with a mysterious stranger, so why drag it down into the mundane world of practicalities and accountability by probing and ferreting around for explanations and provenance?

'What's the matter?'

He was staring at her intently, as if he was the one with all the questions and she was the mystery. His eyes were harder now, and a pleat of a frown rumpled his brow.

'Nothing. I was just thinking about Kat and Greg.' She glanced across at the new tub of spreadable butter, sitting on the worktop minus a proper dish. 'And, um, what they did. I can't help imagining what it must feel like.'

A complete lie until the very instant she voiced the words. But now her innards clenched, thinking of what she'd seen. What *they'd* seen.

'Why, do you want to try it?'

'No! Well ... yes. Maybe sometime, and not with butter.'

Jay's expression cleared. He looked happy and sleekly mischievous again. 'Well, there are much more aesthetic products available to ease the path.' His eyes glittered like sunlight parking off a ferocious northern sea. 'I think you'll enjoy it. A lot. Once you relax it's an incredible sensation.'

What?

For a moment, Sandy struggled to process his words. What was he telling her? That he'd 'received'? That he was bisexual? He seemed so completely male that she couldn't imagine it. But then, he was also obviously an experimenter, and a daring one.

'Well, a man would. Not sure about the woman, though,' she countered. Would he clarify?

That free, sexy laugh rang out again. She loved the sound of it.

'Oh, I've tried most things in my time . . .' He winked. 'If that's what you're asking. I was a public schoolboy, which is probably self-explanatory, and I've been done by a woman, with a strap-on, once or twice.' He held her gaze, dead level. 'So I do know what it's like to "receive".'

It was Sandy's turn to laugh. More a reflex than anything. Images flashed through her brain, hard to compute.

'I can't believe I'm having this conversation. I only met you a few hours ago and now you're telling me all your kinkiest secrets!'

'I don't keep secrets about my sex life.' He cocked his head on one side, as if assessing her reactions. 'And if I did, who's to say that's the kinkiest one?'

'Christ almighty! I've clearly led a sheltered life.' She sipped her coffee, not really because she wanted to drink it, but more as a reflex action, something to do. What the hell else did Jay get up to in the bedroom, or out of it? 'I've done nothing. I feel like a novice.'

'There's nothing wrong with that.' He shrugged his shoulders, his mouth curving, his eyes challenging. 'It just means you have much to learn, Grasshopper.'

What was he offering? Knowledge? Experience? The key to sexual enlightenment? Whatever it was, it amounted to more than just the usual run of a few dates, then into bed, and maybe a bit of oral for variety. Hell, they'd already skipped stage one and majored in stages two and three, and they'd only met today.

'So does that mean you're offering your services as "Master Po"?'

Jay drank the rest of his coffee, then set down the mug with a decisive 'clop'.

'You could say something like that.' Shoving back his chair, he stood up. The movement of his tall muscular body moved air and almost made Sandy flinch where she sat. 'But no more games tonight, eh, Princess? You're tired. You need your rest.' He glanced at the remnants of the sandwiches on the plate, then reached for a piece of buttered crust and popped it in his mouth. 'And sometimes a sandwich can be just as satisfying if you're hungry.'

Strange man.

'Why do you keep calling me "Princess"?'

Dark shutters seemed to come down behind his eyes, and for a moment she thought he was going to go cool on her again. But, after a micropause, he smiled.

'Just a term of endearment. Why, do you actually prefer "Grasshopper"?'

'"Princess" will do.' Hot blood rushed into Sandy's face, thinking of the garden, when he'd murmured the word while he was between her legs. It still beggared belief what she'd allowed him to do within minutes of their first ever conversation.

He loomed over her in a way that seemed to compel her to stay in her seat.

'So, Princess, how do you want to do this?' His hand settled on the side of her face, almost tenderly, and she could almost believe that they were at the beginning of a normal relationship.

Tentative. Affectionate. 'Do you want to do the courtship dance? Dating? Dinner and all that?' His eyes were almost hard for a second, then he smiled. 'It might be fun.'

'What's the alternative?'

'We go straight for the sex, with no shilly-shallying about.'

It seemed honest, and free of the hypocrisy she'd encountered in previous relationship, but a bit stark and bleak. Lacking in romance. Not that she was a great believer in romance, apart from her secret dreams about Prince Charming. The difference between real life and what she fantasised about with him was a yawning chasm without so much as a footbridge.

'Maybe we could have a bit of both?' she found herself saying. Her body was melting for him all over again, but those softer, more sentimental feelings had suddenly got a grip on her. Damn! Jay was someone just passing through, she acknowledged instinctively, so emotional ties were pretty pointless. 'I don't have much time. The café takes up a lot of my life. But dinner out somewhere else might be nice. And I like to go for walks. We could do a bit of that in between the fucking and stuff maybe?'

'It's a deal, Princess.'

His fingertips moved over her cheek, slowly, like a hypnotist working his patsy. His touch was so gentle, so soothing. Her eyelids drooped suddenly, even though she wanted to stay awake and savour every second with him.

'You really are tired. You need rest.' His rough voice was low, gentle, strangely coaxing. Did he actually have hypnotic powers? It almost seemed that way. 'We'll have other nights. Days too. Do you ever have free ones?'

'The Teapot closes on Wednesday afternoons, and on Sundays.'

'Mm. It's Wednesday tomorrow. I think you should get some

sleep now.' He winked. 'Rest up and gather your strength. I'll drop by for coffee in the morning.'

He bent down and his lips settled on hers, just for a second, and then, while she was still reeling from the delicate sweetness of the contact, he released her and glided away to the door.

'Ciao,' he murmured.

And then he was gone.

Sandy touched her face, where he'd cradled her cheek, and her lips, where he'd kissed her.

Oh hell, that'd felt like courtship. And she'd liked it.

Jay stepped into the shower and raised his face to meet the water. It beat down on his skin, and seemed to wake him from a dream.

He could barely remember anything of the drive back to the Waverley from Kissley, except the fact that he'd speeded – something that he'd rarely done since he'd started driving again – and he'd both enjoyed it and felt at one with the car. As he'd crested bends in the dark, and swung the Aston around sharp unknown corners, a confidence and competence had settled over him like a superhero's cloak, and he'd felt 'right' for the first time since the accident.

The other thing he could remember was his hard-on. It still lingered, and he cupped it in his hand now.

'Thank you, Princess.' He smiled in the cascading water, then opened his mouth and let it stream across his tongue.

His penis stiffened even harder at the thought of her, and he couldn't help laughing. How could this be? He'd come on this wild goose chase to find an imaginary woman, and when he'd made contact with her she wasn't his dream at all. And yet the woman he *had* found had given him back a total belief in his potency. His cock jerked, as if it remembered the way it'd pounded into her.

No faltering. No doubts. Nothing but pleasure, hardness, and delicious fulfilment.

Thanks to Sandy. Who was Princess yet not Princess.

Lathering up a bar of soap, he applied the foam to his hard member and worked his fist up and down it, imagining that the silky enclosure was her sweet body caressing him.

Mm ... that was good. So good ...

He pictured her beautiful hair, and in his fantasy it was wrapped around him, like satin to enhance his pleasure. She seemed to kneel in the water before him, offering the long waves to him, inviting him to bring himself off and shoot his semen amongst the glossy red strands.

He pumped and pumped, loving the slide of his own firm flesh and the fantasy both. Now, she opened her mouth and accepted his cock inside it, the wet heat echoing that of the tumbling water around him.

He thrust, she took it all, doing something crazy with her throat.

He dove in, she opened to him, reaching around to caress his buttocks as he came.

His semen jetted and he gasped, 'Sandy', Princess forgotten.

But afterwards, as he shrugged into his robe, the thoughts that sexual euphoria had expunged now flooded back in again.

Why the insistence on straight dealing and no sexual shilly-shallying about, man?

Pouring a whisky, he considered his own hypocrisy. Was his deeper deception the reason he'd suggested honesty? He laughed, then washed away the bitter taste of it with Glenfiddich.

Just forget the lies, man, forget the conflict. Forget that you're

Jason Bentley Forbes and she hates your father's guts, and probably yours by proxy too. Just enjoy, for a little time. Just enjoy, and make sure that she enjoys too.

There would be time to face the hard truths all too soon.

8

'I don't know what it is really. It's not dating and all that. You know, the sort of meaningful relationship stuff that leads to anything.'

Sandy concentrated on the sugar sachets she was shoving in the holder on the end of the counter where the cutlery and condiments were kept. She'd already ripped one getting it out of the box, and had had to sweep the mess up. Kat was putting some of the freshly delivered bought-in confectionery in the display.

'It's more like the beginnings of a rampant shagathon, I think,' Sandy continued, returning behind the counter and stashing the sugar-sachet box beneath it. 'A bit like you and Greg have. Mostly sex.'

'Hey, me and Greg are meaningful sometimes,' the younger girl observed, unoffended. She gave Sandy a wink as she pushed a plate of cake slices into place. 'It's just that we like a lot of bonking too.' She paused and waggled her plucked eyebrows. 'And experimenting, you know what I mean?'

'I do, and I'm sorry about the "meaningfulness" thing. I didn't mean it like that. I know you and Greg are crazy about each other.' She glanced at Kat in her skimpy vest top and tried not to see the image of the other girl half-naked across the kitchen table. But it was hopeless. She kept on seeing it. Until suddenly her mind substituted herself, and Jay with her, instead of the foxy Greg. Would they do that together soon? And other things?

She felt a sort of anticipatory tightening in her middle at the thought of it.

The two of them worked in companionable silence for a while, preparing the café for opening and then, when it did open, serving customers. Wednesday mornings weren't their busiest, it being a non-market day, but there were still plenty of regulars. People who worked in the various solicitors' offices, building societies, travel agents and banks calling in for early cappuccinos to go. Shoppers and young mums desperate to get out of the house. Older folk who enjoyed being able to sit out front on fine warm days, but who weren't able to get up the steps when it was colder and rainy. All punters who might switch to the new fun coffee pub or whatever it was going to be when it opened. She sighed.

But it wasn't really access problems on her mind today. It was Jay. And the crazy way she'd sort of half-agreed to be involved with him.

Yeah, honesty is good. No pretending it's a romantic silk purse when it's a sexy sow's ear.

That was the way to go. No deceiving each other. Just a no-commitment fling while he was in the area doing whatever it was he was doing in the area. As yet, still undisclosed.

Much better for all concerned, she thought, suddenly finding it necessary to scowl at the flower shop they shared the building with as she brought down a couple of lattés for two of her regulars. The bunches of pink rosebuds in galvanised buckets were pretty, but meaningless in a lot of ways. The sort that guilty boyfriends and husbands bought to make their women think they cared when they probably didn't.

No flowers, just fucking with Jay. Yes, much better that way.

The morning dragged. His fault, she supposed, looking up for the hundredth time when a customer appeared at the top of the stairs. If she hadn't been waiting for him, there would have been the usual Wednesday prospect of a free afternoon to look forward to, but instead it was all tension and wild fluctuations in her adrenaline levels.

'He'll come,' predicted Kat cheerfully on Sandy's return from wiping down outside tables that she'd wiped down five minutes ago.

'Well, if he doesn't, it's no big deal. I'll just chalk him down to experience.' A knot in her mid-section seemed to suggest otherwise, but still she winked at Kat. 'People have one-night stands all the time. So I'm entitled to have at least one in my lifetime, aren't I?'

'That wasn't a one-nighter. He really likes you. That was obvious.' Kat sounded confident, but Sandy's doubts were growing. After all, wasn't the longest 'relationship' in her adult life based on a meeting that'd probably lasted barely more than fifteen minutes? Was she forever doomed to have these intense brief encounters that knackered her up for the rest of her days?

'If you say so.'

'I do say so,' replied Kat, sidling over to the window that overlooked the precinct-cum-marketplace in front of the Town Hall. As the other woman peered out, a wide Cheshire Cat grin appeared on her face. 'Well, speak of the devil!'

Sandy resisted the urge to run across the café and elbow her friend out of the way in order to catch her first Jay-glimpse of the day. For a split second she couldn't even picture his face, and her heart raced in panic. Ridiculously, instead of him, she saw Prince Charming, kind and smiling as he calmed her down, his lips soft and sweet as he'd stolen that fleeting kiss. Jay's lips had been sweet last night, but there was nothing soft about him, and even his kindness had a hard uncompromising edge.

Resist. Don't be too keen. He might look up and see you.

The next moment, she was edging her way into the space at the window beside Kat.

Oh ... oh my God. Did I really fuck him?

Jay was strolling around the precinct with a camera around his neck, taking pictures here and there. He looked perfectly at home in the centre of Kissley, even though he was a stranger. A tall, faintly forbidding, beautifully but casually dressed stranger in jeans and dark summer jacket, black T-shirt beneath it.

And other women were watching him as he snapped a shot of the Town Hall, then the War Memorial, then, strangely, the empty supermarket that was such a bone of contention. One or two of the pushchair mothers forgot their fractious brats for a while and stared his way, nudging each other, pointing from a distance. At that range they probably couldn't see the fine scarring on his face, but Sandy doubted that it would bother them if they could see it. Those stigmata of his accident, and the obviously world-class plastic surgery that had followed it, were a part of his dangerous appeal.

Look all you like! she told the giggling women. *I had him last night. He was inside me. He came inside me. He made me come.*

Something inside her cried, *He's mine!* And immediately she told herself not to be silly. Jay belonged to nobody but himself.

But still, he was magnificent, and she couldn't stop herself scoping out the crotch of his strategically worn jeans and thinking about the big warm cock that nestled inside them. He'd be soft now, but still sizeable. Prepared for action at the slightest encouragement. Just as she was, she realised, aware that just looking at him had made her wet, made her ready.

As he stared at the supermarket building, he pursed his lips and frowned. She wondered what was making him angry. He looked irritated. Vexed. It would be nice to think he was cross on her behalf, but she doubted it. He'd probably forgotten all about her tale of woe once they'd got to the heart of the matter between them.

Sex.

The heat and wetness in her pussy seemed to surge and she caught her breath, wondering how soon it would be before he fucked her again. Or did something else to her.

Noises on the stairs broke into her reverie, and she and Kat turned as one to see a group of workmen who were working on resurfacing a nearby car park trooping into the café. Reluctantly she abandoned the window. One last glance revealed no sign of Jay, however. He'd obviously moved on, probably up one of the several streets that led away from the centre of the town.

The next fifteen minutes or so were fun, in a way. The car-park guys were flirty but good-natured, and Kat was in her element. Sandy couldn't help but laugh at the frisky repartee. They were good customers too, apparently stockpiling soft drinks, cakes and sandwiches to last them the rest of the day.

She was just being propositioned herself, asked when she got off work, when a shudder ran up the entire length of her spine. It was like the sensation of a hard stone being dropped into water, sending ripples over her skin.

There was no need to look around. She just knew.

'Customer for you, Sandy.' Kat nodded towards something over Sandy's shoulder, her face wreathed in smiles.

Sandy turned, surreptitiously wiping her suddenly sweaty palms on her jeans. The sight that greeted her was a shock. She's expected Jay, of course. Sixth, seventh and eighth senses had known it was him. But what she hadn't foreseen was the bunch of roses. For a big hard man, he held them lightly and they looked strangely natural in his grasp. Most guys were nervous and awkward when presenting floral tributes or bribes to the feminine object of their interest, yet Jay didn't seem uneasy or uncomfortable in the slightest as he strode towards her, dwarfing the room in the way the car-park workmen never had.

'I hope you like roses.'

Every eye in the café was riveted upon her and Jay, and there was a wolf whistle from the general direction of the work gang, accompanied by commentary.

'Eh up, flowers! What's he after, luv?'

'Get in there, my son!'

Jay grinned good-naturedly and held out his offering, peace or otherwise.

'Thanks, they're lovely.'

And they were. Just a cheapish bunch from the shop down below, but they were soft velvety blooms in a seductive peachy pink, heavily scented.

'They reminded me of you,' said Jay, as she took them. 'All moist and pink and fragrant.' His eyes dead level, commanding hers, he licked his lips, the action slow, drawn out and lascivious.

Oh, way to be subtle, you swine!

So, not romance at all, just a sexual prompt, reminding her of his mouth between her legs. Not that she needed much reminding. The things he'd done to her and with her had been burning in her imagination and her memory since he'd left. She couldn't stop thinking about them, even if she'd tried. And she hadn't actually tried all that hard anyway.

'I'll put them in water,' she said briskly, trying to get a grip. 'What can I get for you?'

His mouth, the one that had wreaked so much havoc, quirked in an evil smile.

'Besides that,' she added crisply.

'A tall black coffee, please, and something sweet and sticky. Whatever you've got. I'll take pot luck. I'll be over here.' He nodded to a table by the window, the one where she'd watched him from earlier.

Face nearly as pink as the roses, Sandy marched away, flinging over her shoulder, 'Right you are. Kat will bring you a coffee and a jam tart over, while I deal with these.'

Male laughter, from the workmen and from Jay, rumbled through the room as she scuttled off along the little corridor to the cloakroom. There was a flower vase under the sink in the W.C. for café patrons.

The odour of potpourri already filled the little cloakroom, and that coupled with the roses meant the confined space smelt like an old-fashioned nineteen fifties call girl's boudoir. Sandy opened the top window a little way, afraid the heady mix would make her dizzy.

'Flowers! Why did you have to bring flowers?' she muttered, fumbling with the stems and slopping water on the marble counter surrounding the sink. The little room had an intimate ambience and, though she'd never before thought of it as sexy, she did now. Thanks to Jay Bentley, she thought of everything as sexy today.

The roses made her think of writhing on a bed, surrounded by their petals, like in that famous film image. She'd be naked and he'd be working his way up from her toes to the zones he'd visited last night.

The water made her think of being naked in a shower with him, bonking hard against a white-tiled wall, tears of relief and pleasure blending with the torrent streaming down her face.

As she stood in front of the vanity unit, bizarre fantasies floated through her mind. Looking in the mirror, she was a courtesan, preparing for her lover, a mysterious man who'd come from nowhere bringing roses and effortless pleasure with him, and offering no background, no explanations.

'What are you doing in Kissley, you git?' she demanded of the absent Jay as she mopped up the spill with tissues and flung them in the bin. 'I know you're here for me today – at least I hope you are – but I still don't know how you came to be here in the first place. Ouch!'

She'd pricked her finger on a thorn. And deeply at that. She sucked hard at the little wound while she arranged the roses haphazardly with one hand.

Aware that she was hiding, she tried to hurry, and then pricked the same finger again when she started using both hands.

'Fucking botheration!'

At that moment the door swung open and Jay appeared, almost filling the narrow space.

'Can I help? You seem to be having a bit of trouble.' In a smooth sly movement he was in the cloakroom before she could answer, and had quietly back-heeled the door closed behind him.

'It's OK, thanks. I just don't get flowers that often so I'm not a very good arranger.'

'Everything looks beautiful from where I'm standing.'

In the mirror his dark flint-coloured eyes were brilliant as they flitted from her throat, to her breasts, to the delta of her sex in her snug-fitting jeans.

Sandy started laughing. She couldn't help herself. He was so blatant.

Jay laughed too, amused by his own clichés. Reaching around her, he took the rose she was holding and placed it adeptly in the vase, then repositioned a couple of others. The result was perfectly balanced, just the arrangement Sandy had been searching for.

'Is there no end to your talents?' Her voice wavered, had no power in it. Her hands were shaking, and she couldn't have gone on arranging the roses if she'd wanted to. She placed her hands on the counter, convinced she'd fall if she didn't, her knees were so jellified.

'Oh, you don't know the half of them, Princess, believe me.'

Powerful arms came around her, hands rising to her breasts, claiming them, cupping them. In the mirror his lush but hard mouth curved in the frame of his dark beard. He pushed his crotch against the cleft of her buttocks, acquainting her with supreme hardness.

Without thinking, Sandy pushed back against him, massaging the solid knot of his erection. He kneaded her breast in return, his grip firm but sensitive, the way a musician might prise the best from a rare instrument.

'I've been thinking of you all night. Imagining myself fucking you again and again,' he breathed in her ear, pushing her crotch against the hard edge of the counter with his hips. In her cleft, her clitoris jumped as if he'd touched it. 'I must have come half a dozen times, lying in bed, fantasising about being in your cunt, and your mouth. The chambermaids at the Waverley will think I'm a sex maniac.'

'Aren't you one?'

Jay growled in her ear, one hand sliding down from her breast to her groin, insinuating itself between her and the counter and clasping her there. She grunted with sensation as he pressed exactly the right spot to rub the seam of her jeans against her clit.

'I am since I set eyes on you, that's for sure.' He pressed again, rocking his finger and his hips in a syncopated rhythm.

Between her legs her body gathered itself, tensing ready to release, simmering ready to boil over. How could he do this?

Get her going so fast? Right here in this tiny room with its atmosphere thick and cloying with floral scents.

Oh hell, the door wasn't even locked!

'Please, lock the door first!'

A low rough laugh seemed to fill the confined space.

'First before what?' He squeezed harder, lifting her up, forcing her own weight into the intensity of the way he rubbed and worked her through the denim. 'What is it you want, Princess? Tell me. Tell me the words.'

Why did he have such a fondness for making her admit to her desire?

Sandy shook her head. Not in negation, but to try to clear her thinking. The smell of potpourri and roses was like an hallucinogen and the sensations between her legs dissolved her reason. She wanted to come and, if he wouldn't lock the door and assure her privacy, she'd come anyway, even if they might be caught.

She set both hands firmly on the counter and swirled her hips against him. He didn't miss a beat, didn't lose contact with her clit through her jeans.

'Tell me,' he growled, his mouth against her throat, and the next moment he was attacking her with a biting, sucking kiss on the tender skin at the juncture of her neck and her shoulder. The soft tickle of his short neat beard was intoxicating.

'I want to come. I want you inside me. I want you to fuck me.'

'I thought you'd never ask.' His breath seemed to boil against her skin and he pushed again, trapping his own hand between her pelvis and the hard marble of the counter. If it hurt him he gave no indication, he just squeezed her harder.

'I'm not asking. I'm telling,' she hissed at him through gritted teeth. The corridor outside was short. They weren't all that far from the main room of the café.

'Ah yes, I love a woman who knows what she wants and doesn't hold back from demanding it.'

Teetering on the brink of an orgasm, she shot back at him, 'Well, I fucking well demand that you lock that door before you do anything else.'

'Your wish is my command.' Still holding her, he backed to the door and, not letting go of her crotch, he reached behind him with his free hand and flipped the key. Then, before she knew what was going on, and while she watched his swift economical actions in the mirror, he reached around and, using both hands now, unfastened her jeans and pushed them, and her panties inside them, down to her knees.

'There, that's better.'

Leaning against the door, he drew her close to him and grabbed her between her legs again in the same hard uncompromising hold as before. Only this time his fingers slid instantly between her folds and found her clit, unprotected now.

Sandy bit back a groan as he began to manipulate her slowly, but with gusto.

It had been a bit like this in the hallway, when they'd watched Kat and Greg, but now the piquancy was to both feel his rough caress, and simultaneously watch her own reaction.

Her face was bright pink and tendrils of her hair were breaking free from her loosely wound plait. Beneath her white T-shirt and her thin bra her nipples looked as dark and firm as a pair of little hedgerow fruits. Like the blackberries in Kat's delicious home-made crumble.

That idea made her laugh out loud, hysteria bubbling.

'What's so funny, beautiful girl?' breathed Jay in her ear. His face wasn't red but it was intense, almost luminous with a kind of raw desire she'd never seen in a man, even in a situation like this. Correction, when had there ever been a situation like this? But still she'd never seen a man want her quite as much as Jay seemed to do, even when they'd been fucking her.

'Weird thoughts in my head. Just ignore me. Get on with it.'

He laughed again, a low rumble that went right through both their bodies and vibrated in the very centre of her sex. Inclining over her, he pushed her forward against the sink, still stroking her clitoris while at the same time rubbing his hand over her bare bottom in lazy circles.

What are you going to do? Smack me for being a greedy, horny girl?

She couldn't voice it, her throat was tight with lust, but he seemed to hear her. As she looked up to see him in the mirror again, he winked. 'Maybe another time. I think I'd prefer to fuck you right now, if you don't mind?'

'I ... I've no objections.' Sandy let out a stifled squeak as a light, almost accidental orgasm set her pussy quivering. It wasn't quite a proper full climax, more a little hiccup of pleasure, short and sharp, gone again in an instant.

'Good girl. Now why don't you push up your T-shirt and bra and let me get a look at your sweet little breasts?'

'They're not that little!'

'Of course they aren't. They're the perfect size.' As if to illustrate the fact, he rearranged his hands, sliding them both between the edge of counter and her chest, underneath her T-shirt, each to cradle a breast, thumbing her nipples through the lace mesh of one of her second-best bras. She'd decided that if she wore her top-of-the-range stuff, her La Perla, he probably wouldn't have turned up today, but she still wanted her body to look nice for him, if he did, and she got lucky.

She almost laughed again. More weird thoughts whilst being

stroked and fondled and fooled about with by a near stranger.

Obeying him, she straightened up, pushed her T-shirt up in a bunch, and then her bra too, nudging his hands aside to free her breasts. The result was so rude and so racy, she couldn't really look at herself, but Jay's warm hand cupped her chin this time and forced her to face the mirror.

Beneath the bundled fabric of her T and her bra, her breasts and her chest looked pink too, flushed with hungry excitement. She'd never seen her nipples so hard, or felt them that way either. They were so crinkled and erect that it bordered upon pain. But it was a good pain. One that made her gasp when Jay cupped her again and flicked each teat with his thumbs.

'Very nice … very nice …' His mouth was against the side of her neck again, ruffling the errant strands of her hair. He pushed her breasts together and in the mirror he admired the deeper channel of her cleavage that way. 'I'd like to fuck you there sometime. In between your gorgeous breasts, slow and easy, then come on your face.'

It was so crude, so vivid, that Sandy's knees went weak and she would have swayed and maybe fallen but for the press of Jay's body against her back. Her arms and hands were like cotton wool, resting against the counter but unable to support her.

'Not now though. Not now. Right at this moment, I just want to be inside you and make you come again, around my cock.'

With a last slow caressing squeeze, he abandoned her breasts and gently laid her forward over the counter and the sink. The far edge of the porcelain basin was cool against her burning face, and it calmed her. She pressed her cheek against it, resting passively while behind her Jay unzipped and took out his penis, quickly sheathing it in a condom from his back pocket.

'Hey, no sleeping on the job!'

The little tap on her bottom was barely more than a touch, but Sandy shot up in the air as if she'd been goosed by a laser. Her sex flurried, ground zero for the jolt. In the mirror she looked into her own face and met eyes that were wide with shock, and dark, oh so dark, with arousal.

And she wasn't the only one who'd noticed.

'Did you like that?'

Jay's own eyes were just as dark, just as intense with desire. And he was doing that evil-delightful thing with his tongue over his lower lip again.

'I . . . I don't know.' It was the truth, although her body seemed to know the score and she realised she was pressing back, pushing her bottom against Jay's erection and rubbing to and fro. He held her wrists, and swung his own hips, pushing and circling, matching her rhythm. In the mirror, he cocked his head, as if assessing her and reading currents of longing she couldn't articulate.

'I think you do. But you're not quite sure you want it today,' he said, leaning close, his voice low and soft, infinitely wise. 'I think that today you just want what I want. And that's to fuck.'

Her face flamed again. Why did he have this habit of making her into a sex maniac? It'd never happened this way with any other man. Yes, she liked sex, and she wasn't a prude, but she'd never wanted to rush at it as voraciously as she did with Jay Bentley.

'OK! I do. Of course I do! But it's *you* that makes me that way. God, I've never known a man like you for railroading me into sex, or whatever, within moments of us setting eyes on one another.' She paused, gasping, as his latex-clad cock slid up and down the groove of her bottom and the thought of what Kat and Gregg had done last night barrelled into her mind.

Thank God there was no butter here in the cloakroom!

'Are you always this rampant?' she demanded, catching her breath as a slippery stream of her honey slid down the inside of her thigh. That was another thing. No other man had ever made her so spontaneously wet. 'Do you always have a hard-on?'

It was as if Jay had been turned to stone in the blink of an eye. And not just his cock. His entire body was still, tense, almost angry.

'What's wrong? What did I say?'

Sandy tried to turn, to see his face, and its sudden raw pain, directly.

'Nothing. You haven't done anything wrong at all.'

But his face was hidden now, down, buried in the crook of her neck, his cheek pressed against her bare skin. She almost imagined she could feel the faint ridges of his scars, although the thought was unlikely really because they were so very fine and carefully crafted.

'In fact, you've done everything right for me, Sandy. Everything.' He looked up again, his eyes suspiciously shining as if some intense emotion, more than lust, had brought moisture to them. 'And I can't thank you enough, because I'm not entirely sure I deserve what I'm about to get.'

The sheen in his eyes seemed to fade, and his face crinkled into a wicked, wry, worldly wise grin.

'And you're dead sure you're going to get it?' Pertly, she pushed with her bottom again, massaging that fabulous hard intruder that was pushing between her soft folds from behind.

'Oh, I think so.' God, that smile, that smile ... 'Or you wouldn't have let yourself be persuaded so easily into pulling your pants down and showing me your pussy. Or pushing your top up and letting me fondle your delightful breasts.' He cupped a breast, massaging it with precise enthusiasm, while at the same time loosely clasping at the delta of her sex. 'I'd say that's a pretty fair indication of your willingness.'

'Brute!'

'Sex kitten!'

'Pig!'

'Horny little minx!'

Sandy giggled, squirming against him. 'Minx? Since when did men ever call women "minxes" nowadays? I thought that was only in old books, historical novels.'

'Suits you. You *are* a minx.'

Grinning, he switched his approach, reaching beneath her from behind to fit himself neatly into her entrance. Realising she'd have to cooperate, Sandy tilted her hips and eased her thighs apart as best she could within the hobble of her pushed-down jeans and panties, trying to give him more room to manoeuvre.

'That's a good girl. Just a bit more.' Bending his knees, Jay adjusted his angle, gave a little shove, and gained purchase by holding her hip as well as her breast. Then he took her breath away with a long hard push, sliding inside her.

Oh, wow!

She'd never been a size queen. She hadn't really been with all that many men. But Jay was big, and hot, and fabulous. And he held still, in up to the deepest point, owning her with the might of his body.

She was a size queen with him.

'Are you all right, Princess?'

His rough voice was soft and edgy, full of ragged emotion.

'Yes, yes, I am . . .' It was difficult to frame words, she was so focused on her body and how he felt inside her.

'Good.' Pushing again with his hips, he swirled his pelvis, taking her with him, stretching her. She shimmered around him, close to the edge already. Subsiding onto one elbow, she reached around and grasped his denim-clad thigh, his tensing backside through his jeans, wanting to be closer, naked, every inch of her skin against every inch of his that she could reach.

'Touch yourself, Princess, not me. I want you to come. I want you to play with yourself, do what you like to do. For yourself.'

He was gasping, quite far gone, as excited as she was. Even teetering on the precipice of her own orgasm, she wanted to please him. Reaching down, she found her clit, then squeaked with pleasure it was so ready, so sensitive. It barely needed a stroke or two to force the issue and bring down her orgasm from on high. Her pussy clenched at his cock and she fell forward, her head dangling in the sink. Jay made a low broken sound, reached around and gently cupped her head while he started to work her with his hips, in and out, in and out.

Within a few moments he froze, then jerked and pounded harder, his big hand still cradling her forehead to stop her bumping her head against the porcelain bowl.

'Oh, Sandy, Sandy, Sandy ... you're amazing. You're amazing ... Thank you!'

An instant later, with a long sigh, he came inside her.

After all the action, and the grunting and gasping, the silence in the tiny room was like a blanket enclosing them. Sandy could almost hear the sweat drying on her skin, and on Jay's. When she had energy again, she pressed her head against his hand, like a cat seeking affection, and almost purred like one when his fingers curved against the bare skin of her brow, as if he really were stroking and petting a beloved feline.

'Oh Christ.' His voice was ragged, rougher even than normal. 'That was something else, God Almighty ... something else.'

Gently, he raised her up from her collapse, and turned her. His eyes were still stormy in his scarred face, but tender with it. His gaze darted from her eyes to her mouth, searching for something, then he kissed her on the lips in a brief light buss, and smoothed the strands of hair back from her face that were swirling around it. Her ponytail was so loose it was bordering on non-existent, the carelessly looped scrunchie sliding out and freeing the wavy auburn mass.

He heaved a sigh, not sadly, but out of a well of deep thought. Sandy didn't know what to say, her own thoughts were deep too, blurred but disquieting. She had a sense of all safety and security in her life shifting like quicksand, all her expectations and everything she'd assumed and believed, liquefying and sliding sideways.

The door handle rattled once, and the pair of them jumped inches the way you did when you fall in a dream.

'Bloody hell!'

Sandy dragged up her knickers and jeans, or at least tried to. How could such simple uncomplicated garments get so tangled and unmanageable? With his own jeans still open, and his softened penis still poking out in its latex coat, Jay brushed her hands away and effortlessly smoothed her panties up her thighs and into place, patting her crotch possessively as he did so, and giving her a wink. Then he did the same with her jeans, covering her efficiently but with tenderness, before attending to himself and disposing of the condom in several layers of tissue.

Sandy wrinkled her nostrils. 'God, this place smells like a knocking shop!'

Jay chuckled. 'Well, I was going to say a Turkish brothel, but yes, I'm afraid you're right.' He reached up and opened the top light on the small window as wide as it would go, making the lace curtains below it slap and flutter. 'There that's better.' His big chest lifted as he breathed in the fresher air from outside. 'Not that I don't love the way you smell,' he added, turning towards her, looking devilish and hungry all over again, even though presumably he was sated for the time being. 'And taste.'

'Don't do that!'

His tongue ... the way he licked his lips. It made her feel devilish and hungry, especially for the feel of his mouth on her, like last night.

'Look, your coffee will be cold and people will be wondering why you're in the loo so long! Get out there, will you?'

'Yes, ma'am.' He laughed, his hand on the doorknob. 'I better had, hadn't I? I don't want anybody to pinch my sticky bun.'

The expression on his face said he wasn't really thinking about confectionery, but, before Sandy had time to react, he'd flashed her a wink, then slid out of the little cloakroom.

Oh God, what did I just do?

A sensation of shock combined with total exhilaration swept through her. She'd fucked a lovely man in the cloakroom of the Little Teapot. Had she ever even *fantasised* about that? It was bizarre. She'd daydreamed about sexy trysts in various locations, but never really on her home turf, the Teapot. It'd mostly been the usual luxe settings she'd imagined. Hotels like the Waverley, holiday scenarios, Club Tropicana, all that. But never in a tiny little loo, inches from the toilet and hanging over the sink.

In the mirror her face was still pink and her eyes were still bright. She didn't quite look like herself somehow. Maybe she *was* 'Princess'? Maybe she'd been transformed into a princess of hotness, brought to life by a kiss between her legs from the horniest and most perverse Prince Charming she could ever have conjured up?

Whatever it was, even though she was still glowing with satisfaction and her pussy was still quietly simmering, there was no doubt she was going to have to change her knickers before she went back into the café.

'Did I really just *do* that?' she muttered to herself as she closed the door, and ran up the stairs towards the flat.

9

Did I really just do that?

Jay glanced up at the window of the Little Teapot, blinking as the sunlight bounced off the glass. It wasn't the window of the little cloakroom. That was around the back, overlooking the yard, but, even so, his imagination took him back there and recreated the feel of Sandy in his arms.

What had she done to him? He'd gone from being a sexually troubled man, unsure of his ability to perform, to being an insatiable unstoppable horn-dog, purely from the sight and touch and even just the thought of her. Right now, simply imagining her lovely round bottom nestling against his groin, and the hot sweet embrace of her sex around his dick, had him shifting uncomfortably on the wooden bench where he waited for her, and hardening yet again.

She wasn't the woman he'd come to Kissley to meet. She wasn't his dream. But somehow this different woman was the right woman for the moment, she was the one to make him whole again.

Well, at least put right the temporary inability to get it up that he'd had. Not even a raw incredible strangely tender coming together of bodies such as the one he'd just shared with Sandy could rid him of his ever-present aches and pains. Now that the endorphins of orgasm were dissipating, his sore bones gouged at him, but at least the effects were filtered through a satisfied sensual glow.

Stretching on the bench, he monitored each limb, each joint.

He was getting better. Had sex really helped? Who knew, but he wasn't arguing with the therapy.

If only other issues were so pleasantly dealt with. Swivelling around, he glanced towards the old supermarket site. He was going to have to admit to Sandy who he really was sooner or later. If he allowed himself to think about it, deceiving her hurt because, when she discovered it, it would hurt her too, and God knew he didn't want that, regardless of whether she was his dream woman or even . . . Well, he hated to pull the wool over *anyone's* eyes.

He'd tell her soon, he swore to himself. Very soon. But not just yet.

Let me have just a little while longer to enjoy being a man again. A little while longer just having sweet uncomplicated sex with a sweet and deliciously complicated woman.

Then he'd face the music. The truth. The fact that he might lose her as soon as he'd found her.

The pain in his bones felt strangely muted when set against *that* prospect.

Sandy stopped at the top of the stairs, just out of Kat's line of sight. Her heart was pounding. She was afraid, but not quite sure what she was afraid of.

Was it Jay? Or herself? The new, strange, sexually voracious Sandy she'd really only been introduced to for the first time in her life last night.

She'd had to get changed and have what her mum would call a quick 'strip wash', standing in front of the sink upstairs this time, in her own bathroom, unable to stop thinking about what had happened in front of a different sink, not so long ago, downstairs. Every time she looked up from the soapy water she'd expected to see Jay reflected behind her, and when she washed between her legs, mopping away the sweat and musk of their coupling, her sensitised flesh had started to rouse again as if he were the one cautiously cleansing her.

There hadn't been time for much more than the swiftest of ablutions though. He'd said, 'See you in ten minutes,' as he'd set off down the stairs. 'I'll wait outside.'

Bossy bugger, she'd thought, trying to feel feisty and rebellious while some soft melting part of her thrilled, imagining all kinds of domination and power at his hands.

At the bottom of the steps there was a mirror, for patrons to check themselves for whipped cream or tomato sauce on their chins before exiting into the precinct.

'God, woman, you still look like you've just been fucked!' she muttered, tutting at the pink flush in her cheeks and the tell-tale sparks in her eyes. Not to mention her nipples, which seemed to have a life of their own, and were already poking through the lace of her bra and the cotton of her top. She'd changed into a fresh one of each, cream lace beneath and wine-coloured cotton jersey overlaying it, a v-necked button-fronted number that looked good with the long black swirly skirt she was wearing on her bottom half. It was all a bit hippy-dippy and Summer of Love, but they were handy and easy to slip into in a hurry. Especially when she'd spent many precious seconds searching for the bra.

It was a push-you-up-and-show-you-off style, and it seemed important that she wear it not only because it made her boobs look great, but also because it fastened in front.

You've planned for easy access, you trollop!

Her cheeks flamed all the peachier for articulating the God's honest truth.

'Get out there! Don't keep him waiting!' called Kat from upstairs, making Sandy jump. 'You're wasting valuable shagging time!'

'We're going to lunch, Kat!' Sandy swept her hair off her face, then flicked it back. 'No shagging!'

Kat laughed. 'You mean *more* shagging.'

Sandy laughed too. 'Have a nice afternoon, Kat. See you later!'

She opened the door and stepped out into the sunshine, and there he was. Waiting just as he'd told her he would. Why did that surprise her?

The thing was, there was still a bit of her that wondered if this whole 'Jay' interlude was some kind of figment of her imagination. Just as much the fantasy as her Prince had been, long ago, if she was honest. Her rescuer had just been a lad who'd been kind for a few minutes, not some perfect paragon of chivalry rescuing a fair damsel. But Jay on the other hand *was* there, sitting on a bench across the way, as large as life and twice as dangerous.

She'd caught him in a split-second moment, unaware of her, looking strangely tense, his face twisted and tight-lipped. He was lounging with his legs stretched out, his camera case beside him and his jacket flung across the back of the seat, but there was nothing relaxed about the way he sat, the lines of his face and his limbs looked hard.

He's in pain.

It was so obvious. High-speed crashes in Aston Martins weren't without their lingering aftermaths. His face and body had been put back together again, but beneath the surface the consequences tormented him.

Yet when he turned her way, every single trace of those consequences vanished. The smile he gave her was hot and focused. Whatever discomforts he'd been suffering were apparently forgotten, and in his expression and body language she saw only desire now. And when he rose to his feet, he moved quickly, sleekly and with purpose.

'You look fabulous,' he murmured when he reached her, inclining his lips to hers and kissing her as if he hadn't just fucked her, less than an hour ago, over a sink. He'd obviously freshened up briefly in the Teapot cloakroom while she'd been upstairs, because he smelt as clean and cool as ever, with that hint of expensive cologne that drove her crazy. It was only in her mind that he smelt of semen and raw sex.

'Thanks,' she murmured when he released her again, feeling desirable, yes, but already hot and bothered in his presence. His dark eyes drifted down her body and she saw him note the fit of her top, and how her nipples were standing out through the cotton and the lace beneath. Rats, she really should have worn something a bit less obvious in public. Admittedly, she wanted to seduce Jay again as soon as possible, but he wasn't the only man in the street who could see the shape of her breasts, and the distinct way they revealed her desire. In fact the beast laughed as a guy who looked as if he worked in one of the banks, and was out for lunch, nearly did a double-take and ogled her openly.

'And I like your top too,' announced Jay cheerfully, ogling her just as unashamedly. Sandy wondered how he'd react if he knew that she'd left off the panties that went with her push-up bra.

He's turning you into a slut, Sandy. Be careful. If you're too available, he'll probably lose interest.

And that was something she couldn't bear to think about. At least for the moment. When he left, he left, and that was the end of it. But while he was here, she wanted him with her and she wasn't going to do anything to screw that up. Which included not bombarding him with questions either, because he was clearly a man who didn't give much away.

'Where to?'

Slinging the strap of his camera and his jacket over one

shoulder, Jay reached for her hand with his free one. It was such a small familiar possessive little gesture, but it made Sandy feel disorientated and panicky. She didn't know him, and yet her fingers did somehow, recognising his touch on the deepest level, in a way that wasn't just to do with sex. Her breath felt tight in her chest and she suddenly needed a drink even though she rarely touched alcohol during the day.

'Let's try the Fox and Grapes in Bank Street. They do good lunches. This way.' She began walking and he fell into step beside her, his hold on her light as air, yet as unyielding as super-glue.

'Isn't it a bit of a busman's holiday for you, eating somewhere like a pub? Fast food for workers and shoppers, I mean.'

A good point. 'Well, yes, but the difference is I get waited on for a change, and I rather like that.'

Casting a glance sideways at her, Jay's eyes danced and his mouth curved dangerously. 'Oh, I'd like to wait on you too.' He did that tongue-tip thing again, the familiar one that made the pit of her belly clench. 'I'd like to tie you naked to a bed and feed you Champagne truffles while I've got my cock inside you.'

'Jay!'

Even though it was Wednesday, quiet and with no market, there were plenty of people around in the precinct. And a young woman, waiting in front of a shop as they passed, swivelled around sharply at the word 'cock'. Jay smiled and waggled his eyebrows at her and Sandy could have punched him. Especially when the girl smiled back, evidently liking the sound of a tall striking man talking dirty, even when it wasn't to her.

'You'd like that though, wouldn't you?' he persisted as they moved on.

It took a supreme effort not to stumble, even though she

was wearing her own flat shoes today and not Kat's high ones. Her knees went weak at the picture Jay painted.

Bound to a bed, bare and vulnerable, open before him. He'd be kneeling, her pelvis would be lifted. She be impaled on his erection, stretched by it, possessed by it. She could almost feel the sensations, and taste the chocolate on her tongue as he fed her truffles from a box beside them. As the rich unctuous confection melted in her mouth, he'd reach between her legs and delicately finger her aching clit.

'Chocolate should be savoured without distractions,' she shot back pertly, trying to banish the fantasy. Not wearing panties, she could already feel silky slippery moisture sliding down her thigh.

Jay just laughed, then looked ahead. 'Our destination, I believe.' He nodded to their left, towards the pub and tables that stood outside under an awning. 'Inside or out?'

'Inside, I think. Sometimes you get mobbed by pigeons when you eat outside in summer here.'

The Fox and Grapes was an old dark traditional pub, and when they stepped inside it took a moment or two for their eyes to adjust to the low lighting. It was popular though, and Sandy recognised a few folk who ate lunch at the Teapot when it wasn't their early closing, and nodded to them. There were no seats at all available in the main bar.

'Shall we just get a swift half and then drive to the Waverley? The food's good there,' suggested Jay, glancing around.

'No, it's OK, there are always spaces in the back.' Tugging on his hand, Sandy led him into the labyrinthine interior of the pub where there was a small 'snug' as well as a few individual booths accommodating just one table. 'Here!' she said, sliding into the one furthest from the main bar, and settling down on the long padded seat.

'I like it.' Jay's gaze flicked around, along the row of booths separated by oaken partitions and stained-glass windows above, with the pub's legend picked out in vibrant colours. When he glanced back at her, his eyes were hooded and speculative, making Sandy's innards dance again.

What was he thinking? Probably the same as she'd been doing, at first subconsciously, and now in the forefront of her mind.

Surely not?

But ... oh ... yes ...

Lust roiled in the pit of her belly, and she felt the slide of her arousal in her cleft as she adjusted her bottom on the seat, unable to sit still.

Jay caught the small movement, and his eyes narrowed as if the table and her skirt were both transparent and he could see the state of her sex.

'What can I get you?' he asked, his face and his voice superficially dead straight.

A glass of wine and an orgasm.

She nearly said it, too. But at the last minute, she bottled out.

'A glass of White Zinfandel and scampi and chips, please.'

Jay pursed his lips. She could see he wanted to smirk, and she suspected it was as much about the girly wine choice as an awareness of what she'd almost asked for.

'OK, so I like sweet pink wine. It's not a crime.'

'I never said it was, Princess. And you can have whatever you want as far as I'm concerned.' The way he let the grin out now said that he was fully aware of her unspoken request too, and might well satisfy it sooner rather than later. 'Right, I'll be back in a jiffy.'

Sandy looked this way and that, pretending to herself that she wasn't checking out whether or not people could see them in their little hideaway. She tried to quash the dangerous thoughts, but it was impossible. Every cell in her body seemed to be vibrating with excitement and anticipation.

Jay returned in a few minutes with drinks and a little white printed ticket for their food. As he slid in beside her, pushing a large glass of wine across the stained surface of the table towards her, she frowned at his own choice of beverage. It was a tall glass of totally clear fluid, crammed with ice and adorned with a slice of lemon.

Gin and tonic? No, it didn't have the oily swirly look of gin. It was water, she realised, still water, plain and pure. Don't drink and drive, she thought. Very sensible. But last night he'd had Champagne and not thought twice about getting into the Aston.

'Cheers,' she said, clinking her glass to his as he lifted it. 'Here's to, um, distractions.'

'Exactly,' said Jay with emphasis, watching her mouth over the rim of his glass as he drank himself.

The Zinfandel was sweet and light, easy to drink. She felt like throwing the lot down her neck and asking for another immediately. The sensation of recklessness was like being on a merry-go-round, and she wanted the ride to go faster and faster and faster.

But when Jay set his glass down, he reached into the pocket of his jacket that he'd set beside him on the bench and drew out a foil blister pack of tablets. Offering no explanation, he popped two and swallowed them quickly with more water.

Painkillers, she thought. She'd been right about the tension in him, something that even with what she suspected were consummate acting skills he'd been unable to hide.

'Is it from the accident? Is it bad?'

Damn, hadn't she just decided she wouldn't pry! She hadn't meant to speak, but it seemed curiosity and concern had more power over her vocal cords than her sense of discretion had.

Jay gave her a long look, and she watched a battle in him too. Macho pride and being the 'big man who didn't give into pain' at odds with an innate honesty and the simple response to sympathy.

'It's not good. Well, not just now.' He drank more water, set the glass down again. 'But don't worry. It's getting better all the time, with every week that passes.'

Sandy didn't quite know what to say, but she sensed that, even though Jay had admitted his 'weakness', he didn't want to dwell on it too long.

'But you could say that's why I'm so fond of "distractions", Sandy,' he went on, leaning back in his seat, looking more relaxed now. Whatever he'd taken, they must be wonder pills, because his grey eyes were brightening in a way that was rapidly becoming familiar to her.

'Like sex?'

He grinned, shaking his head as if despairing of an incorrigible child.

'Yeah, like sex.'

'So I suppose you could really do with something like sex right this minute . . . to help the pills work?'

Jay's face lit with admiration. 'You're an amazing girl, Sandy, you really are. I don't know what I've done to deserve you. In fact I haven't done anything worthy of reward at all. But right now, you're like a gift from heaven. You know that, don't you?'

She wasn't sure what he meant. It was hard to think straight at all. In close proximity to him, in their concealed little nook, she was turning into a mass of hormones and silky fluids, pumping and wanting. She wanted to touch him. And not just his strong thighs, or his big cock inside his jeans. She wanted to touch all of him, see all of him. Stroke her fingers over his face and feel the brush of his dark beard, the tracery of his scars.

She wanted to study his body and see its magnificence, and also the ravages wrought upon it by mangled metal.

And she wanted him to touch her. Where it mattered.

Slowly, she slid closer to him along the bench, until their bodies were in contact through their clothes. Staring into his stormy-sea eyes all the time, she slid her hands under the table and plucked at her skirt, inching and inching it up at the side closest to him, until the hem was against her hip there, even though the fullness of fabric was still trailing at the other side and covering most of her legs. Reaching for his hand beneath the table, she placed it on the bare skin of her thigh. His fingertips felt cool, but only, she supposed, because her own skin was so hot.

He stared back at her, his face composed, his smile slight and mild as if nothing were happening. But his clever hand followed her lead, taking over control. His fingers walked up and up and up, and the corners of his mouth twitched a little. When he reached the side of her hip, he bit his lip and rolled his eyes.

'Now that's what I call a distraction.'

His hand flattened, sliding across her belly, little finger skirting the edge of her bush, then dipping in and tangling. It hugged the gentle curve, still for a moment, then started moving downwards, searching, exploring.

He leaned in close and kissed the side of her neck, next to her ear. 'Ease your skirt up at the back. Pull it out from under you. I want your bare bottom pressed against the seat while I touch you.'

Sandy swayed, slumped against the seatback, suddenly overwhelmed by the rudeness of the idea, the sense of exposure. She'd wanted this game – why ever else would she have come out without knickers? – but the reality almost gave her palpitations.

'You're not afraid, are you?' His mouth opened against her skin, his tongue stroking her in a way that suggested other stroking, other wetness. Then that contact was gone, and he pressed his head against the side of her face in a strange, fondling, almost feline gesture. It was as if he was the cat now, not her, and the rub of his tightly shaven scalp was like fur too, like soft fine suede.

When he looked up again, his eyes were full of fire. Hard. Compelling. She couldn't defy him. She didn't want to. She began surreptitiously tugging her skirt from under her, as per his instructions. His expression softened, became more playful and amused.

She wondered if his pain had gone, or whether he was just sufficiently distracted by her lack of knickers to be able to ignore it.

There was a lot of fabric in her long swirly skirt, and it took some tweaking and shuffling and wiggling about to get all of it out from under her. Sandy kept looking towards the bar, afraid that at any minute the waitress would come with their food and immediately suss out what she was doing. After all, these nooks might have been designed expressly for the purpose of sexual shenanigans.

But it was the pub's busiest time, and as yet there was no sign of the scampi.

Eventually, the skirt was up, and discreetly arranged so that not even if some passer-by climbed under the table for a look would they get an eyeful of something they shouldn't see. The sensation of the rough upholstery against her bare bottom was weird, and disquieting. She wondered how many naked behinds had sat on this same seat before her, playing games. The idea made her wriggle again, involuntarily, and Jay's eyes narrowed.

'Good girl,' he whispered, reaching for his glass with his left hand. It seemed that the devil was ambidextrous, because his other was already going walkabout. 'Now drink your wine. It'll relax you. You've had a trying morning.'

It was a good job she hadn't actually picked up her Zinfandel yet, because she would have choked. And not just at Jay's quaint idea of a trying morning. His fingers were already playing in the cleft of her sex.

She reached for her glass. His forefinger slid up and down, alongside her clit.

She put the wine to her lips. He circled the entrance to her vagina, delicately skirting around with the pad of his fingertip.

She took a tiny sip of wine, and he entered her just a little, just half of the first joint of his forefinger.

When she jerked, and made to put the glass down again, he went, 'Uh oh!' and shook his head, sliding the finger out again and brushing her perineum.

The wine was delicious, such easy drinking, but it seemed bizarre and vaguely obscene to be sipping away at it while she was being played with. It was as if her brain was short-circuiting all the time, unable to compute the two different kinds of stimuli simultaneously. Sweat popped out all over her body, and she could feel heat rising in her face as it trickled and pooled between her breasts and in her armpits. She took a deeper drink, and Jay took her clitoris between his finger and thumb and tugged it.

The glass shook and the wine nearly spilt.

'Careful,' he admonished, still tweaking, manipulating.

'I ... I can't ...'

'Yes, you can.'

She put the wine to her lips, swallowed. Despite its sweetness, a moan bubbled in her throat as he squeezed and stroked, squeezed and stroked, squeezed and stroked. Tears formed in her eyes, not because she was upset or distressed, but just because the rush of strange contrary sensations was close to overload.

'Please,' she muttered incoherently, setting the glass down regardless. It was like being in a match or tourney of some kind, requesting a time out. Immediately Jay withdrew his hand, giving her crotch one last friendly little pat.

'Didn't you like that?' He sounded gentle and concerned, the way he might have done if they'd just tried a ride at the fairground, or a new sport. Maybe it was a sport? If not that, it was definitely a game. Sandy plucked up the glass again and drank nearly all of it in one gulp.

'I don't know. It was weird. I'm not used to doing – feeling – the two things at once.' She twirled the glass's stem in her fingers, trying to quantify the experience. 'I didn't not like it, it was just unusual. A bit intense.'

'Intense is good,' said Jay steadily, swirling his water in its tumbler. 'Intense reminds you you're alive, stretches your senses. A girl like you deserves "intense", no half measures.'

Sandy stared at him, amazed and a little shocked. He'd hit on a nerve somehow. She realised that she'd never really done 'intense', at least not sexually, until he'd kissed her between her legs last night at the Waverley. She'd enjoyed sex, yes, but never felt swept away by it, even during orgasm. But with Jay, she was riding a riptide. All the time.

He sat beside her, sipping his water and looking at her over the rim of the glass, yet it still felt as if his fingers were touching her sex. The impression they'd left on her was indelible. When he'd gone, would she ever forget the feel of him?

'Here you are, sorry you've had to wait.'

The barmaid's voice sounded as if it was coming from another dimension, and Sandy blinked hard, trying to focus, smile and thank the girl, whom she knew quite well. While she fussed with the plates and cutlery and condiments Barbara had set before them, Jay ordered more wine for her, a half bottle this time.

'You'll get me tipsy,' she admonished when the other girl walked away.

'No, just more relaxed.' Jay grinned, reached for a chip and popped it in his mouth. Then, slowly, very intently, he sucked his fingers.

Sandy's sex clenched. It wasn't the grease he was tasting, but her own flavour, lingering.

He laughed and she scowled at him, more excited by what he'd just done than she dare admit.

They ate in silence for a while, and Sandy couldn't believe how hungry she was. Jay seemed less so, and he picked at his food while she devoured everything. When Barbara had brought the wine, and gone again, he leaned towards Sandy and said, 'I want to touch you again. Desperately. Right now.'

Sandy started to fill her glass, but her hand shook so violently that Jay had to take over. He managed it smoothly, without spilling a single drop. As she put it to her lips, sucking greedily at the sweet wine, his hand inveigled its way amongst the ruffled fabric of her skirt, moving unerringly to the delta of her sex.

'Oh, you're so wet. I love that. I love that you're so juicy and so ready. So horny.'

Sandy drained half the wine in one swallow, then set the glass down. It wasn't that she didn't want to do the drinking and being fingered at the same time thing again. No, it was just that she didn't think she'd physically be able to hold onto the glass. Not when Jay's fingertip immediately started circling her clit in a way that couldn't have been more perfect for her if she'd given him written instructions of her preferences, chapter and verse.

Her own hands flopped onto the seat, as if she'd lost the use of them. She could feel the firm muscular line of Jay's thigh where her fingers lay against it, but she didn't seem to have the strength or the dexterity to actively touch him.

Stroking, stroking. Circling, circling. It went on and on, and she felt herself perspiring again as the sense of tension and the need to come gathered and gathered. The underband of her bra was wet through, and she imagined sweatstains on the underarms of her top, but she didn't care. Stirred by Jay's hand, her crotch was a pond, and she was convinced the seat beneath her was saturated and fragrant with her juices.

And he was a devil. An evil beast of taunting and teasing, attack and retreat. Every time she felt orgasm gathering, and she began to pant and shift on the bench, he eased back and played delicately around her folds instead of touching her clitoris directly. Sometimes he just inserted a finger into her again, showing astonishing flexibility in his wrist considering the awkwardness of position and angle, and just left it there, quite still, while he took a tiny sip of water.

'I don't think I can take much more of this!' she gasped eventually, grabbing for her glass regardless of the fact she was convinced she'd spill its contents if Jay moved as much as a muscle. The wine was sweet and flowery in her mouth, a bit too warm now, but she didn't care, sucking it down as if her life depended on it. 'Please, I can't, I just can't ...'

Why couldn't she ask for what she wanted? Jay clearly wanted her to ask. His eyes were narrow and playful, long lashes like black fans sweeping down, slow and teasingly.

'I'll give you what you want, if you ask for it.' He sipped again at his water, then set the glass down as if he might need both hands when she succumbed to him. *When* ...

Sandy didn't know whether to laugh, or get angry. Her feelings were all over the place. She could have done both, easily.

She wanted to be controlled, but she didn't. It didn't make sense, but she couldn't wait to come any longer.

'Fuck you, Jay Bentley, I'll take what I want!'

As if the current powering her body was switched on all of a sudden, her inert hands sprang into action. Beneath the table she rummaged amongst her skirt, knocked away Jay's hand, and replaced it with her own. With her free hand, she held his wrist so he couldn't touch her. Of course, with strength like his, he could easily have reversed the situation, but he didn't. He only watched her face, his own like fire, as she began to rub herself.

It was rough and greedy and inaccurate, but still effective. He'd turned her on so much it took but seconds to come to orgasm. As her pussy lurched and clenched at emptiness, and hot waves of pleasure washed her pelvis and her belly, she dug her nails hard into Jay's hand and gritted her teeth, biting down on the urge to cry out, maybe moan his name.

Even as she came, she knew she was hurting him. Her nails were short, as befitted someone involved in food prep, but they were strong and hard and she'd always had a good grip. Swirling her hips, rocking against her own hand, she was minutely aware of the way her nails dug into his, perhaps breaking the skin.

But he didn't make a sound, or move a muscle.

Except to smile.

10

'But what about you?'

They were walking towards the place where Jay had parked the Aston. In the car park at the back of the Town Hall, apparently, although Sandy had no idea how he'd wangled that. He'd simply murmured something about a petrol-head he'd met at the Waverley who'd given him a pass to leave the car in the secure area there, not wanting such a fine piece of automotive artistry to be at risk from a casual prang, parked at the roadside.

But for the moment, Sandy wasn't bothered about the beautiful supercar. She was more concerned about Jay's equipment rather than his wheels. She'd come in the Fox and Grapes – twice – and he hadn't once.

It was difficult to glance at his groin without being obvious, but she knew he'd sported a hard-on in the pub because, as she'd sat gasping after her own bit of executive action, he'd grabbed her limp hand and pressed it to his groin, and the rampant hardness there. She'd tried to cup him, to rub him too, but he'd put her aside. Very gently, but very firmly.

'What about you?' she repeated, snatching another tiny reconnoitre out of the corner of her eye as Jay disarmed the Aston's security system. He'd got his jacket on now though, which obscured her view. Good job really, come to think of it. She somehow didn't think it would bother Jay very much at all, but she'd have been pink-faced with embarrassment walking across the precinct in daylight beside a man sporting an erection as impressive as his was in his snug-fitting jeans.

'Don't worry about me,' he said easily, opening the door for her and watching her thighs as she negotiated her way into the low body-hugging seat. Despite the volume of her skirt, she was still acutely conscious of her lack of underwear, and the playful draughts that tickled her damp sex-lips as the lightweight black fabric rode up.

'But ... well ... don't you need to come?' she demanded as he slid into the car beside her. Whatever those pills he'd taken were, he at least appeared to be pain-free now, and moved lithely. She wondered for a moment if she should worry about his ability to drive under their influence, then decided not to. At least he'd stuck to water in the pub. As he flung his jacket onto the parcel shelf and stowed his camera behind his seat, she noticed that he still looked pretty hard.

'All in good time.' He fastened his seat belt. 'Unless you'd like to do the honours before we set off?' His teasing eyes lit upon her lips, then his own groin.

Still a little floaty from wine, Sandy let out a little breath, her mouth watering. She'd never been enormously crazy about giving blow jobs, but right now she would have loved to do it. Loved to explore that splendid cock, which had pleasured her so thoroughly, with her tongue. What would he taste like? How hot would he be? Would she be able to get much of him in her mouth? God, he was big.

Her fingers moved of their own volition, but, as they settled on Jay's thigh, he laughed. And when she looked up at him, annoyed that he seemed to be making fun of her, he nodded across the car park to where a little group of office workers from the Town Hall were eating sandwiches and drinking bottled water in a small pocket of garden adjacent to the tarmac. Quite a few were staring in her direction, obviously rabidly curious about the couple who'd just got into James Bond's car.

'Jesus Christ, I nearly did it!' she snapped at him, then burst out laughing as he laughed too. 'You're a terrible influence on me, Mr Bentley. I hardly know you and yet you bamboozle me into letting you feel me up in a pub ... Where they *know* me, I might add. And then you get me so tipsy that I nearly give you a blow job in a public car park!'

'Is it only the wine?' He gave her a crestfallen little-boy pout, which looked bizarrely attractive and at the same time utterly weird coupled with his hard-bitten battle-scarred features. 'I thought it was my sparkling personality and my pretty face that'd won you over.'

The wine had helped, but no, it was him, mostly him, that made her act – and feel – so out of control. There was still a little bit of her that wanted to touch him right here in the car park, even if not taste him. Her fingers itched. She could feel all the nerves and muscles in her hands priming themselves to make a cradling cupping action around his denim-clad crotch area. To hold him, to feel the heat of him through his clothing was like an obsession she seemed to have had for a thousand years.

And his laughing eyes told her he understood every goddamn thing she was feeling.

'Look! Drive, will you!' She clipped her belt, concentrating on a different set of small accurate motions of her fingers. 'Let's get out of here before you make me do something else I could well get arrested for!'

She gave him a fierce look, even though her lips were still twitching to share in his laughter.

They drove for a little while. Kissley was just a small town, and to the north of it, in the opposite direction from the civic hub of the borough, England's green and pleasant was on hand to be enjoyed.

Not that Sandy was quite in the mood for appreciating the glories of nature. Jay was quiet, and seemed to be focused on his driving, even though he kept their speed modest. It was as if he was either deep in thought, or challenging her with silence.

For her part, it was hard to know what to say to him. What did you say to a man who really only seemed to communicate via sex? A dozen times questions about his background, his family, his reasons for being in the area rose to her lips. A dozen times she looked at his hard face and, even though she knew she was being stupid for not asking the questions, she still couldn't. It was as if something unusual, and special, that might never come her way again, would be fractured by who, why and how.

Instead, she kept glancing at his groin.

His erection had subsided a bit, but still it tempted her. She harboured little fantasy scenarios of reaching over and unzipping him, and tasting his cock as he drove. But then, he'd already had one major smash-up driving an Aston Martin, and she didn't want him to have another. Not because she was a prize-winning giver of blow jobs, but perhaps because she wasn't actually all *that* experienced at it and might make a clumsy mess of it.

'What are you looking at, Sandy?'

Oops, she didn't think she'd been so obvious. Jay's attention hadn't been 100% on the road after all then.

'I was just looking at your jeans,' she lied, knowing it was a pitiful fib and he'd see right through it. 'They're very nice. Are they designer?'

'Armani.' He was playing along. Not quite laughing, but not far off.

'Cool.'

'Glad you think so.'

'I guess you've got loads of money then. Designer clobber, flash cars, good hotels and all that.'

Oh, why the fuck did I say that? So much for not asking questions.

'Yes, I've got money. Is that a problem? Would you prefer I was poor, but honest? The salt of the earth, toiling for a crust?'

He didn't sound angry, but she sensed he was testing her.

'Nope, nothing wrong with money in my book. Although I'm not totally hung up on it, of course.' She glanced at him, but he was completely unreadable now, his face almost mask-like. Without animation, the scars were a lot more noticeable. 'I could do with a little bit more of it though. If I could afford different premises with better access, I could move my business and stand a better chance of surviving the onslaught of a bloody Forbes fun pub.'

He frowned. 'What, you mean you'd move the Little Teapot lock stock and barrel? Don't you have a sentimental attachment to where it is now?'

'No, not really. When my gran originally ran the café, it wasn't even in Kissley, it was in another village, the next one along, Otterley.' She stared out of the window, wondering how to explain something she didn't quite understand herself. 'No, it's the "soul" of the café that's important to me. The Little Teapot is a state of mind, as much as bricks and mortar.'

There was a moment of silence. Sandy half expected him to laugh. But instead he said, in a quiet matter-of-fact voice, 'Yes, I get that.' When she looked at him he was frowning again, his face hard and tense as if he were processing some unpleasant fact. Maybe he was? Maybe he had problems of his own, something of which her predicament over the café reminded him?

She couldn't begin to work out what, but who needed to go down the route of fretting and worrying again? Better to face problems when they arose and all that, blah, blah, blah.

She didn't want to see that hard look on his face. She wanted the sexy twinkle, the teasing luscious little smile. Desire in his eyes. She wanted to look down and see the hard-on he'd had before.

'Let's not talk about the Teapot and fun pub and all that stuff this afternoon. It's aggravating and it's boring and I try not to do aggravating and boring on my afternoon off.'

He flicked a glance at her, his fingers light on the wheel. His tension visibly dissipated, and Sandy almost imagined she could see it seeping away, evaporating like an unpleasant miasma. His tongue did that sweet little sweep over his lower lip that turned her innards to honey. It was his 'tell'. His sex tell. Did he know that? Probably. She'd put good money on the fact he did it on purpose.

'So what shall we talk about?' He didn't look at her this time, but he was smiling as he watched the road ahead. They were skimming along with farmers' fields on both sides now, skirted by hedgerows and small copses. The lane they followed branched into smaller ones, unsurfaced, some that looked well used, and others obviously leading to nowhere. The sun was soft in the sky, the atmosphere hazed and drowsy, lying heavily on the skin, even with the swirling breeze from the open windows and the swift passage of the car. 'How about sex then? Shall we discuss that?' Jay appended with a chuckle.

'Oh, that again.'

She wanted to, though. And she wanted to do more than talk. She could barely believe her own horniness, her own body. And she couldn't even blame it on the wine she'd drunk, because she'd been stone-cold sober when he'd come to the café.

'We don't have to,' responded Jay, almost airily. 'I can quote poetry to you and we can waft hand in hand through that meadow over there.' He nodded his head to a big field at the left, with a long slightly winding lane bordering it on one side. Without consulting her, he eased the Aston to a stop at the entrance to the lane, which was little more than a wide track dividing a field from a little wood with overgrown scraggly hedges at either side. Despite its unpaved status, and being out in the middle of nowhere and leading to God alone knew where, the lane was surprisingly well marked.

Sandy blinked, suddenly realising where they were. With a little snort of laughter, she said, 'Well, if we wander through that field, we're likely to get an audience. And they'll probably expect a bit more than wafting and a poetry recital!'

'How do you mean?' He turned towards her, looking interested.

'Well, that's "Adultery Alley".' She nodded towards the lane winding away from them. In the distance, where it widened beside a gate, she could see a car parked. 'It's a notorious local haunt of doggers, bit-on-the-side merchants and general all-round shaggers. There's almost always someone there having a bit of fun in their car.'

Jay's grin widened. 'And how would you know this?'

Good question.

She'd come here once with her ex, in the first fine flush of their relationship, when even he'd been a bit frisky. But he hadn't liked it, and the moment an interested party had driven up behind them, presumably with the intention of watching, or inviting them to watch, he'd started the car and protested a television programme he'd forgotten about.

Sandy could still remember her disappointment, both in him, and at being denied something she hadn't even realised she wanted.

'Oh, it's common knowledge, and Kat and Greg come here all the time, even though they've got plenty of other places to get it on.'

The way Jay's fine dark brows rose told her he knew she wasn't telling the whole story. He didn't have to speak.

'OK! Yes! I came here once, ages ago. But nothing ever happened. The guy I was with bottled out. Turned out he wasn't as kinky as he thought he was. Or I wasn't quite exciting enough.'

'He sounds like a moron.'

'He was my ex-husband.'

'Uh-oh.'

'Another aggravating and boring thing I don't want to talk about.' She tossed her head, her hair flying, shaking away her past. 'So, are we staying here or driving on?'

'Oh, let's stay.' It was tantamount to a purr. This was not a man to bottle out. She could barely imagine the things he might have done in his past. 'I've never "dogged" as such, but I've watched and been watched in my time.' He reached into the glove box and took out a pair of shades, classic standard Wayfarers. 'Shall I pull a bit further into the lane? Then maybe we could get out for a walk, stretch our legs, see what we encounter?' He slipped on the sunglasses, rendering him inscrutable.

'OK.'

Once out of the car, she fished in her bag for her own sunglasses. They weren't designer, just good old Boots, but they did the job. Or sort of. She was well known in Kissley, what with the café and her long red hair, but at least with shades on someone couldn't catch your eye.

'Isn't it a bit risky leaving a car like this in a lane?' The Aston looked completely out of place, halfway into a hedgerow. As completely unexpected as encountering James Bond himself here.

'It'll be fine. The security system is second to none. Come along, I'm feeling curious.'

He took her hand, leading her along the lane as if he might indeed start spouting poetry. Sandy was curious too, about when Jay might have been watched before.

'So, when did it happen, this watching? Voyeurism, and – um – exhibitionism?'

He was opaque. Shaded eyes and expression both, despite his slight smile.

'Oh, certain élite parties. Exclusive resorts. Country weekends. Gatherings of like-minded people. I've experimented.'

'Yeah, you said so.'

'And you also said you wanted to experiment too, so come along.' His hand tightened around hers and he upped his pace a little.

Sandy's heart began to thud, and the fact that she was wearing no knickers suddenly seemed much more apparent. There was no wind, but it felt as if a breeze was tickling her pussy.

In the back of the Ford parked about a hundred yards from where they'd left the Aston, a couple were going at it. As they approached, Sandy couldn't see much except the head, shoulders and upper back of a man, jerking, and female legs sticking up braced against the door jamb and the upholstery of one of the front seats. It wasn't a pretty sight but, judging by the shouts and moans and the choice obscenities faintly audible from the interior of the car, the enthusiastic couple weren't too concerned about the niceties of aesthetics.

When Sandy and Jay were just feet away, the man glanced over his shoulder, as if he'd sensed them. And then immediately redoubled his efforts, thrusting harder. When he threw back his head and shouted, 'Fuck! Fuck! Fuck!' it was obvious he was coming.

Even as the animated performance in the car shuddered to a halt, Sandy felt the tug of Jay's hand and she followed him onwards down the lane by silent mutual consent. She didn't particularly want to get involved, and if they kept moving it maintained at least some sort of pretence that they were simply a couple of friends out for a stroll. A flimsy one, but still.

Around a little bend in the lane though, where an old step stile gave access to the adjoining meadow, they did stop. The low sweeping bows of an old tree now hid them completely from the distant road. Still clasping her fingers in his, Jay pulled off his shades with his free hand and tucked them in the neck of his T-shirt. His eyes were alight with mischief and desire.

When Sandy glanced down at his crotch, his cock was bulging in his jeans.

'Crikey, it doesn't take much to get *you* going!'

Jay laughed suddenly, a harsh noise, almost a bark. He shook his head. 'No, it doesn't, does it?' He smiled, looking down at himself. Sandy could have sworn there was surprise and a sense of wonder in his face. It wasn't the usual smug pride of a man in his own equipment, but more a genuine astonishment at his own condition.

I wonder why he's so surprised he's got the horn? Is it because he's not used to being with girls so ordinary?

Sandy frowned, annoyed with herself for thinking that, yet, even so, with a Bond car he must be used to women of the Bond calibre too.

But why be so negative? He was here, now, with her, not some polished 'It' girl. Seize the day, or whatever. She stared at his crotch.

'What do you want to do about that?' It was difficult not to just reach out and cup him. And the urge spiralled when he reached down to cradle himself, looking for all the world as if he still didn't quite believe his own rampancy. The sight of him fondling himself made her breathless, her heart go light and pitter-pat. Her own sex stirred as if silently offering to receive him and she wished that he'd pull her hand towards him and press it against himself.

'What do you suggest?' He looked her straight in the eye, still holding himself, his thumb gliding over the stretched denim.

'I, um, I could ...' Ridiculously, she couldn't say it, even if she desperately wanted to do it.

His eyes glittered, challenging her mettle as much as the promise of his cock did.

'I could give you a blow job.'

'What an incredibly sweet offer. How could I possibly resist?'

'Don't laugh at me!' she cried, even though she was laughing herself. Dear God, didn't the language of sex sometimes sound completely absurd?

'I'm not laughing at you, we're laughing together.' His voice dropped low, roughened more than ever, and as if he'd read her secret thoughts he drew her hand to his erection and folded his own hand over it. 'There's a big difference.'

Already the shape of him was familiar to her. Dear. Yearned for. She circled her palm over the hard knot of flesh, experiencing a surge of triumph when he let out a gasp and bumped his hips to meet her touch. He closed his eyes and she took a step, bringing the two of them close up against each other while her fingers flexed. She smelt his cologne, and the scents of grass and wheat and wildflowers. What a strange tableau they must present. Two people standing in a lane, bodies aligned, holding and touching. As if he were imagining it too, or maybe just savouring the same odours, he breathed in deep.

'Yes,' he sighed, kissing her brow, rubbing his chin against her almost like a cat again. His beard felt strangely soft as it brushed against her skin. 'Yes ... yes ... touch me.'

She knew what he meant. Touch his skin, not just his jeans. Shaking her other hand free from his, she applied herself to her task, unbuckling his leather belt, then unzipping his jeans. With a tug on his underwear, pushing it down, she freed his cock.

He grabbed her hand then, made her hold him straight away. She would have liked to slide her fingers under his T-shirt and caress his belly, his navel, explore him a little. But it seemed he didn't want that. He wanted to be held.

Jay's cock filled her fist, overflowed it. She was a woman of average size, with slender hands, and her fingers could barely encircle him in their grip. He moaned as she tried to, and she found herself echoing the sound, entranced by the sweet feel of his flesh. He was hot, velvety, hard and clean, yet silky with fluid oozing from the tiny love-eye in his glans. Her mouth watered, wanting to taste him.

Who are you?

That question again, as he stepped back, leaning against the stile, and she followed him, sinking to her knees, still holding him.

Stalks of rough dry grass poked her through her skirt, and she could hear insects buzzing in the undergrowth, but neither bothered her. There was just Jay, and his cock, in her universe, with no other being or thing to disturb her, not even the couple in the car round the corner, who might be compelled by curiosity to follow them any minute.

'Unfasten your top,' he commanded, just as she was about to lean forward, extend her tongue and taste him, 'I want to see your breasts.'

The rawness in his voice thrilled her, as did the idea of

exposing herself to him beneath the sun, and in a place if not public, still with the possibility of discovery. Since she'd first set eyes on him she'd wanted to take risks with this man, even if at the beginning she'd not consciously realised it.

With fumbling fingers she tackled the tiny buttons down the front of her cotton top, and then, congratulating herself on choosing it, she snapped open the front fastening on her bra. The sunshine was mild and diffuse on her skin as she bared herself, but Jay's eyes were burning.

As she knelt before him, uncovered as he was uncovered, he edged sideways, pulling her with him, and sat down on the high step.

'Kiss me.'

For a moment she was confused, wondering whether he wanted her to reach up and press her mouth to his, but then in her heart and in her gut she knew exactly what he meant. Leaning forward, she dropped a tiny kiss on the tip of his cock, with lips closed, just a greeting or a tribute. His hips jerked, pushing him against her face, his sticky glans sliding across her cheek, wetting it. She parted her lips, trying to lick him, but he continued to rub himself against her cheek, digging his hands into her thick hair and controlling the action.

Circling and sliding, he massaged his cock all over her face, as if both exploring and anointing it. The salty smell of man was strong, yet still he seemed clean and good to her. Trying to participate, she reached again for the hem of his T-shirt, wanting to touch and caress him, but he said, 'No!' very firmly, and repeated it, 'No!'

Her lips against his cock, she asked, 'Why?

Curling over her, almost doubled, he whispered, 'My scars are ugly, Princess. Not good to look at. I don't want to repulse you.'

Could he really think that? His body was fine and strong

and his cock was fabulous. How could a bit of scar tissue really spoil all that good stuff?

'Let me be the judge of that,' she whispered and, when he tensed, she delicately licked the side of his cock where it lay against her face.

Jay groaned, but whether it was from the pleasure of her tongue, or the prospect of her seeing his scars, she couldn't tell. The taste of his hard silky flesh made her dizzy.

She kissed him. She licked him. She played him. Not taking him into her mouth, but gently teasing and tantalising and, yes, distracting him. When he slumped back against the upper step of the stile, she plucked at the edge of his T-shirt and this time he didn't stop her.

The scars were bad. At least the ones on his belly and in the area of his groin were. Puckered and angry, they curled savagely over his abdomen, one plunging down, dangerously close to the juncture of his thigh and his crotch. A half an inch further and the twisted metal that had so damaged him might well have emasculated him too.

Sandy tried to imagine the pain, and the fear of that particular injury, but it was difficult. It clearly affected him, but it didn't affect her.

She still thought his body was beautiful. The scars were savage but, to her, not repulsive. Dropping a kiss on his cock-tip, she then tracked her way down his length with more kisses, and progressed from there to his belly and the nearest of his scars.

This she kissed and licked and nuzzled with all the fervour she'd applied to his erection. She ran her fingers lightly up and down it, then plunged in again, with another kiss. A dream, a memory from the past flitted through her mind, and she murmured, 'Kiss it better...' before pressing her lips to the scar once again.

Jay's body shook under her mouth, wracked by a long shiver,

and his hands tightened in her hair. 'Oh God,' he gasped, still trembling, and for a moment Sandy thought he was about to come. Either that or push her away. When she glanced up, he was staring at the sky, his face a strange anguished mask, and his eyes over-bright. Not with lust, she realised, but what looked suspiciously like moisture.

'Jay! Are you all right? I haven't hurt you or anything?' His expression worried her, even though just inches from her face his erect penis was unwavering. 'What is it?' she demanded when he didn't answer.

'Nothing.' His husky voice sounded as if the word was wrenched from his very gut. 'Nothing at all.' He looked down again, his mouth working. Then he smiled, his gaze flicking from her face to his erection, and back again. 'Aren't you going to do anything about that?'

'Do you want me to?' She was still concerned. He was smiling, but he was still tense. Maybe it was just that he had the mad horn and needed to come? But she had a feeling it was something else entirely.

'Need you ask?' Jay shifted his hips, moving against her, manoeuvring his cock close to her lips.

The proximity of his heat, his hardness, was irresistible. Sandy enveloped him, folding her lips around the crown of his penis and starting to lick and tease and suck all over again. His taste was fine and salty, raw but not rank, warm and healthy. More silky pre-come flooded onto her tongue and she went, 'mm … mm …', savouring it.

His jeans fit snugly, and she couldn't reach in to caress his balls, so she slid her hand beneath to cradle them lightly through the denim. Even though the cloth was sturdy, she could almost feel them tensing, crawling, rising, ready to shoot his semen as he came. He was right at the edge and she felt powerful, in control.

Forming tight suction around the tip of his cock, she sucked hard, flicking beneath it with her tongue at the same time. With her free hand around his shaft, she lightly pumped.

Jay cried out incoherently, his hips beginning to work in the age-old jackhammer action of frantic orgasm. He pounded her, his cock knocking the inside of her cheek as he lost all semblance of control, and she lost the ability to control him. His fingers contorting against her scalp, he shouted, 'Princess! Oh – oh God!' as he jerked and filled her mouth with hot sweet come.

Shocked but thrilled, Sandy struggled to breathe, loving the taste of him, and greedily swallowing his essence. She'd never done this, not willingly, but now she wanted to. She wanted to absorb this little part of him into herself, and she would have swallowed more if there had been more of it to come.

After a few moments he began to subside and she let him slip from between her lips, not wanting to hurt him if he was hypersensitive. She felt him release what had become a death grip on her head and, as she drew away, she dropped just the lightest feather of a kiss upon his softening penis, barely a breath, and then another one upon the livid scar. Taking a gasp of air, she laid her cheek against his thigh.

The hands that had almost clawed her scalp now settled gently against it, curved in a gracious arc. She felt his thumbs lightly stroking as he seemed to come back into himself and return from that other place, the realm of orgasm. It was soothing, almost soporific, and she rested more heavily against him, breathing in the blended scents of semen, expensive cologne and grass and earth. High in the tree beside them, an unknown bird sang pure and sweet, and the gentle sun was warm upon her back.

They sat like that for a while, not talking and, in Sandy's case, barely thinking. The presence of Jay was calming, easy somehow, and even the air against her naked breasts didn't feel strange or disquieting. His hands were still against her head now but, even so, she imagined she could sense the very whirls and whorls of his fingerprints where they rested against the mass of her hair.

She felt so relaxed that the question she was afraid to ask seemed unimportant. Kneeling against him, slumped between stile and tree, for the moment it didn't matter who he was.

'Thank you.' As he spoke, Jay leaned down and kissed the top of her head. His fingers slid under her chin, and lifted her face. 'Thank you,' he repeated, then kissed her brow exquisitely chastely.

'Nothing to thank me for. I enjoyed it.' Again, she acknowledged the truth of it. Giving oral sex had never been a favourite of hers, but with Jay it was different, like the divine duty of some sacred priestess. She laughed at the thought, and he looked perplexed for a moment, then laughed along with her.

'I didn't used to like giving blow jobs,' she admitted, touching her fingertips to his cock, still exposed, and watching it twitch and thicken. 'Selfish, I guess. Nothing in it for me. But you seem to taste nicer than most. Very yum, in fact.' He seemed to stir more vigorously, as if from the praise as much as her touch.

Jay drew in a deep breath. 'It wasn't so much the blow job as the other thing.' He laid a hand over his abdomen, pressing the cotton of his T-shirt against the scar beneath. 'Not being bothered by the scar there.' His mouth tightened suddenly. 'Although that's by no means the full extent of the scarring. There's a lot more.' He looked away from her a moment, as if he were physically going away, rather than simply glancing into the middle distance.

'It won't faze me, no matter how many scars you've got. You're strong, you've got a good body. They're just marks, Jay, nothing more.' She laughed softly. 'Everything works, and that's what matters.'

He grinned. Beamed even. He looked like an adolescent boy, discovering the phenomenon of his erection for the very first time.

'Indeed it does. Indeed it does.'

He inclined over her again, finding her mouth for a kiss this time. A deep one, long, and moist and probing. Reaching down, he cupped her bare breast as he tasted her, thumb delicately strumming her nipple.

When she was gasping for air, he broke away from her, his bearded face still alight and happy.

'Look, I want to make love to you. Long, slow, lazy love. But not here.' He nodded to the field, the stile. 'I want to treat you to a bit of luxury, not a roll around in the dust and muck, with grass stalks sticking into our arses and God knows what insects or whatever stinging us while we're fucking.'

'We could go back to the Teapot. I think Kat's gone off somewhere with Greg. I think he's got the afternoon off too.'

Sliding his hands to her waist, Jay lifted Sandy with him as he rose to his feet. While she fumbled with her bra catch, he zipped himself up. She felt a pang of loss, denied the sight of his magnificent cock rising again.

'No, let's go to the Waverley. Get some room service. Indulge ourselves.' Covered again, he reached across and deftly fastened her bra for her, then her top, as if he buttoned up women's clothing every day. 'Would you like that?'

'Yes, I would. That'd be great.'

Yes, it would be fun to see more of the infamous Waverley Grange. She tried to imagine it as he led her along the path. She'd only seen the public rooms so far, but she couldn't forget the blatantly erotic art. Did the rooms and suites have kinky pictures and photographs on their walls, to turn the guests on?

She only really had local gossip to go by, and Greg's tall tales. But then he might have been exaggerating to turn *Kat* on!

When they rounded the corner, the lovers and their car had gone, and the coast was clear. Her heart lifted as they strode back towards the Aston. What could be better? The infamously naughty hotel, a bit of luxury . . . and Jay.

11

Chintz! Good God, she'd never seen so much of it in her life!

The décor of the most notorious hotel in the entire Borough area wasn't quite what Sandy had expected. It was cosy. Almost homely. Intimate but old fashioned. There was a picture of a topless woman on the wall, but it was tastefully bland and conveniently soft focus.

Jay had a medium-sized room, nothing too ostentatious. It had obviously been serviced since he'd left it that morning. There were fresh tea and coffee fixings on the courtesy tray but, as she wandered around, he rang down for a proper afternoon tea to be brought up for them.

Courtesy copies of several local magazines lay on a chest of drawers by the window, along with the *Kissley Gazette*, the county paper and the *Financial Times*. There was also a very plain but obviously expensive attaché case beside the papers, along with a high-end laptop, a personal organiser and two mobile phones.

What do you do, *Jay?*

It was a change from *Who are you?* she supposed. The *FT* and the electronic paraphernalia suggested business to her, and she puffed out her cheeks, feeling uneasy, her stomach crawling inexplicably. She'd wanted to come here, but suddenly it didn't seem quite such a good idea. Suddenly, she didn't *want* to know who he was, or what he did. Not at all. In the café, and down Adultery Alley, things were simpler. Just sex, and maybe a little bit of fondness.

The sound of springs being depressed by a body's weight made her spin around.

Jay was sitting on the side of the bed, watching her intently. She could see he wanted her. He'd been partially aroused most of the way here in the car, even though he'd driven in silence, apparently deep in thought. Once or twice he'd compressed his lips as if grappling with some difficult decision or problematic concept, but, when he'd glanced at her, his grey eyes had still been fiery with sexual heat.

Right now, he looked perplexed, as if his body was tugging him one way – towards fucking her – and his mind was pulling him another, towards something far less pleasant.

'What is it?' Better get it over with.

She walked to the bed and sat down, not touching him even though she wanted to. The knot of his erection, straining the denim at his crotch, called to her fingers, and she wanted to see not just it but also the rest of his body, to assure him that any number of scars couldn't diminish his raw attractiveness.

He didn't reach for her, even though she sensed he wanted to just as much as she wanted him to. His mouth twitched again, and he rubbed quickly at his beard, biting his lip.

What the hell is it? Something was chipping away at what she'd thought was über-confidence. Even his concerns over his scarring hadn't affected him quite this way.

'What is "what"?'

Oh Christ, he's married!

The classic snafu. People did these things. Men on business trips, playing around. Women bored or disappointed with their husbands, seeking solace elsewhere. All kinds of reasons for all kinds of people. She could understand it in some cases, but it wasn't her scene. It *would* fuck things up pretty irrevocably.

She opened her mouth to speak, not sure what would come

out of it. 'You've got a look on your face as if you've got something unpleasant to tell me. Why don't you just spit it out?'

'And if I don't, is that the end of things? Can't we just have our fun, no questions asked?'

Heat twisted in Sandy's chest. She didn't want to feel this way, nagging and needy. She wanted to be sexy and sophisticated, take her pleasure while she may. Jay could be gone tomorrow, or the day after, without a backward glance. It was probably better not to know too much about him, less painful that way.

Yet still she *wanted* to know things. Discover his secrets. Oh hell, she wanted to lay claim, and that made her a bloody fool!

Jay was on his feet beside her, tall and towering. She turned to face him, and he looked strong and rocklike and watchful. Unapologetic too, she noticed, but vaguely defensive.

Why would he feel that way? He was the one who'd said it was just fun between them. Just sexual exploration. The image of him on his knees before her, out in the gardens beyond the window, rose before her eyes. She remembered the feel of his hot mouth and his nimble tongue beleaguering her sex, so real that her clit burned with need. But still she couldn't speak, and Jay frowned at her silence, as if frustrated by it.

'You didn't ask any questions when you let me lick your pussy.'

'Must you be so crude?' How ridiculous a thing was that to say? It wasn't crude. It was true. And she'd loved it. She'd love it again right now too, despite his sudden evasiveness.

'OK, but what do you want me to call it?' he countered.

'I don't know. But I wish you hadn't done it.'

'Liar. You enjoyed it. The fact that we've only just met doesn't stop you responding to what I can do to you, does it?'

'It might do now.'

'Bollocks.'

She glared at him. He looked back, face more masklike than she'd ever seen it. His scars were suddenly starkly vivid, but he was still the most handsome man she'd ever seen. And in his eyes, something . . . something indefinable. Fugitive. Almost familiar.

'Come here,' he said. 'Close the gap between us and let me touch you. And then tell me that you can't get wet for me again.'

'No.'

'Coward.'

'Fuck you!'

'I wish you would.'

Anger swirled, desire coiled into it, indivisible. She'd never been a coward and she wasn't one now. She'd take this strange secretive arrogant bastard of a man and use him. Then throw him away, and try to make the best of her life and her café, chalking Jay Bentley down to experience and the desire to experiment.

She stepped towards him and grabbed his head, dug her nails into his velvety scalp and dragged his face down to hers, almost smashing her mouth against his.

His arms came around her in a perfect smooth movement, like an exquisitely worked mechanism, as if their bodies were a single unit functioning as one. She tried to thrust her tongue into his mouth and assert control, but it didn't happen. Couldn't happen. His tongue pushed in between her lips and subdued her. Effortlessly.

Because, she realised fatalistically, it was still what she wanted, despite everything. She still tried to fight him though, because she knew that was what *he* wanted.

Their tongues duelled, and Sandy grabbed at Jay's T-shirt, wrenching at it, pulling him closer. She grabbed at him, her nails digging through the cotton cloth as she growled at him, trying to mutter 'bastard, bastard' around the intruder in her mouth.

His answer was to haul up her skirt, bunching it with both hands to bare her bottom. Holding her with one big sinewy hand around one cheek, he suddenly slapped the other lightly, once, twice, three times.

'You fuck!' she snarled, tearing her mouth free of him while her heart thundered and her sex beat wildly in incomprehensible pleasure. He slapped again and her clit throbbed, swollen and excited. Unable to help herself she ground her crotch against him, circling, parting her thighs. Anything for pressure.

'I am a fuck,' he purred in her ear, the rasp of his voice raw and thrilling. 'But you still want me all the same.'

She tossed her head, as if that could shake free the feelings. But even if 99.9% of sex was in the brain, she couldn't dislodge the hunger, the pure rampant lust she felt for Jay, right now, and all the time, really. All she wanted was for him to touch her, immediately, and bring her off. Then immediately after that, to throw her on the bed and fuck her to within an inch of her life.

She couldn't look him in the eye, but he made her do it. Dropping her skirt, he cupped her face, a palm to each cheek, and compelled her to meet his gaze.

'What do you want?'

'I want you to stop thinking you can do whatever the hell you like to me, and just leave me alone,' she lied, aware that, if he did leave her alone, she couldn't bear it.

'No can do. Stop lying and tell me what you want right now.'

She couldn't imagine how she'd ever thought his eyes were cool and oceanic. They were metal now, full of sparks struck by his conflict with her. His entire face almost seemed to glow, his glare was so intense, so lit by sex.

'I want you to touch me and make me come and then I want you to fuck me.'

'And?'

'And what? Isn't that enough?'

'Not for you.'

'OK, I want you to spank me and mess about with me, and do all the kinky things you've done with other women in the past. You might think I'm an unsophisticated small-town girl that you can bamboozle and play fast and loose with.' She glared back at him, wanting to do things to *him* – slap, bite, leap on, wrestle to ground, ride to oblivion ... He was strong, but she had fury and lust enough to best him, she knew it. 'But I'm a match for you, you bastard, and you know it!'

Jay laughed, throwing his head back and baring his fine white teeth at her. Infuriated, Sandy raised a hand to land him a blow across the face, but he caught it effortlessly and held it behind her, at the base of her spine. A shiver of raw fear augmented her lust. He could hurt her for real if he wanted to. He'd rehabilitated his damaged body, and probably made it twice as strong as before, and the danger of him losing control made liquid desire well and ooze between her thighs.

Up came the skirt again, roughly, in a tangle, and an eye's blink later his hand was at the delta of her sex. Without finesse, without his usual measured guile, he shoved two fingers inside her, curving them to seek her G spot while he roughly thumbed her clit.

'No,' she moaned, rising on her toes, meaning *yes, yes, yes*! His hand rose with her, relentless, masterful, handling her with uncouth peremptory enthusiasm. He squeezed and rubbed, pressing her clit hard, almost cruelly. She actually shouted,

'Yes!' now, coming helplessly, drenching his hand with her honey.

The rippling clenching pulsations of her orgasm made her head go empty of all thought. It felt light and transparent. She swayed on her feet, falling against him, trapping his hand and reaching up with her own free one to hold onto his rocklike shoulder. Her face, mouth open, pressed against his chest, and she was dimly aware that she actually drooled on his T-shirt. And he held onto her, fingers and thumb, giving no quarter to her spasming pussy, making her come again and again, even when the pleasure was almost pain.

'Oh please,' she whimpered at last, begging for respite while her body surged again.

He stopped. Immediate response to her request. His fingers slid out of her, but stayed between her legs as he gently cupped her sex in a light hold, as if to soothe it. He let go her hand behind her back too, and slung his arm around her, supporting her, holding her safe. Automatically Sandy's arm went around him, holding him far tighter, the lost little girl in her afraid he'd leave. Again.

Again?

She blinked, dragged in a breath. No, that was completely wrong. She was mixing him up with someone else. An impossible dream of a man, a fantasy. Someone so different from Jay's ruthlessness and unstoppable voraciousness that he might as well have been a different species.

'Are you OK?'

His voice was soft and solicitous, and for a moment past and present, fantasy and reality phased and blended again.

'I'm fine,' she said crisply, still shaken, but grabbing for the shreds of her normal self who had issues to face with this man, much as she desired him. As she began to pull away from him, and he began trying to stop her with a firm hand against her back and a sly sweet kiss against the side of her temple, a brisk rap at the door made them both jump.

'Oh hell!' Because he let her, she sprang away from him, flustered. She patted her hair, smoothed down her skirt, and glanced nervously at the door, waiting for it to fly open.

'Relax,' said Jay, with infuriating male casualness. He closed the space between them, brushed the long hanks of her hair away from her face in a way she'd been incapable of doing herself, and cupped her cheek for a moment. 'Relax,' he repeated, then strode to the door.

Sandy darted to the window and made a pretence of looking out, seeing nothing. Her mind was too full of impressions, memories, whirling excitement. When Jay opened the door, she reluctantly looked back towards it.

'Your tea, Mr Bentley,' said the cheery young woman who entered the room. She was pretty, blonde, and had a mischievous twinkle in her eye. She also had a very short black skirt on, which Sandy noticed Jay noticing, typical man.

'Thanks, Maria, could you put it over there please?' He gestured to a space on the sideboard, close to where Sandy was standing. Well, lurking.

Wearing astonishingly high heels as well as her micro skirt and crisp white blouse, Maria glided across the room and set down what was really quite a large and heavy tray laden with tea fixings and an assortment of cakes and biscuits. To divert herself, Sandy eyed them up. Exquisitely fresh and beautifully served, with immaculate white napkins, china, cake forks and the lot. Full marks to the Waverley for their English afternoon tea.

'Shall I pour for you?'

Something about the blonde woman's voice made Sandy frown. It sounded as if she was offering much more than efficient room service. Much, much more. Maria's mouth was very pink and rather shiny, as if she'd been licking her lips. Maybe she preferred the taste of hard but hunky men like Jay to fondant fancies and butter biscuits? It certainly seemed that way. Her trim bottom swayed as she sashayed across the room, heading for the door and, as her blue gaze flickered from Jay to Sandy, her tongue flicked out across her lower lip, and her naughty grin widened.

How the hell does she know?

Surreptitiously, Sandy drew in a breath. But she couldn't smell sex, just the Waverley's light but rather exotic potpourri. Maybe working here imbued the saucy Maria with a more finely tuned detector? It certainly seemed that way when she winked at Sandy over Jay's shoulder while he was giving her a generous tip.

More than we got in the Teapot, I'll be bound! Although maybe you think you've given me mine in kind?

As the door closed behind the retreating Maria, Sandy realised that Jay was watching her, smirking.

'You seem to get on with her pretty well. Does she always bring your room service?'

No, don't do this. He's not your boyfriend. You're not sure you even like him. Well, not properly. And especially now …

Jay's dark brows lifted, the grin widened.

'She's friendly and helpful, and she works on reception and around the place. How am I supposed to act with her?' He advanced across the room and Sandy tried to retreat, but couldn't. 'Are you jealous?' he asked, looming over her as she stood beside the window, pressed against the layers of chintz and floating white nets.

She could smell his cologne, and the scent of grass and pollen from the meadow. There was a hint of foxiness too, sex, desire, and perspiration, totally intoxicating.

'How can I be jealous?' Her chin lifted and she met his grey eyes with all her courage. 'I only met you yesterday, and I'm not even sure I like you. Especially right at this moment.'

'Ah, but we've also made love twice.' He moved closer, his face almost touching hers. She could almost imagine she saw the surgeon's minute stitches along the faint lines of his scars. 'And done other assorted sex things too.'

'Made love? Is that what you'd call it?' She could feel the heat of her own breath, and he was so close, just another fraction of an inch and his beard would be brushing against her skin. 'I'd call it *all* assorted sex things.'

'Whatever.' His voice was amiable as he threaded his fingers through her hair and stroked her scalp. When he exerted light pressure she felt her heart lurch in panic. She didn't fear him, but she did fear herself. 'Want to try something else from the menu?'

Not stopping to think, she dipped and shot out from under his arm and to the side, darting clear of him. 'I'd prefer a cup of tea, actually.'

'Fair enough.'

It seemed he was going out of his way, for the moment, to be non-combative. Which was infuriating because she wanted to get into it with him over his secretiveness, his weird combination of sexual high-handedness and old-fashioned courtship. Either that or she *did* want to make love, fuck, or do sex things. Whatever he wanted to call it. In fact, she wanted that far more than she wanted to argue, she had to admit.

Trying to settle herself, she took a seat, sinking into one of the chintz-clad armchairs. It was deep and softly upholstered, a nice piece of furniture, not just a cheap hotel chair to take up space. There was something strangely decadent about it, despite the homely fabric. She closed her eyes for a moment and seemed to see herself in the form of arty erotic photo images, a bit like the ones in the Lawns Bar. Lingerie, black and shiny, encased her body, and towering high heels her feet. With her legs akimbo, she sat in this very chair with her crotch naked, pubic hair stringently trimmed.

Shaking her head slightly, she opened her eyes again and glared first at Jay, then the tea tray. Let *him* serve *her*. She deserved it. He was a bastard, and in her mind, at least for the moment, she was a sex goddess.

'Milk and sugar?' he enquired, eyeing her as if he'd read her thoughts. When he touched his tongue to the centre of his lower lip, she wondered if he'd seen the art photo thoughts too. Very much his bag, if all his talk was to be believed.

'Just milk, thanks.' She tapped her fingers on the arm of the chair.

'Don't do that.'

Something in his voice made her head come up. He'd not sounded bossy or harsh, but there was a cool metallic timbre to the way he spoke.

She opened her mouth to ask why not, then shut it again. Jay was staring at her, his eyes cool and metallic too, assessing. Challenging. Controlling?

What was this? By rights she should be resisting him, taking a step back and getting some distance, not allowing him to drive her to distraction again with a kind of erotic gamesmanship that she'd never experienced before.

He was certainly playing a game now, she realised, and had begun to without her becoming aware of it. It was the same magic web he'd woven around her in the car last night, leaving her with no control, making her his plaything, his puppet, his sexual doll.

She fell still, her arms resting motionless on the arms of the chair. Remaining immobile was like a conscious act, like effort in stillness, a strain on the muscles. And arousing, deeply arousing. Between her legs she felt the river begin to flow.

Could she speak? She had to try.

'Why were you watching me yesterday? In the Teapot, or at the cocktail party. Why me?'

Pouring tea, adding milk, he didn't answer for a moment. But when he brought her cup and set it on the dressing table at her side, he said, 'Because when I saw you, you were all I could think about. I wanted you.' Dropping to a crouch beside her, he plucked at the dark fabric of her skirt and eased it up her legs, slowly and methodically. The whisper of the soft cloth was like a caress, sending coils of sensation straight to her pussy. He inched it up and up until she was exposed, then folded it neatly in a roll at her waist, baring the dark auburn triangle of her pubic hair.

'Beautiful,' he murmured, slipping a finger between her labia, as if to test her. 'Beautiful,' he repeated, finding exactly what he wanted then bringing his glistening finger to his lips and sucking her juices.

She should have dashed his hand away. She should have covered herself up. But she couldn't. She was hypnotised. Well, not exactly, but somehow enthralled by him.

He's dangerous! He's dangerous! He'll keep playing with you until you're addicted to him, and then he'll disappear. Jump up, run from this place, end it now while you still can. While you can still forget about him and go on with a normal life.

But she couldn't. Maybe she was addicted already? In her mind she bargained with herself, and agreed on one last afternoon – and maybe evening and night – of pleasure with him. Then she'd tell him that it was over, and it'd been fun. But nothing more.

'What are you thinking about?'

Suddenly she didn't want to spoil the moment. She couldn't. It was all too strange. Her body was too excited, sex, breasts, everything, nerves, blood, fingers, toes.

'I don't know. Nothing. Everything.' She tossed her head, as if that were the only part of her he would permit her to move.

Still crouched beside her, he laughed. 'I feel the same. It's like I can't think about anything but sex, and your body, when I'm around you. It's like a spell.' He laid a hand on her thigh, stroking the edge of her pubic mat with his thumb.

'Just my body?' She laughed back at him, both liberated and enslaved somehow. She couldn't work it out. 'No interest at this time in my mind?'

'Touché!'

'Then you admit it?' The compulsion to squirm in response to his caress was out of all proportion to the scope of the action. His thumb was barely moving, and yet nerve impulses were surging as if he was masturbating her, hard and fast.

'It's an integrated package. Body and mind. One with the other.'

'That's nonsense. What on earth are you talking about?' she demanded.

It was nonsense. His mind was whirling. Breathing in the perfume of her sex was like being in an opium den, yet knowing you weren't killing yourself or driving yourself mad, just going crazy in the best of all possible ways.

'I don't know what I'm talking about,' he admitted, still moving his thumb lightly. He loved the heat of her skin just there, the indentation where hip met thigh. The feel of her pubic hair which was softer than that of any woman he'd known, tender and not wiry. Just touching her, and seeing her overwrought response to it, made him dizzy. Opium time again. 'But at the same time I know what I mean and I know what I want,' he continued, 'and what I feel.'

Her green eyes widened, bright yet dark, full of arousal and fear and recognition. But of what? A shared sexual obsession, or something deeper and older? The romantic dream?

Did she still harbour thoughts of their shared moments long ago, he wondered. Did she fantasise, as he'd done, about a perfect fairytale lover? Some kind of mad impossible melding of the ultimate in eroticism and the pure chivalrous ideal?

I'm going mad. She doesn't recognise me. I wouldn't recognise myself. Even without smashing my face up, I'd have probably changed. She wouldn't know me.

Perplexed, he twined a russet curl around his little fingertip and tugged gently, provoking a gasp. He was glad she didn't shave completely down there. He loved the natural look, and the way her neat little bush held her fragrance.

Another gentle pull and she tossed her head. She closed her eyes, in some vain attempt to keep her responses to herself. Well, he would give her that. She couldn't mask her desire in any other way, not with the way she was moving, and the rich odour of her arousal and the way it was glistening on the insides of her thighs.

Her pale hand tensed on the chair arm, even though she'd understood his unspoken command that she stay still. She had neat hands too, with slender fingers. No stupid painted talons, just plain clean nails, pink and natural. He took hold of her hand in his and guided it to her crotch. Parting her labia, he positioned two of her fingers together over her clit.

'Play with yourself for me. Do it now. Show me what you do.'

Her eyes shot open, wide with alarm, pupils a sea of desire.

Heat sluiced through Sandy's body, reaching every pore and follicle. Sweat trickled in her armpits and beneath her breasts. Other liquid grew more copious beneath her fingertips.

'I ... can't.'

'Oh, you can, you can.'

She wanted to look away from him, but she couldn't, he still entranced her. Even as she essayed a tentative rub of her tingling clit, she couldn't stop watching Jay. Folding his limbs gracefully, he sat down cross-legged in front of her to watch the show, but, for all the fluidity of his movement, she caught the clench of his teeth as he settled down.

It still hurts, doesn't it?

He seemed to answer with his eyes, despite the sexy wolfishness of his smile, and it was this acknowledgement of a vulnerability that gave her courage. Daring bloomed, and so did desire. She shifted again in the deep armchair, seeking the perfect position from which to put on a show.

Defying his injunction to stay otherwise still, she quickly unfastened the front of her top and then snapped open her bra. The air in the room seemed warm and heavy on her breasts as she returned one hand to her crotch, and with the other plucked at a nipple, rolling and turning it. Between her legs she was sodden, puffed with arousal.

'Yes, that's good,' Jay encouraged, leaning forward a little as she rolled her clit too, synchronising the two tiny actions. She imagined she could feel his breath, hot and eager on the back of her hand, even though he was nowhere near close enough. She remembered feeling it on her thighs and her pussy when he'd dove in to lick her last night.

Was it only last night? It seemed as if they'd lived an erotic lifetime in the space of less than a day. Astounded, she rubbed and tweaked harder, her breath coming in gasps as streaks of pleasure careened about her body, bouncing from one node of stimulation to another. Tension in her pussy made her part her legs further, pushing against the arms of the chair.

'Here!' he said, plunging forward suddenly, laying hands on

her thighs and parting them so he could drape them over the arms of the chair. 'That's better.'

Was it? Oh God, yes! Better . . . but also worse.

She was totally exposed and displayed, her bottom perched right on the end of the chair, her entire pussy stretched and open, masked a little by her hand, but barely so. A groan of some confused emotion – not shame, but a cousin of it – escaped her lips when Jay reached up to switch on a lamp on the dressing table to give extra light.

'Your cunt is sublime. So pink and juicy. It's exquisite.'

Sandy laughed, despite everything. How preposterous was it to hear such words on a man's lips. Yet somehow they seemed right, and honest, and not unnatural.

'Stick a finger inside yourself. That's it. Work it in and out. Just do that. Don't touch your clit. Just the finger.'

She obeyed him, even though her clitoris seemed to wail silently, missing its attention.

'Now keep it still. Just sit there with your finger in your pussy. And pinch your nipple. Hard. Keep on pinching it until you feel sore, but no touching your clit.'

It was hard to breathe, balancing the tiny pain in her nipple as she pinched and twisted. Her clit quivered involuntarily, and her vagina shuddered and tightened around her finger, almost at the point of orgasm, but not quite. Unable to stop herself, she started hitching her bottom around right on the edge of her seat.

'I love the way you move. I love it that you're so turned on you can't keep still.' He was closer now, she could swear it, even though she could no longer look at either him or her own body. 'No, clench your bottom. That's it, tighten everything up. I want to see that sweet little pucker close then open.'

'No, no,' she moaned, yet still doing it, following his directions as if she were Jean Harlow to his Cecil B. de Mille.

Her sex felt as if it were on fire, poised on the brink of pleasure yet denied it.

'Now stay still. No clenching. Relax.'

How? How the hell could she do that? She was totally on show to him. Clit, labia, perineum, anus, her finger was pushed inside her up to the knuckle. Defiantly she plucked at her nipple and everything surged again, of its own accord, just skirting a climax.

'Stay still,' he whispered, his breath against the inside of her knee.

Please kiss me ... please suck me ... give me your tongue.

But when she opened her eyes, his were glinting like polished stone and a dark little smile played around his lips. Not yet, he seemed to say, without speaking. And a second later, he was up on his feet again, reaching for her teacup.

'You must be thirsty. You need a drink. Have some of your tea.'

With infinite care, he brought the china vessel to her lips. Her body shuddered and fresh sweat popped out in her armpits and her groin. It seemed infinitely more obscene to drink tea, have it fed to her like this while she was half naked and touching herself, than the act of masturbation itself could ever be.

Astonishingly, the tea was still hot. How could that be? It seemed as if she'd been playing with herself for hours, but in reality it was probably only a couple of minutes or so. She sipped obediently, relishing the aromatic liquid and suddenly realising how dry-mouthed she'd become. Probably because every drop of moisture in her body was between her legs.

'Enough?' Jay withdrew the cup a little way. Sandy nodded. 'You're so beautiful. You take my breath away.'

She'd been drifting, but her eyes snapped open. Jay was crouching again, but staring into her face, not between her legs.

'Like this?' she questioned faintly.

'Yes.' His dark eyes flicked from her face to her breasts to her crotch, and back again. 'But in all ways.' He swallowed, seemed to 'go away' somehow for a moment, lost in some imaginary place she couldn't determine. 'And not just visibly.'

'You don't know me.'

'No, I suppose not.'

Time ticked, but not forward, in suspension. Impossible thoughts flitted through Sandy's mind but so fast she couldn't get a hold of them. Then Jay shook his head slightly, as if to clear it, and smiled again, that slow devil-smile.

'Hook your finger,' he said softly, dropping to his knees again. If it hurt him he gave no sign this time.

Pressing on the sensitive pad of her G-spot was agonisingly pleasurable, a blend of near orgasm and a sudden sharp urge to urinate. When she withdrew the pressure, without permission, the sensations faded, leaving only a dangerous echo.

'Too much?'

'Yes, I think so,' she admitted, her voice like feathers.

'OK then,' he answered, reaching up across her body to gently stroke her face. 'Let your body rest a moment. Relax, relax,' he urged again, brushing strands of her wayward hair clear of her sweaty heated brow.

Sandy let her hands drop against her bare thighs. They felt heavy against her skin, warm and almost not a part of herself. Between her thighs, though, she was acutely aware of air against the hot membranes of her sex. Her pose, draped over the chair arms the way she was, remained utterly open, with everything exposed.

With one last pat of her hair, Jay crossed to the tea tray, took his own cup and retreated to the second chintz armchair across from her. Grandstand view of her pussy while he sipped his English Afternoon Blend with obvious enjoyment.

After a while, he put aside his cup and lounged back in his chair, gazing at her sex like a connoisseur appreciating the finer points of a new work. Maybe he was a connoisseur? For all his scars, he was the most attractive man she'd ever encountered, and she suspected he'd been a devastating looker prior to his close tangle with a twisted Aston and the threat of death.

Not for the first time she tried to imagine him with a different face. Something like his current one, but maybe less angular, less hard. It was difficult because, in the space of little more than twenty-four hours, his features, as they were now, were printed on her brain. The only other face she seemed able to conjure, but far more faintly, was her rescuer from long ago, her sweet Prince Charming.

The dizziness she'd experienced drifted back. It was disorientating, a struggle to comprehend the merging of features her brain seemed to present to her.

No, it wasn't possible. They were as unalike as the proverbial chalk was from cheese. And yet still, the stupid notion was pervasive.

Jay drew in a deepish breath, and the spell was broken. Resting his elbows on the arms of the chair, he steepled his fingers and rested his bearded chin upon them.

'Do you play with sex toys?' he enquired, apropos of nothing, and everything.

12

'I beg your pardon?'

Jay laughed. 'Now come on, Princess, surely a sexy woman like you has a vibrator?'

Sandy studied him, eyes narrowed. He stared back. Their eyes locked, and she saw a twinkle in his. It was a silent communication, a tipping point. Their game of cat and mouse, dominance and submission, had just shifted its balance of power. He was in thrall to her, to the sight of her body, lush and sexual, to the supreme feminine power of her pussy.

'Of course I have,' she said, adjusting her position. 'And I wish I had it here now. I need to come.'

'Then make yourself come. You don't need a toy.'

There was admiration in his voice, awe even. His face was alight, he bit his lip, astonished but joyous.

'Why don't you do it? You're the one who's so fond of touching me up. Here it all is. Come and play with me.'

'You come to me, if that's what you want.' He seemed relaxed, but she could sense a tension in him, he was poised.

Suddenly she wanted a change, a different dynamic. Without pausing to think, she slid her thighs off the chair arms and stood up, letting her skirt fall around her as she walked towards him. The fire in his eyes gave her power and, when she reached his chair, she paused in front of him, kicked off her shoes and began to strip. Not for him, but for herself.

Shimmying out of her top, she let it slide down her arms then flung it away. Then she flipped the straps of her open bra off her arms and let that fall away too. A second later she unfastened the button at the side of her full floating skirt, then whizzed down the zip. The black fabric settled like a dark pool around her feet, and she stepped away from it, closing right in on Jay. Imperiously, she nudged his knees together with her thigh and, while he still stared at her as if she was a goddess rising, she settled on his lap, perfectly naked, and swooped forward to take a kiss from his lips.

Jay's mouth yielded to her, moist and warm and tasting of tea. She slid her hands up and cradled his head on either side, her fingertips pressing against the fuzz on his closely shaven scalp. The velvety texture of it was so sensuous, as was the silky brush of his beard against her face as she savoured his lips and the tentative caress of his tongue. When he lifted his own hands to wrap his arms around her body, she silently told him she permitted it.

There was something very piquant about being naked on the knee of a clothed man. It was a strange kind of double nudity that licked across her skin with a special thrill. She shifted across his denim-clad thighs, caressing herself on him, rubbing her sex against the hardness of his muscle, and the other hardness, the solid knot at his groin. Leaning forward, she rubbed her breasts against his chest, abrading her nipples against his dark cotton T-shirt. As she tilted, her loose hair slid around her shoulders and across Jay as he held her. As it brushed against him, he moaned in his throat, transferring the sound into her mouth like the breath of life, as if the feel of her hair moving on his skin was a keen unique pleasure.

The feel of Jay's hands roving over her back and flanks and hips was keen and pleasurable too. He touched her lightly, but somehow found every nice spot, every gracious place. It was more than sex, it was a deep contact, touching on a different level, communication flowing from skin to skin, mind to mind.

Even when the kiss broke, he rubbed his face against hers, his cheek against hers, circling, knowing, silently speaking.

Eventually of course, his fingers gravitated helplessly to her breasts, her sex. She made a soft sound, almost subvocal, of assent.

'Princess, Princess, Princess,' he murmured, thumbing her nipple as his other hand slipped boldly and unerringly between her sex lips. 'You're perfect, you know. Utterly delicious and wonderful. A treasure.'

'Get away with you,' she chided, her voice cracking as he fingered her. 'You must have made free with dozens of fabulous women in your time. You're obviously rich and handsome, they must be all over you, models and It Girls and whatever.'

His caress faltered momentarily. 'Rich, yes,' he admitted. 'And I suppose I was a good-looking guy before the accident.' His fingertip moved again, as slickly as before.

'You're good-looking now too, you fool,' she gasped. 'Kat thinks you're as hot as hell, Greg notwithstanding. And everywhere we've been today, in the precinct and the pub, women were ogling you.'

Jay laughed, but she could tell he was pleased. Typical man.

'I never noticed. I was too busy clocking all the men who were lusting after you.' He backed off a little, but Sandy surged forward, not letting him tease her.

'Now!' she commanded. 'I've had enough of this shilly-shallying about. If you don't get the job done, I *will* do it myself.' Tightening her arms around him, she pressed her mouth to his neck and lightly bit him.

'Yes, Princess!' he growled, his finger circling harder.

It took but seconds, and she howled with pleasure, laughing along with him as she came, her sex pulsing, her legs kicking, her bottom wiggling and working.

He held her, close and quiet, until her body settled and the tension left her, replaced by loose and mellow languor. She moved slowly, still nuzzling against him. Why did it feel, again and again, as if they'd known each other far longer than just a day?

'So, this vibrator,' he said at last. 'What's it like? Where did you get it? How often do you use it?'

'Oh, you men, you always want to know a girl's secrets.' She felt amenable, expansive. She could tell him a few little tantalising titbits, couldn't she? He'd just given her an exquisite orgasm, the latest in what seemed like an endless stream of them.

'Indulge me.'

Was the balance tipping again? He sounded determined. His arms were still light around her, but she sensed his dominant spirit rising. It was as intrinsic to him, and as hardcore, as the erection that still jutted, poking against her bottom.

'OK. It's pink and it's plastic and it's not very sophisticated. Just a cheap buzzing tube, really.'

'But it works, I assume, doesn't it?' His mouth opened against her neck, just as hers had opened against his.

'Yes. You could say that.'

'Good orgasms?'

'Yes, very good. It's cheap, but it's a bit of a beast.'

'Splendid.' He started kissing, nuzzling. He was just playing, she could tell, but it felt good. Sort of semi-sexy. 'So where did you acquire this inexpensive treasure?'

Sandy smiled, remembering a fun night.

'Oh, Kat had a sex-toy party. Just a few mates around, to choose from catalogues and play with samples. Several bottles of wine and a lot of nibbles.'

Jay sighed happily. 'Ah, like a sexy college girls' sleepover party?'

'A bit like that. But no skimpy pyjamas or pillow fights. Just a lot of boozing and giggling but no funny business.'

'What, no girl on girl?' Mock disappointment.

'No!'

'OK, so what else did you buy? Any other naughty knickknacks you can tell me about?'

There had been plenty of choice. Dildos, vibrators, alarming-looking butt plugs and beads. Some fairly soft porn videos, directed by a woman for women. Lots and lots of extremely trashy underwear, none of which she'd bought.

'Knickers.' She giggled. 'I bought some naughty knickers and a bra with peepholes.'

Jay's hands tightened on her, pressing her down on his cock through his jeans. Ah, men, they were such primitive beasts really, even the mysterious ones with pots of money and fancy cars. Show them a bit of sexy tat and they got the horn. Or even more of the horn, in the case of the man beneath her.

'Details, woman, details!' he ordered, growling.

'Um ... they were red. Nylon. With black lace and marabou trim. Kat didn't have my size, so I took a chance on a smaller set. When I got them on they were very tight.'

'Better and better.' A large warm hand cupped her breast, gentle but hungry. 'Did your nipples poke out of the little holes, because of the tightness?'

'Yes, a bit. Well, a lot actually. And the lace tickled. It made my nipples harden every time I wore it.'

'And what about the panties? Were they little too? Did they fit your perfect little pussy like a glove?'

Sandy smiled, her face hidden from him. She knew what he'd probably like to hear.

'They were split up the middle, and they gaped open because they were tight. They didn't cover much.'

'I think I just died and went to heaven,' Jay purred. 'Did you wear these luscious items often then? Did you wear them when you were with men? To tantalise them, just the way you're tantalising me now?'

Should she compound the lie, or tell a sort of truth?

'No, I never wore them for a man.'

'Would you wear them for me, next time we're together?'

She shot up on his knee. He was laughing. He knew she'd been fibbing, that was obvious.

'Oh, all right already. I haven't got any split-crotch knickers or a peephole bra.' She felt hot again. Her entire body seemed to be blushing. When she looked down there was a pinkish bloom to her breasts and her belly and limbs.

'You're such a little fibber,' he said equably, sliding his hand behind her neck and pulling him back to her for a kiss that was slow yet not probing. Almost quizzical. When they parted again he was frowning a little.

And just what are you fibbing to me about, Mister?

She stared at his face, searching for something, anything. Even while she still wanted him.

'What is it?'

The words 'who are you?' balanced on the end of her tongue, but remained unspoken. Instead she said, on the spur of the moment, 'I was just wondering what you looked like without the beard.'

Jay cocked his head on one side, rubbing the side of his goatee. 'Just the same. Only with less whiskers, and a few more scars on show.'

Sandy frowned, scrunched up her eyes, peered at him. There was something. A fleeting likeness. Even though she'd just blurted out the notion, she did try to imagine him clean-shaven. Younger. Unscarred. Different.

No, it was ridiculous. There was probably no likeness at all.

And it was a weird place to go too. They needed a distraction, and she knew where to find one. She massaged her bottom against his thighs and his erection again.

'Don't you ... um ... need something?'

She adjusted her weight on his lap and reached down to curve her fingers over the bulge beneath the denim.

'Yes, I do, Princess, I do. All this talk of sexy lingerie and sex toys has made me hornier than I was before.' He placed his large hand over hers, exerted pressure. 'If that's possible, given that around you I'm automatically in lust.'

'Shall we ... um ...' Under her hand she felt a jerk, a slight surge as he thickened even more.

'Fuck?' Jay's grin widened. 'My dear, I thought you'd never ask.' His mouth settled on hers again, the kiss quick and deep this time, the opposite of before. 'But I think I need a shower first. How about you? Would you like one?'

'Together?'

Again the frown came. She got the distinct impression he was reluctant to let her see his body and its scars. Were they worse than the ones on his face, that had obviously had a lot of fine work done on them? She suspected they were, if the ones she'd seen near his groin were anything to go by. Would he insist on switching out the lights before they finally got naked, skin on skin, in a bed?

'Maybe not, then,' she pre-empted. With a last pat at his equipment, she rose from his lap as gracefully as she could. He caught her hand as she rose, and let her fingers trail through his as she moved away in the direction of the bathroom. The sensation was slight, but strangely poignant and stirring.

She turned at the door and he was staring at her, his eyes intent, his body still roused, his lips pursed and thoughtful.

Sequestered in the bathroom, Sandy peed, then just sat on the toilet for several minutes, thinking. What was she doing here with this man? Involved so intimately. Again and again, the words 'who are you?' tolled in her brain. She'd plunged deeper into sex with Jay than with any man she'd ever known, even her ex-husband, whom she'd married too young and without really knowing. They'd separated amicably, long before she'd experienced anything like the craving, the yearning, the raw lust she'd felt for Jay in little more than twenty-four hours.

The shower refreshed her. The hot water was copious and the shower gel and other toiletries luxurious. She coiled her hair into a loose knot, bound it up with the sash from one of the robes hung on the back of the door, and tried to keep the curls that dangled and trailed from getting too wet.

As she wound one of the bath sheets around herself, and rubbed a bit of moisturiser from one of the complimentary sachets on her face, she studied the toiletries that belonged to the man whose bathroom it was.

High-end cologne and skin balm, a razor that looked as if it'd been designed for NASA, rechargeable battery toothbrush, hand-made soap from a fragrance boutique in Bond Street. The man lived well and cared for his battered body with the finest grooming products money could buy.

Questions, questions, questions batted around in her head, ones she knew she should get answers for, but really didn't want to. The only way to stop thinking was to get back out there, and start touching and fucking and communicating in the way that worked perfectly for them.

'Your turn.'

Jay opened his eyes at the sound of her voice from the bathroom doorway. He'd been dozing, floating lightly on troubled seas of thoughts and desires, his mind switchbacking from rampant lust, and fantasies of kink and exploration, to tender feelings of yearning, remorse and almost adolescent confusion. He spun from being the Jay of now, damaged but worldly wise, to the Jay of yesteryear, who'd been entranced by a fairytale beauty whom he'd met for mere moments.

What would have happened to his life if he'd been able to stay back then, not had a girlfriend or an itinerary? Sandy and he could have been together now, legitimately and with no secrets.

Fucking hell, they might even have been married!

He'd never wanted that until now, never thought about it. But now it had smacked into him like a pile-driver and left him lying there, reeling.

And now she was here, a vision of innocent femininity, despite all they'd done together. Bundled in a thick white robe and with her magical hair tumbling around her shoulders. His cock kicked and his heart slowly turned over.

'Thanks. Enjoy your shower?' He had to force the words out. His throat was tight, and he couldn't think straight. He wanted to throw her on the bed and ravish her. He wanted to hold her and cherish her and keep her from all harm. Bloody hell, he wanted to be anybody but Jason Bentley Forbes, who she'd probably hate when she came to know his true identity.

'Yes, thanks.' It was all comfort and no comfort that she seemed to be having similar problems. Jay sprang to his feet, vacating his place on the bed. He felt as awkward as a youth, and made a vague gesture for her to take his place. It was like battling his way through a storm, trying to stand by, looking casual and normal as she slid past him and sat down on the side of the bed.

'How about a drink? What would you like? More tea? A glass of wine?'

Get a fucking grip, man! What's wrong with you?

'A water, please. I can get it myself.' She sprang to her feet again and he grabbed her hand, urging her back onto the bed.

'No, I'll get it. Why don't you have a snooze? Rest up for ...'

What the hell is the matter with you, half-wit? What are you, fifteen now?

'OK. Thanks.'

The small action of pouring the water into the glass and adding ice calmed and centred him. But he knew he had to get into the bathroom and sort himself out before he did something completely gauche, insane. God alone knew what.

'Won't be long.' He gave her a smile he feared looked half mental and strode into the bathroom without looking back, closing the door with infinite care behind him.

'Jesus, what's happening to me?' he whispered as he leaned on the door and wished he was back in the room, holding her in his arms, and, fuck, climbing on top of her.

Fully dressed, he dragged the shower screen along the side of the tub and turned the water on, running icy cold. His arm and the shoulder of his T-shirt were drenched, but he barely noticed it.

He stared at his face in the mirror and didn't recognise himself. It wasn't the first time he'd had that feeling since his surgery, far from it. But today, he knew himself less than ever before.

I look wrong. This isn't me.

He felt a surge of horror, a panic that he squashed with difficulty. Turning away, he unzipped and urinated, trying not to think. But as he flushed, he stared back at himself, at his face. And suddenly he knew there was something he could do. He crossed to the mirror, reached for his razor and fiddled with the settings until he found the required one. Applying it to his face, he began to remove his beard.

* * *

Sandy lay on the bed, sipping her water, trying to relax, as Jay had urged.

Fat chance of that.

He'd been weird, slightly spaced out, and had as good as run into the bathroom. What was the matter with him? One minute rampant sex god, the next, a distant and distracted stranger. OK, he *was* a stranger, but a few minutes ago he'd seemed even more unknown than ever.

From her spot on the bed she perused his belongings again just as she'd checked out his toiletries in the bathroom. A couple of beautiful jackets hung over the front of the wardrobe, and what looked like hand-made shoes were lined up against the wall. On the chest of drawers his laptop sat, intriguing her. It was probably crammed with his personal information but not even her raging curiosity about him could compel her to open it and have a snoop. He probably had it password-protected anyway, even if she could overcome her qualms.

Set beside the lappie, the pigskin attaché case was closed but its latches were popped open. Curiosity brought her to a sitting upright position. She bit her lip, then set aside her drink.

She listened to the sounds from the bathroom. The shower was running and had been for a while, and before that she'd heard the loo flush, and a buzzing sound, obviously the razor he used to trim his neat goatee.

She slid to her feet and stood beside the bed.

No, no, no!

Which was more dangerous, the attaché case? Or the bath-room, where the man himself was? She wanted to know about him, desperately, but she couldn't bring herself to spy like a cheap little cheat.

Another, greater curiosity flared, one that made her feel even more uncomfortable. She thought again about his scars.

Obviously they bothered him, but she wanted to show him that they didn't bother her.

But what if they *did*?

The only way was to face them. If she wanted more from him, and suddenly she did, his scarred body had to be dealt with.

Padding to the bathroom door, the thud of her heart almost deafened her. She dragged in a breath and placed her fingers on the handle, but lightly, so as not to rattle it. Looking back at the bed, she hesitated. She could return there, switch in the television, distract herself that way. Instead, she turned the handle and slid into the steamy room, stepping quietly and easing the door shut behind her.

Beyond the frosted screen, the figure in the shower turned towards her instantly, blurred by the pattern of the glass, but looking not quite as she'd expected. She could see marks on his body, even through the screen, but it was the face that made her frown, confused.

'Well, come on then, now you're here.'

Jay's rough voice echoed around the tiled room, bouncing oddly.

'Er ... it's all right. I'll leave. I just wondered if you were OK. You've been in here a long time.' No longer than she had, but she didn't know what to say.

'Liar. Are you afraid? Afraid my body might freak you out?'

Shit, he was so clever. He'd sussed her out completely.

'What's to be afraid of?' she called out, flinging off the robe and marching towards the tub. When she reached it, she stepped around the edge of the screen and joined Jay in the streaming water.

'Oh my God!'

But it wasn't his scars that made her eyes widen. She noted

them subliminally. They were extensive, and looked fierce, and spoke of agonising pain. No, it was his face, which she'd thought was becoming familiar to her, that caused her shock.

'You've shaved your beard off!'

She almost swayed in the water, and instantly Jay anticipated it, and stepped forward, slinging an arm around her, holding her steady.

'Give the lady a lollipop for observation.' His dark eyes glittered, their brilliance refracted through droplets of water that hung on the tips of his long black lashes.

'Why? Why did you shave it off?'

She could do nothing but stare at his face, tracking every detail, every feature.

The beard had been a small one, and not really covered a great deal of his chin, but he looked astonishingly different. Younger. Less ferocious, yet still uncompromising, and strangely beautiful. Yes, there were scars, and some newly revealed ones around his chin, mostly on the left, but somehow they only highlighted the evenness and perfection of his features.

This was a face that had been quite literally sculpted and reshaped. And while doing so, a great surgeon had naturally created the best work that he could. High cheekbones, firm jaw, a nose that was almost unnaturally straight. He'd have the face of a fairytale prince when the scars eventually faded, as she guessed they would.

She really did sway then, but he held her, held her hard against the firm packed muscle of his chest and torso, the long strength of his thighs and, yes, the thickening jut of his erection.

Sandy drew in a deep breath, gathered herself, then put a hand onto Jay's wet shoulder, further steadying herself.

Why had she thought that? Jay wasn't a bit like *her* Prince Charming. No, not a bit like him. And yet why, when she looked up into his grey eyes, did the strange impression persist?

'Hey, are you all right?' he said softly, smoothing the water-logged hair back from her brow and slicking it over her shoulders.

'Yes, I'm fine.' Still holding onto his shoulder, she took a step back, looked into his face and then down his body, at his scars.

They were fierce and reddened, twisting over his chest and flanks and belly, and across one thigh. Not pretty. Not pretty at all. The thought of what he'd gone through, the pain and presumably immobilisation while he healed, made her heart twist with sympathy. And when Jay frowned suddenly, she knew her face had shown her feelings.

'Not a pretty sight, eh?' he said, his mouth hard as he spoke, as if there was more than just this moment making him bitter. 'Enough to put even the horniest bitch off.'

Her knee-jerk reaction was anger, and she cried, 'No! They're not pretty, but then I'm not just some horny bitch. I like you. And I thought you liked me. I thought we had something.'

Jay glared. But just for a second. Then his face twisted, playing out a complex series of emotional shifts. All even clearer now for his features being shorn of the beard.

'We do have something. I don't know what. It's early yet.'

Sandy stood on tiptoes and reached up to kiss his face, pressing her lips to his chin, the corner of his mouth, his cheek, feeling it, knowing it. She ran her hand down his body, exploring raised and crimped skin, touching it lightly in case there was pain, but not flinching from it.

Cupping her hand around his cock, she felt it throb and thicken and grow.

'I don't want a pity-fuck,' he breathed roughly, mouth against her wet hair.

'Why the hell would I pity-fuck you?' she growled back at him. 'What I'm interested in is a "best sex of my life", "never realised what I was missing" fuck, that's what.'

He bucked against her, rubbing his cock against her hip, circling his pelvis.

'OK, you've got scars. And yes, they look like pretty bad ones.' She looked up and met his eyes, making hers as hard, and uncompromising in their own way, as his. 'But there's nothing wrong with this, is there?' She ran her fingers up and down his cock, astounded that it could feel hotter and harder than ever before. 'This bloody great thing is in perfect working order as far as I can tell.'

Jay's laugh was a broken, bitter bark, and he shook his head. 'If only you knew, Princess. If only you knew.'

'What do you mean?' She strummed the head of his penis with her thumb, caressing the groove beneath, and then smiling as he hissed through his teeth, his fingers gouging her shoulder involuntarily as he rolled his head.

'Jesus, Sandy . . . Oh God . . .'

He pumped his hips, then stilled, clearly fighting for control. 'What did you mean?'

'Fucking hell, Sandy, if you want me to admit, I will!' As she looked up at him, he closed his eyes, and a muscle in his jaw jumped. 'The first time I was with a woman after my accident, this "bloody great thing" wasn't in such perfect working order as it is now.' He gritted his teeth momentarily in an obvious battle with his every alpha male instinct. 'I was pretty much a non-event, a dead loss. I wasn't a man.'

A wild clamour beat in Sandy's chest. Awe. Wonder. How much had it cost him to admit that to her? A man's greatest fear, and yet he'd shared it, with her. A woman he'd known less than a day. A woman he wanted to impress.

She wanted to kiss him and hug him and tell him everything would be all right, but that probably wasn't the response he wanted. Instead, she gave him another long lingering stroke with her thumb, cherishing the supreme hardness that hadn't wavered despite his confession.

'Well, as far as I can see and feel it's an insatiable monster now, Jay, and that's a fact.' She pumped him, slow, slow, then faster. 'Whatever happened before must've been a post-traumatic blip. There's nothing wrong here now. Nothing at all. In fact everything's right apart from the fact we don't have a condom handy.'

'Damn,' Jay growled, but it was a happy sound. Confident and primal. 'I've got condoms aplenty, but they're all in the bedside drawer.' He laughed, thrusting with his hips again, sliding her grip. 'And the way you touch me makes me want to come. And now, you sexy little tease, right now!'

'What are we doing to do?'

'Here, hold onto the rail,' said Jay suddenly, turning her in the stall. 'We'll just have to improvise.'

She grabbed the chrome handhold with one hand while Jay manoeuvred behind her, pressing his erection against her hip and swirling it against her skin. He too gripped the hold with one hand, and the other arm he slung around her belly, holding her tight.

'Touch yourself,' he commanded, his mouth against her hair as he began to work himself against her. 'Make yourself come as I get off rubbing against you.'

The words were raw and no-nonsense, but they excited her, as did the feel of his hot slippery penis, gliding against her bottom and her flank, coasting on the streaming water and its own lubrication. She swirled her own hips, trying to follow his, and stay in sync.

'Touch yourself,' he repeated again, his arm tightening

around her as he moved in an up and down jerk, right in her bottom cleft.

It was rude and delicious, and her clitoris pulsed as she pressed a fingertip against it. Jay's cock was tantalising delicate sensitive forbidden areas, and he was hard. It was like having a warm silky dildo rubbing and teasing her. The sensations were delicious and perverse, but now, with this man, she was hungry to try anything while the fires were hot, before they parted.

A little pang, a prefiguring of the loss she knew may well come, made her lose her thread a moment, but, when Jay kissed the side of her wet face, she found it again. Gyrating her bottom, teasing him back as he teased her, she got their groove back.

She barely needed to touch her clitoris. It felt as if it were simmering beneath her fingertip, ready to detonate. That was the way she seemed to be always, around Jay. As her pussy jerked and fluttered wildly, she cried out incoherently and pressed her forehead against the tiles. They were still cool despite the tropically hot water sluicing down.

Her orgasm was rough, hard, too soon really. She'd wanted to last out longer. Moaning, she pressed forward, jamming her hand against the wall with the weight of her body, still circling, trying to drag out the last pulses of pleasure as long as she could. Jay followed, pressing and moving too, rocking against her, not with all his weight, but adding force and more momentum. He was pleasuring himself, but working with her, sensing her needs.

This was a strange way to fuck, have sex, make love. But then nothing about Jay was common or usual. He'd blown into her life like a volatile dark storm, gathering energy and yes, with every hour that passed, wreaking havoc.

'Come again,' he urged, his penis sliding rhythmically in the cleft of her bottom. 'Come again for me, baby. You can do it!'

'I–I'm not sure I can,' she gasped, suddenly feeling exhausted. Hellfire, she'd had so much sex in the last twenty-four hours, more than she'd had in the previous twenty-four months. Slumped against the tiled wall, she seemed to have no energy in her.

Whereas Jay had enough for two.

Manhandling her, he took the pair of them down onto their knees, and set her facing the side of the bathtub. There was a towel on the rail just in reach, and he snatched it and slid it underneath her as a makeshift pillow. Following his lead, Sandy folded her arms on top of it and rested her face on them, the natural dishing of her back bringing her bottom up.

The tub was wide, but Jay was a big man, and space was tight. But somehow he slid behind her, rubbing himself against her thighs and her bottom as before, but this time with hands free to reach around and beneath her, to give pleasure.

Sandy drifted, didn't try to rouse, just let Jay 'happen' to her. It was a gentle liberating state, free from responsibilities and expectations, no performance stress. Floating and listening to the water and to Jay's breathing and occasional grunt of pleasure, she closed her eyes and surrendered to the moment.

His touch was light, incredibly measured and circumspect given what must be happening within his own body. It was like being stroked and gently roused by some incredible computer-driven sex robot. Or maybe cyborg, formed of warm human flesh but with the millimetre-perfect accuracy of a machine. An image that had amused her before made her grin. Surely only a Terminator was capable of operating in the face of such conflicting forces.

'What is it?' he purred, leaning over her. She could hear a smile in his voice, just as he seemed to read the slight smile on her face. He couldn't know what had provoked it, could he?

'Nothing. Just crazy thoughts. All this sex is making me mental.'

Jay paused, his fingers stilling between her thighs, at her breasts.

'No! Don't stop!' she cried, the stillness making her realise that her arousal was winding up again and she wanted – no, desperately needed – him to work her up to its conclusion.

'Your wish is my command.'

His fingers started slicking, slicking, slicking again, in her sex. But as he did so his mouth started moving in a track, down over her shoulder and on down her spine.

Before she knew it, suddenly the pleasuring was all about her again. Jay moved back in the tub, presumably still as rampantly erect as before, but now his mouth was kissing the small of her back, then her tailbone. And below.

And then he was kissing the pucker of her anus. Tickling it with his tongue, lightly probing and flicking with the furled point.

'Ooh ... no,' she crooned, years of inhibition speaking for her while every nerve and desire in her body screamed, *yes, yes, yes*!

'Yes!' confirmed Jay, his breath searing hot against the cheeks of her bottom and the little vent that pulsed with excitement in time to the tremors of imminent orgasm that shimmered in her vagina.

He prodded her with his tongue. He gently squeezed the bud of her clit with his thumb and finger. With the power of his mind, he somehow silently said 'Come!'

And she did. A massive wrenching orgasm that sent waves of dark transgressive bliss surging through her pussy and her entire pelvis. Incoherent, she let out a raw uncouth cry and slumped hard against the side of the porcelain tub, her sex pulsating and her anus pouting against his tongue.

For a few moments he held onto her, sweetening the sensations with his fingers and his tongue. And then he let go of her where she rested against the side of the bath and reared up over her. Summoning her last energy, Sandy twisted, craning to watch him behind her as, like a scarred and pagan god of sex, he pumped his cock in rough, almost angry strokes, then spurted semen over her bottom, shouting and snarling as incoherently as she had.

But as he slumped back, and took her with him, he whispered, 'Princess ...' and as the water swirled around them, he held her close.

13

In her dream, Prince Charming was leaning over her, his glorious features full of concern, his dark shaggy hair dangling forward over his brow. His grey eyes offered comfort and sympathy.

The fear and shock slid away, and she reached up to touch that dear face. But he receded, speeding away from her as if on a camera dolly, down a long menacing tunnel.

She called out to him, 'Jay! Please come back ... Jay!'

A hand touched her face, but *not* Prince Charming's, and she sat bolt upright in a strange bed in a room smelling of potpourri, her heart thudding and her pulse racing, totally disorientated.

But the arm that came around her felt just as good as the one that had encircled her all those years ago. And it was probably far stronger.

'Hey, are you all right, love? You were shouting and thrashing in your sleep.' Jay's fingers curved round her cheek and he made her look at him. With his other hand he brushed back her hair where strands of it had fallen across her face as she slept and into her mouth. 'You shouted my name. I hope I wasn't a monster in your nightmare.'

Sandy gave him a cautious little smile, still not quite sure what she was feeling. She glanced around the room, at all the chintz. Ah yes, the Waverley. The bathroom door was open and, seeing the gleaming white tiling beyond, she felt a rush of heat, and a blush rising in her face. She seemed to feel the slick of his tongue, licking her skin and probing wickedly between the cheeks of her bottom.

Oh boy . . .

Unable to look at him for a moment, she continued her perusal, and blushed more. At some point while she'd been taking the nap that she hadn't realised she'd needed until she'd laid her head down, someone had come and taken the tea tray, replacing it with a trolley laden with sandwiches, cold cuts, bread and cheese, wine, coffee in a cafetiere. They'd seen her sleeping in a guest's room. Sandy focused in on the beautiful presentation of fine food in an attempt to stop thinking about that. And about Jay's wicked tongue. And the deeper implications of her dream.

It'd been Prince Charming, she was certain of it, his face clearer than usual in her memory. But Jay had been the one she'd called for as that face had sped away.

Why do I keep linking the two of them? Surely, it's not possible that . . .

She shook her head. It was ridiculous and unlikely, and even so, if it was true, *she* hadn't changed all that much in the intervening years, even if Prince Charming had. Her face and her hair were just the same, and he must have recognised her, even if he was unrecognisable himself.

'Sandy?'

He was staring at her in concern, and perhaps a bit of suspicion. Was he really PC and even now realising that she'd sussed his true identity?

What the fuck is your true identity?

'Just a weird dream. I'm OK. Nothing to worry about.'

He frowned at her. For a face that had been stitched together by a surgeon's skill, his was extraordinarily expressive, especially now the goatee beard was history.

She decided to test him.

'It was about something that once happened to me, and someone I once met.' Shaking herself free of him, she slid off the bed and went to the tray, poured some coffee into a cup, then added milk. 'I was at the seaside, and someone tried to mug me on the sea front and steal my bag. They knocked me over, and this young man helped me.' She took a sip of the brew. It was rich and aromatic. Under normal circumstances she would have sighed with pleasure and made a point of remembering to ask at Reception about the brand, but instead she went on, 'He was kind and sweet and he sat with me until an ambulance came. But then he had to go and catch a ferry with his friends, and I never saw him again.'

'And he never tried to contact you again? Or you him?' Jay's voice was neutral, unrevealing. He wasn't PC, obviously. Disappointment stabbed her, even though she'd not seriously thought it was possible.

'No, alas, we never exchanged names.'

She heard him get up, come to stand beside her. Almost felt the heat of his body as he approached, even though he was wearing a hotel bathrobe, just as she was.

'But you still think about him.' It was a statement, as he too poured coffee, black and strong.

'Yes. Somehow in my mind he's become some kind of perfect fantasy hero. A kind of Prince Charming. The very embodiment of nobility, of chivalry . . . and romance.' She put down her cup, picked up a sliver of cheese and nibbled it. 'I know it's ridiculous. He's probably not like that at all. He could have turned out to be the most horrible, lying conniving git, a total bastard.'

'You're probably right.' Jay reached out and took some of the same cheese. 'We men are like that, mostly.'

'Maybe so. But it cuts both ways. If he met me now, he'd

probably find that I'm not a bit like the girl he remembers. There's nothing I need rescuing from. I rescue myself.'

There was a long silence. No sips of coffee. No nibbles of cheese. It was as if they were frozen in time, preserved in amber.

'Yes, I get that. I admire you for it,' said Jay eventually. Sandy half-expected him to reach for her, but he didn't and her body cried out for him. And not just her body.

Don't be stupid, she told herself. You've only known him a day, and he's obviously not here for long. It's like a one-night stand, but without the night. Just quick, but wild and gorgeous sex. Nothing wrong with that.

In fact, as she looked around, she saw things had changed.

A sombre charcoal-grey suit hung alone on the wardrobe door now, along with a shirt in anthracite and a tie in the same shade. The laptop had been stowed in a case that matched the attaché case. When she glanced back at Jay, she saw that beneath his robe, where it gaped open, he was wearing grey jersey jockey trunks.

He was leaving.

'Time to go now?' she said as lightly as she could, giving him what she hoped was a casual untroubled smile.

His eyes tracked over her face, as if he were assessing every feature, just as the Terminator would, and making calculations based on the configuration and tension of muscles to assess her mood and her responses.

'Just for a couple of days. I have some meetings down in London, but I'm coming back here at the weekend. I've retained this room.'

She forced herself to stay cool, but Jay must have seen the response on her face because his own expression morphed into a smile, smug and male.

'OK! I'm pleased,' she admitted, her head coming up. 'I . . . I like the sex! We have fun. I'd like a bit more of it. So, yes, I'm glad you're not leaving for good just yet.'

Jay touched a finger to her chin and looked down into her eyes. 'You're a special woman, Princess. Your fantasy hero guy was an imbecile not to stay around and get to know you. I'm going to try to not be quite so stupid.'

Sandy's heart leapt, wondering what the implications of *that* were.

But as he brought his mouth down on hers, she saw shadows in his eyes.

'Why the hell don't you just Google him and be done with it?' demanded Kat, gesturing wildly with the breadknife the next morning as she and Sandy made sandwiches for the lunchtime trade.

It had occurred to her. In fact, last night when she'd returned home late from the Waverley, Sandy had fired up her laptop, put Jay's name into the search engine and had her finger hovering over 'Enter' for several seconds. But when it had come down to it, she'd closed the browser and opened email instead to send a few messages to her family and far-flung friends.

It came back to that hunger for more of the sex, the close-ness they were sharing. The pleasure that might come to a standstill if she found out something about him that made her dislike him, or be disillusioned in some way. Her gut said there was some secret or other, and that it wasn't a very good one, but her body and, yes, her pussy, said don't pursue it.

And not just her body. Her mind preferred to remain in their special bubble of time together too. He was intriguing, unusual, intelligent, and also profoundly and mysteriously glamorous in his scarred and troubled way. How likely was she ever to be involved with a man who drove an Aston Martin again? Her ex had been quite well off, but nothing like in Jay's obvious league. The car, the beautiful clothing, and everything about him really, screamed that he was wealthy in a way beyond her modest world.

'I don't want to,' she told Kat, tamping down a tuna salad sandwich with a polythene-gloved hand. 'I don't want to know anything about him, really. It's just a brief "thing" while he's in the area, nothing more. Why complicate it by knowing who he is and potentially spoiling everything?' She sliced the sandwich neatly, and slid it into the plastic container, then sealed it. 'This is the first time I've had a full-on, just sex and pleasure relationship, and I'm going to make the most of it. You of all people should appreciate that, the way you are with Greg.'

Kat gave her a long look. 'Greg and I talk, and have fun out of bed as well as in it.' Unable to stop herself, Sandy glanced at the replacement butter dish, and when their eyes met again, Kat laughed. 'You know what I mean. Non-sex fun out of bed. I like him, I really do. And you could probably like Jay that way too, if you knew you could trust him, by knowing more about him.'

'No. I've made up my mind. Why mess with a good thing?' Something in her heart told her that Jay's entrance into her life would be followed fairly quickly by his exit again, and she was determined not to muck up the intervening days.

'Fair enough,' conceded Kat. 'But if you won't find out more about him, and he's going to remain a mystery man, you're completely free to tell me all about his kinky sex preferences.' Sandy's mouth dropped open, but Kat went on blithely, 'And don't try to tell me he isn't kinky, because he's just got that look of a delicious pervert written all over him.'

'How can you say that? He might be totally conservative in bed for all you know.'

Sandy felt hot. Memories were already flooding in. She felt prickly and embarrassed to be thinking about all the things she and Jay had crammed into their so-brief acquaintance, right here, in the company of her friend. She wasn't Kat. She'd always been more the willing listener, not the one to tell every lurid detail about herself.

'Well, we didn't do anything all *that* pervy and fetishy. It was more a kind of vanilla, but intense, you know what I mean?' Which she supposed was a true representation, thus far. Not to say that Jay hadn't talked about such things, whispering outrageous scenarios in her ear while he'd fucked her fiercely, face-down across the chintz duvet cover after their improvised congress in the shower. He'd murmured of erotic toys and spanking, of bondage and erotic games, but the sex itself had been straight, hard and workmanlike. He'd obviously been thinking ahead, planning his London trip and his business, whatever that was, while he'd been thrusting inside her. Men!

'Early days, hon, early days,' observed Kat sagely. 'A man like him, he's a dead ringer for a master. The sort of guy who'd dress you in leather lingerie, tie you up and spank your bottom, then fuck you senseless until you couldn't see straight, and begged for mercy.'

'How do *you* know all about leather and masters anyway?' Sandy demanded, going on the offensive. Kat was far too close to the truth of what Jay had whispered about. 'Does Greg do all those things to you? As part of the "experimenting"?'

Kat's grin was creamy. She tapped the side of her nose. 'Yes, he likes to experiment. But you know that.' She paused, then seemed to make a decision. 'We've been to "special nights" at the Waverley. Held in the private function suite. You know, leather, bondage, erotic punishment and whatnot. Just the sort of thing I swear your bloke is into.'

'He's not "my" bloke. I barely know him.'

'He looks as if he's yours.' Sandy looked hard at her friend.

Kat had a serious expression on her face now, thoughtful, almost worried. 'He has the look of a guy who's been obsessed with you for years. I don't know, but he stares at you as if you're the woman of his dreams.'

'That's ridiculous!' Shaken, Sandy started fiddling with the tuna filling, stirring it in its bowl even though it was already well mixed. 'You've only ever seen him looking at me on a couple of occasions, how the hell do you come to that conclusion?'

'Hey, simmer down, love. It's just an impression I get. Maybe I'm wrong?' Kat laid down the breadknife and patted Sandy on the arm. 'You just enjoy him for a while, eh? He's obviously a classy man who knows how to treat a woman. You make the most of him. He's obviously got pots of money too, so you'll probably get lots of pampering and lovely pressies out of it, even if it is just a temporary thing.'

'What kind of a person do you think I am?' Sandy protested, guilt pricking her. The luxurious facilities at the Waverley and the room service had been nice.

'A woman, kiddo. That's what I think you are.' Kat took up her knife again and nodded towards Sandy and the bread, the butter, the fillings. 'Now get a move on, or it'll be sandwich time and there'll be nothing to sell.'

'OK, boss,' replied Sandy with a laugh. But as she buttered and filled and passed the finished sandwiches to Kat, her mind was whirling with thoughts of Jay, and of obsession.

And stupid notions that she might have been obsessed with him for years too.

On Friday morning, to the accompaniment of an 'I told you so' nod from Kat, a parcel arrived.

It came via courier delivery at about ten o'clock and, once she tore off the outer wrapping, Sandy discovered a beautifully constructed package from a world-famous London lingerie house. The box was white and gold and adorned with soft pink ribbons and, despite the fact that Kat's eyes were out on stalks, and she protested bitterly about the 'unfairness and mental cruelty' of being denied a glimpse of the parcel's contents, Sandy excused herself and sneaked away into the flat to open it up.

Inside, swathed in layers and layers of tissue in multi-shades of pink, was a collection of the most exquisite beauty: several bra and G-string sets in sumptuous combinations of colours and fabrics, not to mention a number of cellophane packets containing gossamer-fine hold-up stockings, and a gorgeous black camisole in heavy satin with matching knickers.

Sandy handled the lovely things, full of wonder. A set in a sweetly virginal white net caught her eye. It was trimmed with delicate lace edging and cheeky little embroidered daisies with smiley faces that made her want to smile back at them. Next, she pulled out a coffee satin confection, encrusted with elaborate chocolate lace and appliqués of autumn leaves and sea shells. There was even a racy red and black set that was the high-end version of the naughty but imaginary peephole and split-crotch ensemble that she'd described to Jay.

There was no card with the extravagant goodies, but she'd have bet a year of the Teapot's takings that they were from him. Who else could have sent them? There was nobody in her life, in her *sexual* life, other than him.

When the hell did you have time to choose all this lot? Weren't you going back to London on business?

A rather horrible thought occurred. Perhaps he had a faithful secretary or P.A. who he sent out to exclusive knicker boutiques to buy presents for his latest conquests?

Sandy threw the red and black fripperies back into the box as if they'd burnt her. Emotions churned, and the vilest, greenest and most shaming of them was jealousy. She imagined the secretary, seeing Jay every day, working with him closely. Maybe even having a drink after work with him. Dinner. Perhaps more.

Fuck, you don't even know if he has got a female secretary! Maybe it's a bloke?

Was that worse?

Or maybe Jay had slipped discreetly into the exclusive shop during evening opening hours, carefully choosing all these beautiful things for her himself, picturing them on her body, and then getting hard as he put himself in that picture and imagined taking them off her again.

Picking up the white bra, she imagined the feel of the delicate net against her nipple. Abrading the sensitive crest when it was hard and erect, just the way it was now. And Jay's hand would close around her breast, cupping it. Still rubbing the fine white fabric between her fingers, she cupped herself with her other hand, trying to make herself believe that her narrow fingers were Jay's bigger, stronger ones. He'd lift the weight of her breast, roll the flesh a little, then perhaps pinch her nipple in that infernal way he seemed so fond of, inflicting a pleasure-pain that shot straight to her clit and made it swell.

She was distracted, turned on, horny, just from looking at a few bits of posh underwear and thinking about the man who'd sent them to her. Low in her pelvis, the heavy weight of desire gripped like vice. Gripped her like Jay's hand. Not knowing when it'd started, she found herself breathing heavily, almost panting. She wanted to touch herself. Pincering her nipple, she clenched the muscles in her pussy, her bottom, working herself without actually giving in to using her fingers. Her chest felt hot, her crotch moist, her head light as thistledown.

Collapsing onto the kitchen chair, she closed her eyes,

fantasising that Jay was here, lifting her skirt, bending down to slide his hand between her legs and then slipping his fingers under the elastic of her knickers. The white bra fell to the floor. Her fingers became his, wriggling into her panties to seek and find her clit.

As she stroked herself, she became the director of her own shadow-play as well as the star performer. While she masturbated the tiny sensitive little organ in a complicated rhythm, Jay assumed the role of servant, for once, doing her bidding. With his clever curving fingers at her command, he filled her vagina and – ooh – her anus, a living sex toy.

Sandy's heels dragged along the kitchen floor. Two more flicks, here, there, and she was tumbling over the edge into orgasm. Her pussy rippled like a flame. She chanted 'Jay, Jay, Jay,' under her breath, in an agony of soundless stolen pleasure.

Still touching herself, she sat gasping for a moment or two, barely able to believe the effect the man could have on her without even being there. He just had to send her a few bras and pairs of knickers and she turned into a voracious lust-monkey, unable to keep her hands off herself, desperate for pleasure at the slightest provocation.

'Sandy! We're getting a bit busy!'

Kat's voice echoed from the café, making Sandy jump and wrench her hand out of her knickers.

'OK, won't be a minute!'

After stuffing the lingerie back in the box and cramming down the lid, she darted to the sink and washed her hands, then drank a glass of cold water to calm herself. At the door, she turned and looked back at her gift, shaking her head.

What have you done to me, Jay Bentley? What have you done?

* * *

Fortunately, the second parcel arrived late in the day, almost at closing time.

Sandy had let Kat off early to go around to Greg's place, to do God alone knew what. With her boyfriend on her mind, Kat seemed to have forgotten the first parcel and, as she clattered down the stairs whistling, Sandy experienced a 'grrr' of female envy. Kat would be getting some tonight, and lots of it. And those lots would probably be wild and kinky and experimental. Fabulous fucking, and who knew what else.

I wish you were here, Jay. I wish I was lying on my back on the kitchen floor, with my legs wide open and you between them, pumping hard.

The image was vivid, and kept morphing and morphing and morphing.

Fingers, tongues, Jay's cock, her pussy, all in infinite combinations and with infinite diversity.

Sandy shook her head to clear it and, as she did so, a rather cute looking UPS man suddenly walked into the café, bearing a clipboard and another large parcel.

'You all right, love?' he said cheerfully as he set the box down and proffered his board for her signature.

'Fine, thanks.'

Was she? Her face was pink and her heart was thudding, and it certainly wasn't anything to do with this bloke, even though he was nice looking. She hustled him down the stairs with unseemly haste and locked the door behind him. OK, so it was a bit early. She and Kat had already brought the outside tables and chairs in, and there were no teatime customers.

Charging up the steps two at a time, she nearly tripped and the shock of it pulled her up sharply.

What the hell was the matter with her? She'd known a man two days, tops, and he'd turned her into a madwoman and a nymphomaniac. She had to get a grip. She had to get a grip.

But the second parcel sat on one of the red and white chequer-clothed tables. If the first had been hot lingerie, what the devil was in this one?

Sandy lugged it into the bedroom. Out of sight, out of mind. In the sitting room, Kat was likely to 'accidentally' flip open the lid and take a look inside. And Sandy knew without a doubt that this box had come from Jay just as much as the other one had.

This time the inner carton was black, and tied with red and scarlet paper ribbon. Ah ha, the classic sex colours. Her heart thumped harder as she teased open the bow.

Inside, again, tissue paper. All black this time. And several printed leaflets, all bearing the logo 'Personal Indulgences', and all bearing details of, guess what, sex toys.

But judging by the prices, whatever lay swathed in the layers of tissue paper was a world away from the stuff that Kat had been flogging at her Naughty Girls' Party. Sandy pulled a delivery note from amongst the paperwork, and even though there was no price on it, and no indication of who'd ordered it, the words 'Custom Box' were intriguing.

So the items were specially chosen, but by whom? By whom?

She turned away, not sure she wanted to look, yet dying to.

'Bugger it!'

She stomped through to the kitchen, opened the fridge and found the open bottle of wine she'd been saving for this evening. So what if it was only six o'clock? She poured some into an old glass on the drainer and marched back to the bedroom. And the box open on the bed.

After burrowing into the tissue paper layers, she brought out a small package, wrapped in stiff black paper and more red and black ribbon. Heedless of the care that had been taken to wrap it, she tore off the covering and revealed a mask.

It was a beautiful confection of off-black suede with wide black ribbons to hold it in place. The lining was satin and very soft. After taking a swig of wine first, Sandy tried it over her eyes, shaking in the darkness it created.

What would it be like to be lying on the bed in darkness like this? Waiting and wondering what Jay was going to do to her? Where he would touch her first, and would it be a gentle touch, or a harder one? She had to breathe deeply, not knowing which she really wanted.

The second item she unveiled was, *quelle surprise*, a vibrator. But not any old vibrator, and a world away from the tacky plastic tube she'd bought at Kat's party. It was in the form of what she could only describe as a thoughtfully shaped stone, not like any toy she'd even seen before. But she could instantly and instinctively see how it was used. There was a button to press, but it yielded no buzz.

Ah, batteries, Mr Knowitall. I need batteries.

But as she set the vibrator aside, and rummaged around a bit amongst the other as yet unknown items, her fingers alighted on some more familiar shapes, secreted at the bottom of the box.

Energiser Ultimate Lithium, half a dozen packages of them. *Bloody hell, Jay! What kind of insatiable sex freak do you think I am?*

The sort who had sex about half a dozen times in the space of twenty-four hours with a man she barely knew, and that wasn't counting cunnilingus, fellatio and general unspecified fiddling about, that's what.

She took a long swig of wine before tackling the rest of the box's contents.

*   *   *

At ten o'clock, when the phone rang, Sandy had long ago sworn off wine for the rest of the evening. Who needed it, when the contents of her 'custom box' were enough to make any red-blooded woman's head spin. Vibrators, dildos, silk bondage restraints and an eye-watering selection of plugs and beads and other insertable objects. Not to mention nipple clamps, lubricants and a beautiful glass jar full of supposedly proven herbal arousal balm.

Jeepers creepers, I know we talked about experimentation, Jay, but I wasn't expecting to receive an entire tactical war chest devoted to it!

With the contents of the box spread out around her on the bed, she stared at the phone's display.

'Number withheld.'

But there was only one person it could be.

14

'Hello, Princess, how are you? Had a good day?'

Sandy pulled a face at the receiver. Cheeky sod! Giving her the 'everything's completely normal, let's chat about stuff like the weather' line, when he'd just sent her hundreds, maybe thousands of pounds' worth of exclusive lingerie and designer sex toys.

'Yes, fine thank you. Quite busy. How are you? How was your day?'

Two could play at that game.

But she didn't expect to hear a sigh. Then a long pause.

'Hellish, to be honest. A lot of arguing with people and trying to make them see a different way to do things.'

In the short time she'd known him, it'd become obvious that Jay had suffered some kind of injury to his vocal cords in his accident. His voice was husky and gravelly, a real bedroom voice if ever there was one. But tonight he sounded tired, ragged around the edges.

Despite everything, she felt a strange melt of sympathy. She barely knew him, but she wanted to reach out across the distance between them and soothe his stress.

'Who've you been arguing with?'

It was way beyond their unspoken no-go area, but surprisingly he answered quickly and unguardedly.

'My father, the old bastard. I thought we'd come to an accommodation recently, found a way to work together, but now I'm wondering whether I was wrong.'

'I'm sorry about that. I've always got on well with my parents. It must be tough.'

'Don't worry, love. We'll muddle through somehow. I'd rather talk about you.'

She could hear the smile in his voice, that devilish grin that made his grey eyes shine like metal. When was he going to ask about the parcels, she wondered.

'So, this busy day. Anything exciting to report? Any strange men accosting you in the café and hustling you into the cloakroom for a desperate fuck?'

She smiled her own devilish grin, wishing she had a glass of wine again to sip while she played silly buggers with him a bit longer. 'No, not today, alas. But there were a couple of delivery men who gave me the eye. You wouldn't believe how hunky the UPS guys are nowadays.'

'UPS, eh? Did you get anything nice?'

'Nice? Not really. Some anonymous pervert sent me a bunch of sleazy lingerie and a whole load of sex toys. There really are some sick and depraved weirdos out there nowadays.'

'*Sleazy* lingerie?' Mock aggrieved.

'Well, actually it's quite nice. I think I'm going to keep it. Especially the red and black number. Although that *is* sort of semi-sleazy. Great if you like the classic split-crotch and peephole look.'

A low gritty chuckle emanated from the speaker.

'Oh, you mean like the set you had, then suddenly didn't have?'

Giving herself a moment to think, Sandy set the phone in its cradle and pressed the button for hands free.

'Yep, that's the one.'

'Really? Well, maybe your anonymous perverted friend realised that you really *did* want a red and black sleazoid set after all and was pandering to your every whim?' There was a slight click, and Sandy realised that Jay must have switched to hands free too. He'd read her mind, or maybe he'd been planning to use his hands for other things all along? 'So, what about the other parcel? The sex toys? Have you tried any of them yet?'

Sandy stared around, looking at the items nestling in their wrappings. She'd hardly dared handle most of the things, shaken up by the weird unstable breathless feelings in her stomach at the thought of actually using them.

'No! Of course not. And who says I'm going to?'

'Tut tut, bottling out, are we?' Jay's voice was arch and amused. It made her bristle, but also wish he was there so she could jump all over his bones. That sort of macho cleverness should in theory make her want to tell him to get lost, but instead it made her go all strange and want him in that very alarming and very submissive way she didn't quite understand.

'I thought you were the girl who wanted to experiment,' he reminded her, and she half wanted to kill him, and half surrender to him in those deepest darkest ways.

'I do.'

'So experiment then. Pick something and try it.'

'All right then, I will.'

She rummaged about and pulled out the thoughtfully shaped vibrator in which she'd thoughtfully fitted a set of batteries.

'You do realise this amounts to phone sex, don't you?' The device was quite weighty in her palm but it fitted nicely. Ergonomically designed, oh yeah. Not like the gruesome pink and black and red plastic jobbies that had been on sale at Kat's party. This was class, and the softest smoothest milky pearly-blue.

'Oh no, not phone sex. Perish the thought,' Jay replied, laughing. 'That had never occurred to me.'

Ignoring him, Sandy turned on the vibrator. Its purr was low, discreet, nearly silent at its lowest setting. Could he hear it? She didn't ask, but she imagined him in his own bed somewhere, stretched out against a mountain of luxurious pillows, settling down to touch himself, if he wasn't already. Weirdly, she also saw him having difficulty getting comfy, as if the tiredness she sensed in him was due to pain as well as work and parental aggro.

Why do I keep getting these nurturing feelings for him? He can take care of himself, and it's not as if we're a big long-term deal.

Banishing troubling thoughts, Sandy wriggled against her own far less sumptuous Tesco-bought pillows. She spread her legs, tweaked up her mini nightshirt, and rested the humming vibe against her thigh.

Dare she do it?

There was a big difference between occasionally indulging in a little zizz with a vibrator in the privacy of the bathroom or under the covers of your strictly solo bed, and pleasuring yourself with one for an eagerly listening and very horny male audience.

'Well, you've turned it on, Princess. That's a good start. But it's doing you no good just sitting there buzzing. You've got to do something with it. Press it against your pussy. That's how they work.'

'I know how vibrators work, thank you very much.'

Cautiously, she eased her thighs further apart, pointing her toes a little in the way that seemed to work for her. On a deep breath, she let the pearly-blue shape rest against her cleft, through the buffer of her pubic thatch.

Oh, it was so smooth. Deceptively gentle. Insidious. It barely seemed to be doing anything, and yet the frequency of the buzz set up a resonance through her sex that made her gasp. And she hadn't even touched it to naked skin yet.

'Good?'

How the fuck did he know? Good God, had he tried the thing? But no, the box had been packed by the sex-toy company. He'd just ordered from a catalogue or something. Unless he had one of his own, or he'd borrowed a girlfriend's.

'*That* good, eh? Left you speechless.'

'It's all right.' But it was more than all right, and the waver in her voice only confirmed that to him. The subtle silky vibrations seemed to flurry through her entire body. She could feel them in her brain, making her ears tingle. And in her toes, making them point more than ever. Greedy for sensation, she pressed the device harder against herself then, biting her lip to keep from crying out, she dove her fingers down into her bush and parted a way to give the vibe access.

When it touched her clit she cried, 'Oh God!' She couldn't help herself.

'That's it, Princess. You know you want it. Do yourself for me.'

'Well, aren't you just a prince of sophistication?' Sandy gasped through gritted teeth, trying to control her movements, and her own voice, as Jay laughed.

Her hips seemed to want to grind of their own accord, circling and rocking against the mattress. Every part of her pussy and bottom was sensitised, nerves firing, muscles gathering ready to release again in the pulsations of orgasm. She closed her eyes, unable to look at herself, but that only created a shadow vision of Jay, sitting up in his own bed but watching her. Had he got his cock in his hand? Surely he had? How could he *not* have?

'You. What about you? Are you wanking?' she demanded, pumping her hips, her hand, and the pretty vibrator, riding the action.

'Now who's the sophisticated one?'

But his voice gave him away too. A hint of a gasp. Not quite panting, but not too far off. He was breathing heavily, fighting for control. Just as she was.

The muscles in Sandy's thighs were rigid. Her clit tingled. So close, so very, very close. In a supreme effort of will, she backed the vibrator off a little, letting it lie to one side, still buzzing away, but not quite at the heart of the matter. It was a blessed respite, but her pleasure centres still screamed back at her, 'now, now, now!'

'Tell me what *you're* doing, Jay. I want to imagine it. Are you in bed? Are you naked?' She could see his body, magnificent yet tattooed with the marks of pain and suffering. Somehow his scars didn't seem to matter, because they made him what he was, a tempered man, not a pretty boy.

There was a long pause. A breathing space. Sandy frowned, wondering if it was those scars that were making him reticent. The pretty boy would have been happy to describe his body, and embellish its attractions no doubt. But maybe the scarred man didn't want to remind her of his flaws?

'Yes, I'm in bed,' he admitted at length, 'and I wish you were here, so you could be doing what I'm doing now.'

'What's that?'

'Rubbing my cock, Princess, rubbing my cock. And alas, my big old mitt isn't nearly as tantalising and delightful as your little hand.' He made a little grunting sound, quite endearing really. 'But it's doing the job, I've got to admit, and not too badly.'

Oh, that beautiful cock! Thankfully, it was one of the few parts of him that was totally unscarred and she could vouch for its effectiveness and then some.

'Do you wear pyjamas?'

'No, I've got my robe on. But open, so I can touch myself.'

'Robe colour?'

'Grey.'

'Like your eyes. And the Aston?'

'Sort of.'

'Bed sheets?'

'White cotton. Nothing exotic. No chintz.'

Sandy laughed. He'd still looked hard as nails when swathed in the Waverley's fussily patterned bedding.

'Are you close?'

Jay laughed. 'Yes. Are *you*? I'm not hearing much action from your end of the line any more.'

'I'm trying to make it last.' She edged the little vibrator nearer to her clit, then edged it back again when the urge to wriggle and buck and grab for pleasure like a kid gorging on sweeties became overwhelming.

'But why?' Jay's voice was staccato as if he too were fighting the same greed. 'You girls are so lucky. You can go again straight away.'

'I'm not sure I always want to. Sometimes what I want is the one great big one that sweeps me away, totally satisfying.'

She could almost see him pausing mid-stroke, his close-cropped head cocked on one side. Despite the pleasure, she was thinking, thinking too.

One great big one, that sweeps me away, totally satisfying.

Sandy wasn't really sure she was still talking about an orgasm.

One great big one, that sweeps me away, totally satisfying.

Yes, that was what he wanted. What he'd always wanted.

And Sandy was still it. She'd always been it. Always would be.

My beautiful Princess. I wasn't wrong. You are *the one.*

But it was stupid, crazy, irrational and so incredibly messed up by circumstances that it almost seemed like some kind of punishment for his profligate ways and his intransigence in his relationship with his father.

Fuck, fuck, fuck, the woman he'd always dreamed was perfect for him, *was* perfect for him. But unfortunately she'd soon have more than ample reason to despise him. For who he was, and for him not *telling* her who he was. Either as her long-lost rescuer or Jason Bentley Forbes.

He opened his mouth, to spill forth all the truths and take his chances, but a sudden sweet little half-gasp of suppressed pleasure from the speakerphone stilled his tongue. And his cock – which hadn't drooped, but which had lost some of its aching urgency while he'd turned thoughts and revelations over in his mind – leaped and stiffened harder in his fingers.

He closed his eyes, imagining her beautiful pink lips parted on that gasp.

She was miles and miles away, and yet she was with him, writhing, responding to his touch, or his mouth, or the thrust of his cock. He wanted to do everything with her and to her, and to freely offer her the same gifts. Submission had never been one of his kinks, but with Sandy he could imagine the balance tipping sometimes. Tipping and provoking intense thrills.

'Jay, are you still there? Are you OK?'

'Yeah, I'm fine, love. Just imagining you having that great big orgasm that sweeps you away. Hell, I'd like to be there to give you your next one.'

She didn't answer. But he could sense her breathing. Almost hear her panting. A vision of her moving uneasily against her pillows, her bright mane of hair like a tousled cape of ruddy silk against the white cotton fabric. In his dream she was naked, her skin like honey, moist with sweat, and between her legs, moister still.

The high-tech vibrator was pressed against her pussy.

'Are you still using your toy?'

God, he wanted to be there, to be the one using it on her. Driving her to extremes of pleasure, making her come and come and come until she couldn't see straight, and just clung to him shaking and compliant. For once. She wasn't the delicate flower of his skewed dreams based on a few moments' contact. She was fit and feisty and wild and full of will and self determination. Which made her moments of surrender all the more precious, like rare cosmic jewels.

When she was half out of her mind, half fainting with more orgasms in an hour than most women had in a week, he wanted to mount her, ride her, open her heart and soul to him utterly as he compelled her to rise again from the depths of utter submission to that one last great climax that would bond them together.

Oh fuck, oh fuck . . . Just two days of knowing the real Princess and I've fallen in love with her.

As his cock spurted, he knew the impossible was true.

Sandy heard the tell-tale groans, and for a moment it distracted her from her own rise to climax, not quite sure what the emotions she was feeling were. This didn't seem like the pattern she'd expected at all. Should the masterful man be the one to tease her and tease her and tease her, withholding his own culmination until he'd coaxed come after come out of her?

Selfish, she thought, then immediately, *not selfish*. It was as if he'd given her a gift. His vulnerability and his surrender to his senses, and to her.

'Oh God, Sandy,' he murmured after a few moments. His low raspy voice was barely audible across the miles, but the weight of emotion in it rang clear. 'Sorry, love, I couldn't wait. I was thinking about you. Thinking about touching you and making you come and being in you, and it all got a bit too much for me and I climaxed.' She heard the rustle of bedclothes and the sound of him adjusting his position, and at the same time a sharp intake of breath. Was he hurting? 'I wanted to tease you and tease you and tease you, you know? Play it out a bit.'

Despite her concern, Sandy had to smile. How perfectly she'd read him there. What he'd intended and hoped for – and what, on this occasion, he'd been unable to achieve. The fact that he wasn't always all conquering, all control, was somehow exquisitely amazing.

The sounds of more movement came, and then Jay's voice, different, back in command.

'Your turn now, Princess. I've come for you, you've got to come for me. You owe me your pleasure.'

Her belly shuddered. This Jay thrilled her too, in a different way. Against the smooth surface of the vibrator, her sex heaved like a wave and the moisture down there began to well.

'Turn the power up, Sandy. Do it now. I want you writhing. I want to know that thing is throbbing against you, driving you insane, tormenting your clit.' He paused, as if for effect. 'Do it now and, as you do it, pinch your nipple.'

Sandy silently moaned 'no' while meaning 'yes'. There was such power in his voice, such compulsion. What weird perversity inside her made her want to be tortured with pleasure by him? It seemed so deeply kinky a thing to crave, and yet she did.

'Are you doing as I say?'

'I'm trying.'

She shuffled down the bed until she was lying flat, took the crest of her nipple between her fingertips, and squeezed. The little pain, combined with the vibrations, made her whine.

'Better. Now come on, try harder,' Jay urged, as if he were

there in the room, observing every twitch, every wriggle, every jerk of her hips. 'Open your legs very, very wide. Expose everything, make sure the vibe touches as much of you as possible. And pinch your nipple hard, baby, no playing. Make it hurt.'

The hard ache in her teat made her clitoris feel as if it were sizzling. Her pelvis rose involuntarily, cramming her tender pussy against the buzzing hardness of the unforgiving vibrator. She thumbed the power slider, twisted her nipple. And screamed out loud as a white pulsation wrenched at her sex.

Arching like a bow, riding the huge hard clenching orgasm, she gasped and moaned, her voice uncouth as her heels dragged against the bedding. Behind her closed eyelids she saw Jay's face, his triumphant smile, his burning eyes.

'Jay! Oh God, Jay!' she shouted, still jerking, still coming.

'Oh yes, Princess,' she heard him say, as if through fog.

Over-stimulated, she flung away the vibe and collapsed back against the bed, cupping her simmering crotch and, instead of arching now, curling up, making herself foetal. A great well of emotion seemed to burst inside her and she found herself sobbing like a child.

'Sandy? Sandy? Are you all right? Talk to me.'

The fog cleared, and she could hear the real concern in his voice. And that only made her emotions surge and bubble. Her heart ached and ached to have him beside her. Her entire body seemed to cry out for *his* warm body, tight against her. Not fucking, just holding, just being there.

'Sandy!'

'It's all right. I'm fine. Just a bit orgasmed out, that's all.'

Struggling, she dragged herself up again, to sit against the pillows. With a shake of her hair she tried to tidy herself, just as if he'd been there, dragging down her nightshirt that had got pushed right up into a bundle above her breasts. Trying to steady her breathing and not snivel, she tweaked the cotton fabric down modestly over her thighs.

'Was that a big one?' he asked, sounding strangely tentative.

'Um, yes ... pretty big. You could say that.'

'I wish I'd seen it.'

'I wish you had too.' The words just popped out, without her consciously thinking them, but it was true. She would have liked to have given him that intense experience.

There was a moment of silence and, gritting her teeth, Sandy fought not to cry. She wasn't sad, not really, and she wasn't normally a baby, but the whirlwind of what she'd just been though had her at sixes and sevens. Surreptitiously, she reached for her bedside box of tissues. Maybe it was a good job Jay wasn't here, or he'd see the tears and know how wimpy and girly she was being.

'Don't cry.'

Her hand froze, tissue half out of the box.

How the hell do you know these things?

'I'm not!' She rubbed furiously at her eyes. He'd probably be able to see their red rims now too.

'Oh, I think you are, and I'm sorry if I've upset you in any way. I just thought you'd like a bit of sexy fun.'

He didn't sound too sure of himself either. To Sandy, his voice seemed huskier than ever.

'I did. I do. It's just sometimes ... post-coital *tristesse* and all that, you know?'

He sighed. He felt it too, she just knew he did.

'I wish I was there, Princess. I wish I was next to you so I could hold you and kiss it better.'

Sandy's head seemed to float. She went hot and cold. Felt almost faint. She'd heard him say those words before. And not just in the garden at the Waverley when her feet had been killing her in those stupid shoes. The voice was so different. And yet the same. The same!

She'd told him the story. He knew she remembered him. He *must* remember her, he must! But why not say so?

Prince Charming had been beautiful. Jay was beautiful in his own savage way. But it was a beauty crafted by a surgeon's knife out of cruelly damaged raw material. Could they be the same man? Dare she ask? Would he admit it? And where did that leave them if he did?

More silence stretched on, heavy across the airwaves. But she couldn't take it.

'Are you him? Prince Charming?' The words came out tiny, as if she hardly dared speak them, as if she was allowing herself an opt out and she could claim he'd misheard her.

She heard a great drawing in of breath. Shocking somehow. And deeply revealing in such a hard unflappable man. He'd started this by using the words 'kiss it better', but was he now regretting that and wishing he hadn't?

But either way, he'd told her all she needed to know.

Jay Bentley and Prince Charming were the same man.

'Are you him?' she prompted.

'I was once.' He sounded so weary now, and she could hear the pain in his broken voice. But was that from regret, or his injuries? That was less clear. 'But I've changed too much to ever be that man again. I've done too much.' He sighed. 'I wasn't an admirable person then, and I'm far worse now.'

'Let me be the judge of that!' Sandy cried. She was on that strange merry-go-round of panic and confusion again, trying to reach some intangible goal, some half-imaginary person. He kept floating into reach then being snatched back away from her. And now she had a feeling he was gone for good. The tears she'd suppressed before flowed freely down her face.

'I've destroyed your dream, haven't I?' His voice was cool, flat. Oddly emotionless. 'You've spent all these years fantasising about your pretty saviour and now you know you'll never find him. Not in any form that's recognisable as the man he once was.'

'Do you think I'm so shallow that I only dream about someone because they look cute? Looks aren't everything. And anyway, you look fine to me as you are.'

A bitter jag of laughter.

'Well, that would be fine. But I'm not chivalrous and high-minded like your dream guy. You don't know anything about me, and it's probably better that you never do.'

Sandy flung away her mushy crumpled tissue and grabbed another one. It wouldn't come out of the box, and she bashed and smashed at the cardboard, aware that she was behaving like a child having a tantrum but needing some kind of release for the pressure cooker of her emotions.

'Is that it then?' she demanded. 'Just a few incredible shags and a bit of sexual experimentation? And fifteen years of dreams stomped to pulp into the bargain.'

'I'm sorry.'

'I'm sorry.'

The words were simultaneous, and so was the laughter that followed within a heartbeat.

'I'm sorry for being a drama queen there,' said Sandy at last. A strange calm settled over her. She felt tired, but not unhappy. 'How can I possibly expect anyone to be like somebody I just dreamed up? And indeed, why should they be? Prince Charming was just a figment of my imagination really, based on someone I met briefly, who was kind to me.' She paused. 'And please don't try to deny you were kind, because you were.'

'OK,' he conceded. 'But you're not a drama queen, you're Princess.' His rough voice sounded unexpectedly tender.

'And you're not the only one who can lay the weight of un-realistic fantasies on the shoulders of an unknowing stranger.'

What was he trying to say?

Panic started to geyser up again.

'Oh shit! Now I get it. *I'm* a huge disappointment to *you.*'

A cold hand gripped her heart. How could she have been so stupid? And so arrogant? Jay had harboured expectations of his dream person too, and she didn't match them.

'No-fucking-way,' he said steadily. 'There's nothing disap-pointing about you, lady. You're exciting and beautiful and you arouse me in ways you can't imagine.' He laughed softly. 'Hell, here we are having a row and I've got a hard-on all over again. I'm going to have to wank myself to sleep at this rate, imag-ining all the things I want to do to you.'

It had been a long, long night. One in which she'd travelled across an ocean of time, revisited a dream, lost it, but somehow recovered it again. Sandy felt tired, confused and suddenly very sleepy. And yet at the same time, the seductive vision formed again.

Jay in his grey robe, stretched against white sheets, handling himself. It seemed so simple and so straightforward to just concentrate on that, and push to one side the perplexing and puzzling issues of identity, not to mention the insidiously gath-ering curiosity at how he'd found her. It couldn't be coincidence, surely?

Bollocks to it. Concentrate on now. Thrash all that stuff out another time, when you're sharper.

The picture of a gorgeous cock wrapped in long dextrous fingers eased the mind as much as it stirred her sticky body. It was so simple and so relaxing just to think of it.

'So, are you going to do that?'

He laughed again.

'How do you know that I'm not doing it already?'

In her imagination the hand moved, began to pump. Narrow male hips lifted, thrusting the reddened shaft through the sticky gripping hand.

'How do *you* know that *I'm* not doing it already too?'

Jay's breathing was rough now. 'Oh, please say you are.'

'I might be.'

'There's no "might" about it, Princess. Touch yourself for me.'

Sandy smiled. It was so easy. Unbelievable, but easy.

The weight of dreams and memories and suspicions lifted as she touched herself.

15

Sandy stared around but she couldn't see any sign of the notorious Waverley Grange 'behaviour' that Kat was forever telling tall tales about. But then, this was the restaurant, and perhaps people were only interested in eating here. Other appetites were probably catered to elsewhere.

She was on edge. She was tired. She felt out of place. She wished she'd never said she'd meet Jay here. But after his revelation the other night, she wanted neutral ground. With people around, she had a buffer against emotions that were huge and confusing. With people around, she could control her desire and her thoughts, see things more clearly.

Saturday-night dining at the Waverley was clearly a gala affair and, judging by the lack of vacant tables, the restaurant was probably booked up well in advance. But Jay obviously had the clout to secure a reservation at short notice.

She reached for her glass and took a sip of wine. The bottle had already been on the table in a cooler when the handsome hotel manager, Signor Guidetti himself, had seated her at the table. He'd poured for her and assured her that 'Mr Bentley' would be with her shortly. In other circumstances, she might have gone a bit girly under all that Italian charm, but she was so distracted, all she could manage was a nervous smile.

The wine was soft yet light, quite sophisticated for a rosé. She didn't think in a million years that this was the sort of thing Jay would drink, but he'd clearly ordered it for her because he already knew her tastes.

She put down the glass, frowning at it.

Just because we met fifteen years ago, Mister, it doesn't mean we've known each other for fifteen years. You know nothing about me, and I know even less about you.

On Thursday night, lulled by orgasms, the impact of Jay's identity had been blunted somehow. But since then, she'd done nothing but turn the revelation over and over in her mind. She almost felt angry with him for negating her cherished dream of all those years, by being a strange scarred troubled man who rigidly denied his own chivalry. And yet she knew she was probably as far from his dream of her as he was from hers of him.

Fuck you, why did you ever come to Kissley?

Which begged another question.

Why *had* he come to Kissley? For her? And if so, *how* had he found her here? How had he known to come here?

She stared around the room, her eyes idly flicking over other diners, in an effort to distract herself. But everywhere there seemed to be couples who looked happy and relaxed. At a corner table she noticed the young blonde woman who'd brought room service the other day. No embargo on the hotel's staff becoming patrons on their days off, then? The vivacious blonde was holding hands and laughing with an older thick-set guy who gazed at her with a combination of fondness and clearly simmering lust. Lucky bitch, to have such a sexy, affectionate and probably straightforward relationship!

Sandy straightened her already immaculately set-out cutlery, and glanced in the other direction. Narrowing her eyes, she peered at another couple sitting by the window. She could swear she knew the guy with glasses from somewhere. Handsome as an angel and with a mop of black curls. Wasn't he on the telly, some history guru? It didn't matter though, whether he was the celeb or not, he was clearly spoken for.

His companion, a curvaceous tawny-haired woman with a rather magnificent bosom, was giving him looks far more intense and intimate than a mere fan ever would.

Life *seemed so straightforward for some people.* But then, so had hers been until a certain scarred hard case had walked into her life, screwed her senseless, and dislocated a dream she'd harboured in her heart for fifteen long years.

'Fuck you, Jay Bentley,' she muttered, then swigged her wine again.

But as she set down her glass the hairs on the nape of her neck all came to attention. Turning to the door, she saw him there, paused momentarily and staring at her. How could he possibly have ever been Prince Charming? He was so tall. So steely-looking. So intimidating. And yet he already looked different, as if seen through a new filter.

As he threaded his way between the tables, walking towards her, his dark lightweight jacket seemed to float from his broad shoulders. He dominated the room. Women at other tables stared at him, not in the least put off by his scars. Sandy didn't blame them. God, he looked even better now that he appeared to be letting his hair grow. Even in a couple of days it had thickened, and was looking extraordinarily dark. The same black as Prince Charming's shaggy mane.

'I'm sorry I kept you waiting,' he said, sliding into his seat. 'I meant to be here much earlier, but I was detained.' He sighed and poured himself some water from the bottle of San Pellegrino on the table. 'More wrangling with the old man. He's a bloody stubborn old git.'

How odd. He talks to me as if we have known each other fifteen years. As if we're old friends. Old lovers.

And for all his strangeness, she felt his body call to hers with a familiarity out of all proportion to the hours and days that she'd known it. Following the way he moved his fingers over the stem of his glass, she shuddered as if they'd left permanent tracks on her skin, on her breasts and her sex, ley lines that were suddenly irradiated anew by his proximity. Her own fingertips tingled too, as if his skin, his scars and his cock had left their brilliant spoor on her.

She wanted to talk, ask questions, set ground rules, but an electric field of pure lust short-circuited her brain.

'It's OK. I haven't been here long and it's nice. And the wine's nice. Don't worry.'

She blushed, aware that she was babbling and that she couldn't stop looking at his fingers, his strong wrists, and then the wedge of tanned skin in the open neckline of his black silk shirt. She saw a peppering of dark hair deep in the V, and the thin but angry line of one of his body scars.

'You're too forgiving,' he said. His husky voice sounded tense and tired. Was that from aggro with his father, or something else?

They stared at each other. Sandy's brain seemed to grind thoughts and information slowly, and it was hard. Looking at Jay's body in his beautiful clothing, the strong shape of his chest and arms, was easy. It seemed a coward's way out, but the temptation to shove issues aside in favour of sexual attraction was so strong she could almost taste it.

She wanted to taste *him*.

His grey eyes glittered as if he understood her perfectly. And concurred.

'So . . .' He sipped his water again. Sandy reached for the wine bottle, to pour him some, but he shook his dark head slightly. She set it back in the bucket and stared at him.

'So . . .' she echoed.

Jay laughed and shrugged his shoulders. 'There's too much to think about, isn't there? Too much to process.' He leaned forward in his seat, his forearm on the table. 'Why don't we just enjoy the moment for a while? Instead of raking over the past.' He paused, his mouth tightening. 'Or prodding at a future that'll bite us in the arse?'

What did he mean? Sandy opened her mouth to ask, but Jay reached for her hand and folded it in his. The action should have been innocuous, but the way his finger stroked her palm was electrifying. Delicious energy shot from the tiny caress, careering along her nerves at light speed to settle and bubble in her sex. Within a couple of heartbeats, she felt her body moisten and bloom like a tropical flower.

The fingers of her free hand tensed against the tablecloth and Jay's glance darted towards the tiny movement, monitoring her. The hard line of his mouth curved now, becoming mellower and more sensual. His nostrils flared as if he'd caught the aroma of the juice that drenched her panties all of a sudden. It was impossible, of course, but she could still half believe it. Had they given him bionic powers when they'd put him back together?

'So,' he said again, his voice low, 'have you played with all your toys yet?' His eyes scanned downwards, as if he had more superpowers, and he could see through the table, its cloth and her clothes. 'Are you wearing some of your new lingerie tonight?'

She was. The coffee and chocolate ensemble. She'd nearly chosen the black and red high-end stripper set, but right at the last minute she'd chickened out and gone classy rather than overt beneath her simple black heavy silk sheath dress. It was her other 'best frock' besides the dress she'd worn to the Chamber of Commerce cocktail party, but this time she had on her own shoes, elegant, but not too high.

'Could be,' she answered, finding it possible, and easier, to smile back at him. He was right. They should play now, and face the thorns when they had to.

'I suppose I have to guess which?'

She nodded, and he narrowed his eyes, and with his free hand stroked the beard that wasn't there any more, as if pondering.

'The leaves and shells set. *Café au lait* with darker lace?'

'How the hell do you do that? Have you got X-ray vision or something?'

Jay laughed triumphantly and, leaning towards her, raised her hand to his lips, lavishing a kiss on the back of it.

'So, what's my prize for guessing right?'

Sandy began to shake, already knowing the award he wanted. Which was her, completely and unconditionally. He didn't even have to name his price.

'Who said there is a prize?'

'Oh, I think there is. I'm convinced of it.' He kissed her hand again, touching his tongue lightly yet lasciviously against her skin.

A soft cough made them both glance to the side, and Sandy wanted to laugh at the way Jay looked genuinely startled for a moment. He'd been so into her, no one else had existed.

It was the waiter with the menus but, when they began to peruse them, Sandy realised she wasn't hungry. Jay's impatient eyes told her he felt the same.

'Look, what say we just have a starter here and then shoot over to the Teapot for the next course?' she suggested. Her own boldness made her feel drunk, giddy, voracious. She'd only had one glass of the pink wine, but she was already floating.

'Perfect.'

A few moments later, they were eating the chef's special paté with crisp hot melba toast and delicious little accompaniments. It was sublimely unctuous, the best Sandy had ever tasted, and yet it almost seemed as if someone else were eating it, some other person's taste buds sighing over the seasoning.

All *she* could think of was what was to come after. Herself and Jay, locked in a bubble of time and sex where neither the past nor the present nor any element of the outside world could touch them. When finally they were finished, and he came around to draw out her chair as she stood, her heart pounded as it had never done before.

Jay focused on the road ahead. He had to. It took all his powers of concentration not to stare at the woman beside him like a starving hound slavering over a T-bone.

His chest felt tight. Sandy was like grace and salvation to him. Almost three days spent arguing with his father had wrecked him far more than the old Aston ever had. The old bastard was stubborn and domineering – traits Jay knew *he'd* inherited – and set on his original plans. He'd wanted Jay working in his business empire, wheedled him into it, and Jay had accepted even though he'd known they'd end up at logger-heads sooner or later.

But now he was away from all that, even if only for one night. Truths would have to be faced, but not tonight, please God, not tonight.

He risked a brief glance at Sandy, and his groin tightened instantaneously. Her profile was pure, her beautiful hair piled high in a messed-up chignon, her mouth soft and glossy, natural pink yet shiny with some cosmetic. He imagined his come on those lips, and in her let-down hair, and splattered across her beautiful breasts, so shapely beneath her classy black dress. She was wearing the lingerie he'd chosen, and the idea of that excited him in a way that made his cock excruciatingly hard if he allowed himself to think about it. He wanted to press his face into her cleavage, feel the heat of her through that fine coffee-coloured satin. He wanted to slide up her skirt and then slip his fingers beneath her tiny

G-string. Was she wet? He wanted to think so. He wanted to play in her moisture, or watch her play in it instead.

His erection stirred in his shorts, pushing against his fly, aching, aching. The need to see and touch and kiss and stroke her was messing with his head, making it dangerously hard to drive his performance car.

Recognising a lay-by he'd passed before on the quiet stretch of rode, he flipped the indicator and pulled up, his heart pounding.

'What's wrong?' demanded Sandy as the car rolled to a halt.

Jay's face was taut, his eyes brilliant in the darkened interior of the car. Without saying anything else, he unclipped his seat belt then reached across to unfasten hers. Still leaning half across the car, he cupped her face and pressed his lips to hers, hard. As his tongue plunged into her mouth, his hand slid down, finding her breast and cradling it hungrily, without finesse.

There was nothing else to do but respond. She couldn't have resisted, even if she'd wanted to. And she didn't want to. She was melting, flowing with lust, and he squeezed her nipple through her dress. Kinetic energy in her pelvis made her wriggle.

'You like that, don't you?' he growled, his mouth half-open against her face as he pinched and twisted the little crest of flesh. 'A little bit of pain with your pleasure.'

Sandy gasped, loving it, hating it, confused with herself for wanting it, yet knowing that she'd been waiting all her life for a man to know what she wanted even when she couldn't quite work it out. Reaching down, she cupped her own crotch, rubbing herself through her dress because she couldn't stop herself and her clit was burning to be touched.

'Oh, you're so magnificently horny, Princess. Always ready.'

His voice was a low rasp in her ear, like claws scratching leather. 'I bet you're wet as hell, . . . saturating that sexy little thong with your juices. Oh God, I swear I can smell you. I swear I can.'

Sandy gripped herself, twisting in the embrace of the car's racing seat as Jay worked on her breast and possessed her mouth again, stabbing with his tongue. Her body was on fire for him, her pussy wet through, puffed and aching, silently screaming for his hand or her own.

'Pull your skirt up,' Jay gasped as their mouths broke apart. 'Pull it up and show me your cunt. Now.'

It's a public road, protested the wimp inside her.

Who cares, countered the woman dying of lust and ready, willing and able to do anything for this man, and give him anything.

As Jay continued to kiss her so hard she could barely breathe, she struggled with her skirt, hitching it and tugging it while she hefted her bottom around in the seat and tried to get the lined black silk from under her. Jay helped, abandoning her breast for a moment to pull at her skirt. Even as they grappled, the light from headlights swept across them.

She was in too deep to stop now though, and she knew Jay was. Her hemline came up, exposing the patterned tops of her stockings and her crotch, barely clad in lace and satin the colour of cappuccino. While she bunched her skirt at her waist he was already plucking at her G-string, pulling it aside, stretching the elastic to get at her.

His hot fingers found her and started working on her clitoris.

'Pinch your nipples while I play with you. Go on! Do it!'

Sandy complied, squashing her swollen little teats hard, groaning at the pain but shifting her hips as it excited her.

Jay pressed her clit hard, and her heels dragged against the carpet in the foot well.

It was all unreal, surreal, hyper-real. Sex play in a supercar at the side of a country road. 'Kiss me while I come,' she commanded, suddenly taking the power from him. Or at least a bit of it. He laughed, as if deigning to indulge her as he crushed his mouth down on hers again.

His tongue fought hers as his finger flicked her clit. She growled into his mouth, then grabbed for him, clutching frantically at any bit of him she could reach as her orgasm beat her on the rocks of pleasure and threatened to wash her away.

More headlights swept over them as she clung to him, her sex clenching and clenching, her clitoris pulsing beneath the pad of his unyielding finger. Sandy's head rang with the sound of her own cries, grunts of passion, unladylike and revealing. She babbled profane nonsense, appalled by it, yet free. Her movements were crude too, thrusting and writhing, unfettered by shame or fear.

'Yes ... yes ... yes,' gasped Jay, as if applauding. His fingers were wet and slippery but he kept the pressure constant, coaxing and nursing her to new heights, without pause or respite.

Eventually, she croaked, 'Enough! No more!' And he withdrew his finger, but cupped her entire pussy in a gentle soothing hold.

More cars swept by. How had this road suddenly become a major thoroughfare? Had people followed them here, subconsciously seeking a show? Sandy didn't care. She was aware only of Jay's touch, the scent of his cologne, and his hot breath against her skin as she rested her forehead on his shoulder. She was leaning in towards him just as he was inclined across the car to get to her.

Still she held on. He was the rock now, solid and sure. She could cling on forever. But as her breathing steadied, all that had been unreal and out of the world slowly became real and normal again.

She was sitting in a car with her skirt around her waist and a man's hand between her legs. Passing motorists probably couldn't see her, but if anyone came by on foot, they would get an eyeful of far more than they'd bargained for.

'We'll get arrested,' she said, pushing at Jay's chest and arm. He seemed reluctant to let go of her at first, but then withdrew, settling back into his seat. In the darkness his eyes were stormy yet inscrutable. Sandy tugged frantically at her skirt but it seemed tangled somehow. He reached back across, slipping his hands under her armpits and, even at such an awkward angle, lifting her effortlessly so she could slide her skirt beneath her.

'Better?'

She nodded but she wasn't sure. Something dark and perverse inside her mourned the exposure. She liked showing herself to him. Exhibiting her thighs, her sex, allowing him total access to her, to do whatever he wanted. She liked giving him dominion over her pleasure too. The power to give it, the power to withhold it. Freedom to use her like a plaything, and handle her intimately.

We may not have this 'thing' for long. But tonight we've got it. And I want more.

She stared at his mouth, and in the darkness of the car's interior it looked reddened as if he'd bitten his lip. Her body stirred once more, as if those lips were pressed between her legs, and the tongue that had owned hers was licking and tasting her. As she started to get excited and wet again he smiled. Why was it always so bloody easy for him to read her?

Exerting a dominion of her own, Sandy reached out and

placed her hand over his crotch, assessing his erection. Dear God, he was hard. She could feel the heat and the shape of him clean through the silk worsted of his suit trousers. As her fingers tightened experimentally, his cock kicked against her touch, and he muttered, 'Fuck!' beneath his breath, while his insanely long black eyelashes flickered down and his head tipped back.

There was a contrary thrill to this strange see-saw they seemed to be on tonight. One minute he was in charge, the next, she was. She knew he'd take back the power any moment, any second. But right now, it was hers, and as heady as the wine she'd sipped.

Slowly, she circled her palm against the bulge of his cock, her fingers curving, exploring, cupping. Jay rolled his head, his white teeth digging into his full lower lip.

'You know you're going to make me come if you do much more of that,' he warned, but he didn't brush her hand away.

'Would that be such a tragedy?' She moved her thumb, strumming it from side to side, and his breath hissed.

'I don't suppose so, really,' he said, through gritted teeth. 'Especially if you like the idea of men so helplessly aroused by you that they sticky their shorts in your honour.'

'I've never thought about it before.'

His erection stirred. How could he get any stiffer? Any bigger? He was already enormous, tenting his elegant trousers and pushing against the zip.

Jay let out a harsh laugh, adjusting himself in his seat. 'Good God, woman, it must happen all the time. With your face, your hair, your body, men must get hard over you all the time.'

Sandy frowned. She was pretty enough, she knew that, but she knew prettier and sexier women who she imagined did induce hard-ons aplenty. Kat, for instance, was much more of a siren than she was.

'I'm not so sure.'

'Then be sure, you sexy little tart,' Jay growled, moving uneasily, his hips lifting a little to push himself into her hold. 'I've developed a raging hard-on every time I've even set eyes on you. And I do mean every time.'

It took a moment for the penny to drop but, when it did, Sandy tried to snatch her hand away. She felt confused, a bit appalled, but also ridiculously pleased in a way. But before she could properly retreat, Jay's stronger hand grasped hers, clamping it in place.

'Yes, I admit it, I'm a disgusting sexual pervert, and I was fifteen years ago. Even while I was trying to comfort you and calm you and be the perfect gentle knight, I was still fancying you at the same time and getting hard for you.'

That was sick, wasn't it? Sort of . . . Well, a bit.

'I never realised. I just thought you were trying to be kind.'

He sighed. 'I *was*. I *was*. But I was twenty, and you were utterly gorgeous. You still are. That's why you affect me in a way no other woman ever has.'

Sandy's heart lurched. Could she believe that? Jay's erection was still as rampant as ever, but suddenly there was a peculiar quality of resignation, of weariness about him. He seemed almost bitter. Did he resent her somehow for this supposed power she had over him?

'I don't believe that.' She stared at him, trying to divine what it was that had changed his aura so abruptly. 'A man like you, so accomplished and so attractive –' she ignored his grunt of derision '– and who's obviously got a bob or two. You must have woman throwing themselves at you right left and centre. And don't tell me they've all been dogs and they haven't turned you on!'

To her surprise, Jay laced his fingers with hers and lifted her hand away from his body. In the low light of the car's interior, his eyes looked dark and troubled. He drew her hand to his lips and kissed the palm, then leaned across and set it in her own lap.

'Seat belt,' he instructed crisply. 'Let's get back to your place. I want to try out a few of those sex toys. Experiment a bit.' As he clipped his own belt, his expression lightened, eyes glinting playfully.

So that's the way it is? Play first, discussions afterwards.

Sandy fastened herself in, all the time on the point of opening her mouth and demanding answers, illumination. She sensed he'd been about to admit to something, she knew not what, but serious somehow. But now he'd set it aside, shut it in a box, sequestered the less than palatable in favour of pursuing pleasure.

Was that selfish? Evasive? Typically male? Was she going to force the issue? Be typically female at the expense of pleasure for herself too?

No, I fucking well am not, Jay Bentley! No way!

He could be gone again tomorrow. Why screw up the chance of a lifetime with a sexy and mysterious man, just to get a few answers she might not like anyway?

'Yeah, so do I! Let's go. What are we waiting for?'

His eyes were full of admiration as he stabbed the starter and the car roared.

16

'Where are you going with it? What are you doing?'

With the box of exotic goodies in his arms, Jay was already heading for the café when he answered her.

'Indulge me. I have this perverse desire to have a little fun in your workplace, Princess.' He elbowed open the door into the main serving area. 'I like the idea of you thinking about me touching you and tasting you next time you're serving tea and a doughnut to some horny workman who's eyeing you up and fancying you.'

'You're twisted, you are,' she muttered as she followed him in. He was already sifting through the items in the box, and a vertigo of anticipation gripped her as she mentally catalogued its contents.

'Alas, yes.' He flashed her a glance out of the corner of his eye, lifting out the vibrator she'd used while they'd spoken on the phone. She swallowed, knowing, just knowing he was going to raise it to his nose to see if he could smell her on it, even though she'd washed and soaped it pretty scrupulously.

But Jay being Jay, he didn't. He just winked and set it back in the box.

'How about these? Have you tried these?'

Unfolding one of the small black paper parcels, he showed her a pair of delicate nipple clamps, each adorned with a prismatic Swarovski crystal pendant.

Sandy's reaction was strong and instant, a primitive automatic urge to cross her legs and cringe at the same time.

She hadn't tried them. She daren't. But she wanted to. When she pinched her nipples while she was playing with herself, or being played with, her level of arousal nearly went through the ceiling. But the idea of clamps made her throat go dry, and fear grind with the desire low in her belly.

'No,' she said in a small voice, part of her praying he'd put them back in the box, most of her praying that they'd taken his fancy.

'Why not?'

Oh boy ...

Delicious apprehension crawled across her skin, but then without warning Jay smirked and held the little clamps against his ears. 'Do they suit me?'

Despite the tension, Sandy laughed.

'Uh-oh, this is serious business,' he reproved, his face not quite straight as he held the jewelled toys out in front of him, swinging the little pendants.

Christ, they looked heavy.

'Why not?' he asked her.

'I daren't. I once tried some makeshift nipple clamps after I saw a woman wearing them in one of the magazines that Greg lends to Kat to get her going.'

Sandy blushed as Jay's dark eyebrows rose. 'So you like to read erotic magazines, do you? I wish I'd known, I'd have sent some of those too.' Obviously they'd got far beyond any kind of pretence that it wasn't him who'd sent the sexy booty.

'I was curious.'

'So am I. What do you mean by "makeshift" nipple clamps, Princess? I'm dying to know here.'

Sandy blushed furiously. This was far more embarrassing than anything they'd done together. Stupid, really. She stared at her toes and almost fidgeted like a naughty child, then wondered if Jay would find that amusing.

'Um ... well, I tried a clothes peg, but it hurt so much I screamed and kicked over the bathroom stool.'

Jay's eyebrows shot up.

'Bloody hell, I'm not surprised. Clothes pegs are very blunt tools to use on tender little nipples like yours.' Without warning, he brushed the back of his hands against said tender little nipples and the surge of pleasure that induced almost made her sigh. 'I like playing kinky little games, but I'm not into brutal pain like that, love, and I've a feeling you aren't either.' His fingertips swept lightly across her breasts again, still holding the jewelled clamps. 'I like pleasure and experimentation, a bit of pervy exploratory fun, nothing heavy.'

She looked at him again, into his eyes. They were steady and bright, and she felt safe with him. He was a horny highly sexed man, but he was caring, not a selfish domineering brute.

'Now these ... These are much more suited to the purpose.' Palming one of the clamps, he showed her the other more closely. 'They screw on, and we only have to tighten them sufficiently that they stay in place. No sadistic torture involved, and they certainly wouldn't keep the washing on the line.'

Sandy let out a bubble of nervous laughter, her heart beating wildly. God, she wanted to try them. They were pretty, and she had a feeling that they weren't quite as mild as Jay was making out, but she could still take it.

The way he smiled at her, slowly, and creamily, told her he was as keen to play now as she was. If not more.

'Take off your dress.'

The words were low, intent, almost mellow, but Sandy felt so excited she was afraid she might sway on her feet. Dragging in a breath, she braced herself and lifted her chin. Not in defiance, but to try to fool him she wasn't afraid. She probably wasn't fooling him one bit, but the act of attempting to gave her confidence and strength.

Reaching behind her, she whizzed down the zip of her dress, acutely aware of cooler air hitting her back. It wasn't cold in the room, but her skin was so heated there was an appreciable temperature difference. And even more so when she shook the dress off her shoulders and allowed it to slide off, down her body, until she could step out of it. In a show of bravado she kicked it away, sending it coasting along the wooden floor and beneath one of the chequer-clothed tables.

Aware of Jay's eyes scrutinising her in the minutest detail, she glanced quickly towards the window, and saw her own reflection.

A shapely girl with piled-up hair, wearing a gorgeous bra and a tiny G-string that barely hid her pubes. Her thighs were bisected by bands of dark lace, the tops of her stockings, but her bare hips and flanks gleamed exotically in the soft lamp-light of the ordinary room where she spent so much of her working life. The darkness outside seemed to enclose them in a bubble out of time, and yet at the back of her mind Sandy was aware that anyone in the upper chambers of the Town Hall across the precinct square could look in and see her in her undies. They'd have to have binoculars to see any details, but that didn't mean there couldn't be someone lurking in a darkened room up there, watching the show.

The thought of being observed while playing some perverse little game of pain and pleasure with Jay made her clit ache.

'What are you smiling at?' enquired Jay, smiling too.

'Someone might be watching us, from across the precinct.' She nodded towards the darkness outside, beyond their zone of light and intimacy. 'With the lights on this place is like a beacon.'

Jay moved in, close enough for her to feel his breath on the side of her face. His hand settled against her flank. He was still holding the little clamps and they were cool and sharp feeling against the surface of her skin.

'Does it excite you? The idea of being on show? It does me. I like the idea of others looking, but only *me* touching and exploring.'

Closing her eyes, Sandy melted, leaning against him like a magnet attracted to its polar opposite, its match. It was so easy to be soft with him, pliant. His presence granted her the freedom not to have to fight and struggle.

'Let down your hair,' he purred, his mouth touching her skin now, tongue sneaking out, pointed and insolent, tasting her cheek. Then, as suddenly as he'd approached, he dropped a kiss on her neck and spun away towards the nearest table. The little clamps tinkled as he dropped them on a place mat, and he dragged a chair out, reversed it and sat down, his elbows folded across the top of its back.

'Let down your hair, Princess,' he said again, more firmly.

She pulled out the pins, and the little band, and flung them away. Her hair slithered down over her shoulders, long, but not long enough to cover her body, her breasts. Tipping her head, she flipped the mass of it back, exposing her shoulders.

'Exquisite. The woman of my dreams.' His voice was rough, like a metal comb dragged over suede. 'Literally.'

'So you say.'

'So I know,' he growled. 'Don't argue with me, woman. Show me the goodies.'

For half a heartbeat Sandy stuck her tongue out at him, which made him laugh, then she straightened her face, closed her eyes, smoothed her hands over her hair again and then slid them over her shoulders and on down to cup her breasts.

'Good ... good. Now, strum your nipples, tickle them through the satin.'

Sandy complied, biting her lip. How could the tips of her breasts already be so sensitive, so aroused? She'd done nothing to them yet, maybe just brushed the cloth of her bodice against them in the course of stripping off her dress.

It's you. The way you look at me. The way you talk to me. You don't even have to touch me . . . although God, how I love it when you do.

Thumbs moving slowly, she shimmied her hips, shaking her hair again. She was a dancer now, a burlesque performer, a goddess of sex. Rolling her shoulders, she thrust out her chest, plucking at her nipples through the soft cups of her bra.

'Excellent . . . better . . . but I need more. Flip down the cups of your bra and show me your beautiful breasts.'

Sandy felt as if there was a band around her chest, making it tricky to breathe. She swallowed hard. Jay's grey eyes upon her had weight, they were a heavy desiring beam cruising her neck, her shoulders, her breasts. Her hands felt heavy too, and her fingers were difficult to control. But she obeyed him, reaching into first one satin cup then the other, pushing them down, prising out each breast and letting them rest on the pushed-down fabric. Unable to look down at herself, she glanced across to the darkened window and saw herself looking lewd and sleazy, but also high class. Like a two-thousand-dollar-an-hour call girl, going through her moves for her client. Against the pallor of her skin, her nipples were smoky smudges, pert and dark.

'Touch them.'

There was no question about what he meant.

Jay's eyes were fiery, and the way he didn't hide that heat made her confidence surge and rise. She loved him as Mr Cool, but she adored his ardour more. Looking at him steadily, she licked the middle finger of each hand and then applied them to her teats, and made naughty little circles.

His eyes just as steady, Jay laughed, rising to his feet, closing on her. Sandy circled faster, gyrating her hips in a mock bump and grind. As if unable to hide his admiration, Jay let out a gasp. He was beside her now, and she realised that he'd snatched up the little clamps as he'd approached.

'Be still now,' he whispered, his cheek against hers again, his breath making the shorter strands of her hair around her face feather and lift.

Dashing her hands away, he brought one of the clamps to her left nipple and, pulling out the stiff little peak of flesh, he slid it into the tiny metal jaws. And then began to tighten it.

Pressure. Light at first, then firmer, more noticeable. Not painful, not in the beginning. But hinting at it. Then hinting more acutely. Starting to hurt a little, but still not awful. Starting to hurt more, and *be* a bit awful. But also breathtakingly dark, perverse and wonderful.

Sandy groaned, her hips moving again, not in a dance, but because she couldn't keep them still.

'How does that feel?'

He let the Swarovski jewel dangle and swing. She bit her lip, feeling her sex react to the stimulus and silky fluid well between her labia.

'Not bad,' she hissed, as he flicked the pendant crystal.

He gave her a slow smile that told her he knew she was lying. It did feel bad, but also transcendent, and altering, and she wanted more.

'Indeed,' he observed, then, in small neat movements, he dressed her other breast with sparkling brilliance.

'Oh my, oh my,' he murmured, flicking the gems again and making her gasp and want to clasp at her crotch, rub herself, slip her fingers beneath the narrow band of silk there and manipulate her clit. When her hands moved uneasily, heading that way, Jay's sharp glance noted and recorded the action.

'Oh no, no, no, young lady!' he chided and, within a moment, he'd fished around in the box and drawn out a long length of gleaming black satin.

Her bonds.

Catching first one hand then the other, he drew them behind her, and secured them lightly but firmly at the small of her back. The tails of the bow dangled down, floating against her bottom and the backs of her thighs, light as thistledown.

The clamps hurt. They really did. But what they did to her between her legs was so intense she barely noticed the pain. It was as if silken filaments, black silk filaments like the ribbons around her wrists, were stretched from the tips of her breasts to the tip of her clitoris. Every slight movement, even a breath, was excruciatingly exciting.

When Jay took her by the upper arm and pulled her close to him, the jewels swung and she drew in a harsh breath, fighting the urge to rub her thighs together. As she gasped again, Jay kissed her voraciously, plunging his tongue into her mouth, drawing the gasp into his mouth with the force of the kiss.

Sandy wanted to hug him, hold him, rub herself against him, abrade her clamped nipples against his jacket and drag the gems to and fro. She wanted more. More pain. More stimulation. More everything.

More Jay. A lot more Jay.

The kiss went on and on. The need to grab and hold and rub and rock went on and on. Sandy wanted to scream, but he was controlling her voice with the force of his lips and tongue.

Even as she melted, though, she wanted to fight him. How could that be? It certainly hadn't seemed that way in those mags of Kat's she'd glanced at. You were either submissive or dominant, clear-cut, black and white. But she felt like she was both. A handmaiden *and* a combatant. Her spirit rising, she battled his tongue in her mouth, pushing back, giving as good as she was getting. And when Jay laughed, she laughed too, the mirth blending in the searing wet kiss.

'Princess, you are amazing,' he growled as they broke apart. 'You don't give up, do you?'

'Never!' she shot back at him, then darted forward, nipping at his jawline and the lobe of his ear.

Without warning, his hand grabbed her crotch, squeezing. He tightened the grip, massaging in a fast hard rhythm. Press, press, press. One long finger rubbed against the narrow band of fabric, pushing it against her entrance, her perineum. He prodded her rudely, tickling and teasing.

Sandy breathed hard. Him touching her there was gorgeous but aggravating. She wanted more direct pressure on her clit, solid stimulation. Good, hard, solid rubbing to bring her off, fast and furiously, like a chain of fireworks. But he denied her, loosening his hold and just patting the gusset of her G-string, over the hot zone.

'Not yet ... not yet ... We're playing, remember? I want to wind you up and wind you up before you come.'

'You're evil,' she hissed at him, trying to bear down. 'Bastard!' she added when he withdrew his hand.

Jay gave her an odd distant look, the expression in his eyes suddenly a million miles from their fierce erotic contest. Then in one blink of his long black lashes it was gone again, and he was laughing and leering at her once more.

'Aren't I just?' Then he kissed her again, all tongue and moisture and muscularity, while he slid a hand between their bodies and played devilishly with the clamps.

Sandy's hips jerked. Her clit thudded. She was almost there, but she needed contact. Perhaps just a whisker of a touch. She tried to rub herself against his thigh, but he sidestepped her, and began to walk her towards the table to her rear.

When they reached it, he broke the kiss, gave her a demon smile – and suddenly lifted her off her feet, his hands at her waist, and sat her down on the table.

Sandy's heart pounded and she felt breathless. It shouldn't be easy to forget how strong he was, but she had. And to be lifted up bodily thrilled her anew, triggering memories and responses, both new and old. She was Princess, but he was her Prince. Her Prince Charming. The man who would always sweep her away.

His eyes holding hers, he pushed her a little way across the table, wrinkling the cloth. Impatiently, he moved the little bowl of flowers and the condiments, dumping them on the counter. Sandy could have sprung up at that moment, but she just sat there as if he'd stapled her to the wooden surface beneath the chequered fabric.

He returned to her and brushed the hair away from her face again, arranging it, caressing it. Then with spread fingers on her bare midriff, he pressed her backwards, forcing her to rest on her loosely bound hands. The position wasn't exactly comfortable, but perversely she didn't want it to be. She was vulnerable, off balance, and it excited her more than ever, if that were possible.

Jay spun away from her and shucked out of his elegant black jacket, flinging it over a nearby chair. Beneath it, his silk shirt clung to his shoulders. He was a strong man. He could do anything to her. Anything he wanted. She wriggled on the table, silently begging him to begin.

What would it be? Fingers? Cock? Tongue? Toys?

Would it be pain? Or more pleasure? Much more pleasure? *I want all of it! Goddamnit, give me the lot!*

Clasping his hands, Jay rubbed one thumb across his other palm, obviously thinking and scheming. His eyes darted from her body, awkwardly displayed, to the box of toys, then back again. Around his firm mouth, a little smile played, wicked and contemplative.

'All these toys,' he said, crossing to the box, 'and we've barely sampled any of them yet. What shall we try next?' Still glancing at her as he worked, he sifted through the packaging, his scarred face animated as he assessed the items. From time to time he quirked an eyebrow, but he didn't show her whatever it was that interested him.

The perverse devil . . . Sandy had examined most of the toys in the box, and her chest tightened in anticipation. What would it be? There were beads and butt plugs, and a diabolical selection of vibrators. Some were sweet and aesthetic and efficient, like the thoughtfully fashioned one she'd already tried. But others were bizarre and unlikely and elaborate. Constructions shaped like rabbits and penguins and God alone knew what else.

'How about this?'

Sandy swallowed hard. 'This' was a slyly innocuous-looking egg-shaped object, marbled rosy pink, with a silver woven cord attached. She'd seen something similar at Kat's sex-toy party, and the idea of it had made her squirm. Jay swung it by its cord, letting its weight make a pendulum of it. It looked heavy and unyielding. Her belly surged and she couldn't speak, but her silence made him smile.

He understood. God how he understood. He knew she yearned for the tricky little thing, even though she feared it.

'This, then,' he confirmed, giving the egg one last twirl before reaching into the box and pulling out a tube of lubricant.

She tried not to cringe as he placed the egg and the lube on the table beside her, then ran a hand up the inside of her stocking-clad thigh. Carefully, he drew her legs apart, forcing her to adjust her position and adjust the placement of her hands on the tablecloth behind her. Lifting one of her legs, he pulled a chair close and set her foot on it. With narrowed eyes, he studied the arrangement of her limbs, and then adjusted the chair a little to one side, making her thighs stretch wider and her pussy open and pout.

Sandy closed her eyes as her feminine fragrance filled her nostrils.

'Gorgeous,' pronounced Jay, touching her belly, then her thigh, pushing and inching it further from the other one. He nudged the chair a little way, opening her wider, then reached down and slid two fingers beneath her G-string.

'Oh Princess, Princess, I'm not even sure that we'll need this.' He touched the lubricant tube with his free hand while he paddled in her cleft, stretching the now saturated coffee-coloured satin, and fingered her entrance.

Licking her lips, biting them, moving uneasily on the table, Sandy tried to bear down and wiggle his fingers onto her clit. But he wasn't having any. He pushed one finger into her vagina as far as the knuckle, and just left it there while he kissed her again, running his tongue softly and teasingly over her lips. When he whispered her name against her mouth she clenched down hard on him.

'Sexy girl,' he whispered, 'sexy, sexy girl. Do you want me to put it in you?' He kissed her again. 'It's big. It'll stretch you. It'll jiggle about as you walk, and by God I'm going to make you walk. I promise I will.'

Sandy turned her face away. It was flaming. Heat flared through her body, focusing on the tingling-burning tips of her breasts, her aching clit and her vagina where his finger possessed her. Suddenly she wanted to be stretched. Filled. Stuffed. Penetrated by toys, because it was his will, his pleasure. And hers.

'Yes.' Her voice came out as tiny little bleat. She swallowed again, breathed deep. 'Yes, I want it in me. Put it in. Put it inside me.' Just the words made her juices flow, trickling over his fingers.

Jay withdrew his hand and licked his finger slowly as if he were savouring a lollipop. Sandy felt empty, even though he'd stretched her but a little. She hitched her bottom a few inches across the table, closer to the edge, tilting her hips, making her sex more inviting.

Smiling, Jay tapped his finger on his lower lip. 'My, you are in a hurry, aren't you? Are you sure you can take it? It seems much bigger than I anticipated.'

Sandy licked her own lower lip, and narrowed her eyes at him. She'd never thought herself a practised seductress, but he seemed to bring out the Jezebel in her.

'You're big, and I can take you.'

He looked pleased. Men! A bit of praise for their cocks and their prowess and you could get them eating out of your hand. Sandy contained her own satisfaction at this fact, and just regarded him steadily, adjusting the position of her bottom to facilitate his next move.

'True,' he said with a smug smile as he caught up the tube of lubricant and flipped off the cap.

After loading his fingers with the silky gel, he tweaked aside her G-string with his other hand, then pressed the stuff to her pussy. It was cold, and the contrast between that and her fever-hot flesh made her gasp. And gasp again when he worked the lube into her entrance, with not one finger but two this time.

He repeated the process. And again. She felt slippery, awash with moisture, her entire sex swimming in it. The excess gel trickled down the inside of her bottom cheeks, coating her anus too.

It was a rude feeling, but it excited her, made her feel twitchy. She shook her head, sending her hair flying around her again.

Jay grabbed a hank of it while he massaged the gel over her perineum, holding her not unkindly but imposing his will upon her. Slowly, slowly he drew her face to his again for more kissing.

Sandy sighed into the kiss, excitement spiralling. Something it would have done even if he hadn't been touching her sex. There was something about kissing Jay that was different to kissing any other man she'd ever kissed. And it was stronger now, more potent than ever now that she knew he was her long-lost Prince Charming.

Maybe he could indeed kiss *anything* better. A little dark shadow crossed her mind as she wondered if he'd need to.

'Ready?' His breath was hot against her face as he murmured the words into her hair, nuzzling the wavy red mass.

'Ready,' she confirmed, feeling her heart rise nervously in her chest, seemingly into her throat.

Still holding her lightly by her hair, he picked up the love-egg and pressed its surface against her.

God! It's big! Much bigger than I thought ...

Pressure. Relentless pressure. Impossible pressure. It wouldn't go inside her, surely? It just wouldn't. She opened her mouth to protest, then shut it again, biting her lip. Behind her, against the table, she made fists of her hands.

But Jay seemed to know her limits, her size, the resilience of her body. He kept pressing the damned thing against her, steadily, relentlessly, and while he did so he started kissing her again, making her concentrate on their mouths with complicated little licks, probes and darts. Voluptuous tasting and exploring that both thrilled her and calmed her at the same time.

As he swirled his tongue around hers in a swift wicked dance, her body relaxed and granted entrance to the love-ball.

She groaned into his mouth, tensing again, flight or fight reflexes making her want to pull away from it, expel it. But he persisted, kissing harder and looping more of her hair around his fingers as he pushed the little ovoid right up inside her, directing it with the tip of his finger until it settled in the natural niche within her body.

'Grip it. Play with it. Use those strong clever muscles down there to work it.'

'I can't! I can't!' she cried. She could feel the weight of the love toy pressing on the root of her clitoris from within. The strange presence inside her was unnerving, disorientating. Areas of stimulation were being fired that had never been fired before, creating sensations that she wasn't even sure she liked. There was a sense of needing to urinate, even though she knew she didn't really need to. She started to make noises, little grunts and gasps of protest, whimpers of arousal she was help-less to contain.

'Would it be easier if I gagged you?' he asked softly, reaching beyond her, searching in the box again. The way this rocked her body, and the intrusion within it, made her gurgle low in her throat. The sound was uncouth and alien in the familiar surroundings of her café.

Sweating, the tips of her breasts aching from the clamps, and her entire pussy in chaos, she nodded. There seemed an awesome symmetry about being stoppered at both ends.

The gag that he fished out of the box was a black sphere with long black ribbons. Before she could change her mind, Jay slipped it into her mouth and secured it in place, tying it over her hair. She'd expected the taste of rubber from the ball, but it was surprisingly neutral.

'Are you OK with that?' His voice was serious, concerned.

Sandy nodded. She felt again that sense of reassurance, of safety with him. He might be entranced by sexual games, and revelling in the perversity of what he could do with her, and to her, because she let him. But at the bottom of that, at the heart of the play, her welfare was paramount to him. If she didn't like it and she didn't want it, and if it didn't give *her* pleasure, they wouldn't do it.

Gagged, clamped and filled with the love-egg, she felt both objectified and exalted. A surrendered being. Her arousal soared, and she wanted more, more, more. Prepared like this, she wanted to rub herself against Jay, work her crotch against him. She wanted to part her thighs and rock her pussy against *his* strong thigh until she came. She wanted him to handle her when she couldn't handle him. She wanted him to play with her in every way he wanted to. Perhaps spank her? Perhaps hurt her and expose her and exalt her in strange new ways that expanded her perceptions?

Wild thoughts made her gurgle again around her gag. Her clit seemed to swell between her legs, shouting silently for service. Contact.

'Walk for me,' said Jay, taking her by the upper arm and setting her on her feet. The way the egg rocked inside her made her eyes start in her head, and a wash of her own lubrication joined the pond between her legs. Perspiration poured from her, trickling down her back and gathering in her armpits and soaking the band of her bra beneath her breasts. She panted continuously around the rubber ball in her mouth as he led her to the open space in front of the counter and, sliding his arm around her waist, guided her into a slow and silent close-dance.

How bizarre. How strange. How intense.

For moments on end, they swayed together, and with every tick, tick, tick of her heart, Sandy grew more aroused, more excited. The egg rolled and churned inside her, caressing her inner pleasure centres. She wanted to moan, she wanted to sob, she wanted to holler blue murder.

She wanted to be pushed to her limits, to fly apart with pleasure, then be made whole again by sharing it with Jay.

You are 'The One', she told him silently as a tear born of extreme sensation and emotion slid down her face. She nearly swooned when he captured it with his tongue, then kissed its track. She knew it was insane to have fallen for a man she'd known, in real terms, for just a few days. But she had. It was a done deal. She loved him.

How could she not love Prince Charming now she'd found him again?

As he kissed her face, Jay's hands slid down and settled on her bottom cheeks, holding her there. His fingers cupped the rounds of flesh and began to massage them.

'Your arse is beautiful, Princess,' he murmured against her brow. 'Magnificent. Sumptuous. A work of art.' He swooped down and nipped her earlobe, inflicting a delicious little pain. 'I'd love to spank you now, do you know that?' He paused. 'Would you let me?'

Sandy's knees went weak, but he caught her, one arm snaking around her waist, holding her up, while the other continued to knead her bottom cheek. His fingertips were dangerously near to where the silvery woven cord dangled out of her.

'Would you let me spank you?' he repeated, then snagged her earlobe for another little nip.

When he kissed her lobe better, she nodded her head, wanting and needing to be spanked, although not knowing why. Turning, she caught a twinkle in his eye that seemed to dance into hers. They exchanged grins, as best she could with the obstruction in her mouth.

Spanking? It was an absurd game to play really, wasn't it?

She knew it. He knew it. And yet *that* was the fun of it, the sharing.

Then it was all seriousness. Sort of . . .

'Lean across the table, Princess,' he instructed her, swirling her around and pressing on the centre of her back.

Sandy started to comply, then balked. She nodded down at her breasts, at the jewels dangling from the clamps. They'd dig into her, and that wasn't the kind of pain she wanted, no way.

'We'll take them off then. But you might regret it, sweetheart, I warn you.'

She had a feeling she knew why, but still her head came up, daring him to do his worst.

Swiftly, deftly, Jay unscrewed the first clamp. And Sandy squealed around the gag. The pressure released was far worse than the pressure first inflicted, and double when he unfastened the other one. Sandy danced from one foot to the other, then gasped again as the egg moved inside her. It was overload, too much. She didn't know whether she wanted to rub herself, or come, or just yell as best she could with the gag in her mouth.

But Jay held her close again, pressing her freed nipples against the solid wall of his chest. At first Sandy moaned, but within moments she began to purr and shimmy, loving the pressure and the delicate scrape of his silk shirt against the tender tips of her breasts.

'Better?' he asked, his hands firm on her back and her bottom.

She nodded, still moving, circling, and working herself against him, nipples, crotch, belly, thighs.

He buried his face in her hair, and she felt him breath in deeply, as if intoxicated by the scent of it and her herbal shampoo.

'We don't have to do the spanking thing,' he said, pausing to kiss her brow. 'Not if you don't really want to. You don't have to pander to my kinky whims. It's just a game.'

Sandy looked up into his eyes and gave him an old-fashioned look, telling him silently that she was damned if she was going to let him bottle out on her and not satisfy her curiosity, her desire, her expectations.

Jay stared down at her, his eyes unfathomable. He wanted her, she knew, and he wanted them to indulge in erotic fun together, and experiment, but there was more going on, much, much more. Strange tiny tensions played across his face, and she couldn't decipher them. Then he smiled.

'You're a remarkable woman, Princess. Why is it that I know you can take anything I can dish out?' His raw voice was almost velvet for once. 'Now lie across the table and prove it to yourself.'

She obeyed him, trembling and yet smiling to herself. She pictured her pale bottom gleaming in the centre of the café, like a choice dish on display, a kinky naughty buffet. Especially with the silk ribbon of her thong bisecting her buttocks, and the silver cord of the love-egg hanging down. Just the image of it in her mind made her sex melt and moisten, delicately flexing and clenching around the silicon egg. When Jay touched her there, right on her entrance, as light as a feather, she moaned out loud. He was monitoring her body, its every response.

'You're so hot, Princess, so hot. I've never known a woman quite like you.' He flicked at her labia, the tips of his fingers floating over her, sweeping up her perineum, tantalising the rose of her bottom. They slid over her cheeks, touching and testing, assessing the resilience of flesh, of muscle.

Then, in a sudden, breathtaking action, he lightly spanked her left buttock.

Sandy jerked, her legs kicking, her bound hands trying to fly to the point of impact and pain.

She breathed hard, surprised by the spank, shocked by other sensations, hitting in different ways. The sudden tightening, then releasing, tightening, then releasing in her sex.

Cause and effect. Pain and pleasure. Astonishing. But true, oh so true.

He spanked again, and the blow was hot, dark, exciting. Sandy circled her hips against the edge of the table, rubbing herself, trying to get some action and some pressure for her clit.

'Naughty, naughty! Stay still,' he chided, mock stern.

Sandy tried, she really tried, but it was as if there was a motor inside her making her move, winding her up, making everything tense and hum and gather. She worked her hips, and Jay laughed and slapped her harder.

Involuntarily, Sandy's hands jerked, trying to get to her buttocks and her crotch. Trying to get to Jay and drag him to her and force her to touch her again or fuck her. Or just do anything ...

Slap! Slap! Slap!

She whined behind the gag, wanting more.

Slap! Slap! Slap!

She jiggled her hips, rubbing, working.

'What do you want?' Jay demanded, staying his hand and moving in close, fitting himself against her flaming buttocks, his cock like an iron knot prodding her anal groove. In a swift efficient action, he pried open the bow on her gag and flung it away. The ball bounced once, then twice, then rolled under the table. 'What do you want?' he asked again, one hand in her hair now while the other slid over her back and her shoulders and her bound arms, curved and caressing.

Connections in Sandy's brain weren't working properly. Was

it more pain she wanted, or pleasure? The ultimate pleasure she could get from Jay's big cock?

She had no idea. She couldn't speak. Maybe she wanted both? Maybe she wanted both *at once*?

Articulating with her body, she pressed back against him, inviting him, stretching against her bonds with her fingers to try and caress his cock.

Jay leaned right over her, his chest against her back, his groin pressed to the heat he'd created, and she felt his forehead touch the back of her head, as if it were bowed. As if he was awed by her.

'My Princess, my Princess,' he whispered.

For a moment he just rested there, as if lost in a fugue, frozen in time. Then with a swift sharp movement he reached down and snagged the twisted silken cord dangling from her body. He pulled, slow and firm and steady, unwavering, and Sandy groaned, her body quickening from the tug and the rolling pressure of the egg being withdrawn.

'Oh God! Oh God!' she whimpered, starting to come wildly just as he reached under her and stroked her clit as he continued pulling on the cord.

Immense pulsations of blinding pleasure swelled and crested in the cradle of her belly, sparkling and centring on her clitoris. Jay swept his fingers in circles, and she tossed her head, overwhelmed and sobbing, loving his touch.

With a pop, the egg was out of her, and Sandy soared again. As Jay flung it away and it bounced in the general direction of the gag, she rocked and struggled beneath him, uncoordinated, uncontrolled. Tugging at her bonds, she felt the restriction sudden loosen, and the silken ties were a thing of the past too.

Her hands went to herself, to her needy clitoris, and to him, clasping and grasping at his thigh, his hip, scrabbling for touch, contact, any way she could hold him. Still over her, still pressed against her, she felt him searching in his pocket, and she gasped, 'Thank God!' when he drew out the item she'd been hoping for.

Free at last, she wriggled and squirmed around until she was perched on the edge of the table, then opened her thighs, as wide as they'd go, in a blatant invitation. Jay's face was a dark mask of concentration as he rolled on the condom. The fearful set of his mouth was both thrilling and alarming. When he was covered, he grabbed her by the thighs and pulled her forward, positioning himself. Sandy felt herself sliding along the cloth from the force of his thrust, and she scrabbled for purchase, but he leaned over, gripped her by the shoulder, and started fucking her, hard and fast.

His expression was intent. His eyes were wild, and almost black. He was ferocious and he was wondrous, powering into her.

'Touch yourself,' he commanded, his raw voice barely more than a gasp.

She barely needed telling. Holding onto the table for dear life with one hand, she reached down and found her clit with the other, loving the fact that his magnificent cock was sliding to and fro, barely an inch or two away from her questing hand. She let a couple of her fingers glide along the latex as he moved, caressing him as he caressed her, from within, with his long thick shaft.

Just looking into his eyes made her rush to climax again. Yes, the touching and the fucking helped, but somehow it was those crazed grey depths that triggered her. She shouted, 'Jay! Oh God, Jay!' as her pussy clenched and gripped and clutched at him, the pulsations so intense they were almost painful. Dimly, she felt the echoes of pain in her bottom where she'd been spanked and, even though it stimulated her, it seemed to belong to another woman.

All she was about were those eyes, and her spasming sex, and Jay deep in it. And as she drowned in him, his face contorted, and he came.

17

Afterwards, they staggered to bed.

Sandy wasn't quite sure who was supporting whom, and at the back of her mind she made a note that she'd better not leave the box of toys just lying there in the café, or forget about her dress on the floor and the gag and the love-egg under one of the tables. Some of her customers were a tad on the conservative side. For the moment though her compelling need was to get to her bed, get on her back again, and get Jay inside her. Again.

It seemed she just couldn't get enough of his hands, his cock, his face, his body. Even his scars. He opened his mouth to protest as she as good as ripped off his shirt and pulled open his trousers again, tugging at them for him to take them off. But she wouldn't be gainsaid, she wanted the entire package and she wanted it naked, scarred or otherwise.

Like a battle-damaged warrior he loomed over her. Stripped of his clothes, he now seemed to want to impose his imperfections on her, and he drew her hands over the red twisted marks that covered his chest, his torso, his belly. He seemed to be saying, face it, this is what you wanted to see, so see it and feel it all.

Sandy caressed him, each and every line and gouge. She felt sorrow for his pain, but also awe at his courage, his fortitude. Returning from this hell to be a man, a virile, fucking man who was more, far more than normal men who'd never suffered.

She kissed each scar, and rubbed her own body against his, like some priestess absorbed in a rite, healing his hurts.

Finally, she pushed him onto his back, reached into her bedside drawer, and got out a condom. With slow deliberation, she rolled it onto him, leaning over to kiss his latex-clad cock as part of the process.

Then she straddled him, sinking down on his fine sweet erection, down, down, down until she felt as if she were bursting, crammed right to her throat with his length and girth. And when she was squatting down on him, full to the brim, she sat there, getting her breath and absorbing the sensations of being stretched and totally possessed.

Jay lay back, battered but beautiful, surrendered to her, almost. He was still total man, but somehow hers to ride and use and love.

'Oh God,' he murmured as she touched his nipples, pinching them as she'd pinched her own. He muttered again, low in his throat, when she reached back and between his legs and stroked his arse-hole.

'Whoa! Too much attention to me, and not enough to you,' he said at length, and reared up to kiss her, and then fondle her breasts with a strange rough tenderness, tweaking as she'd tweaked, then almost doubling himself up to suck and bite her nipples.

Now it was Sandy's turn to murmur, to whimper, as her vagina stirred around him.

And then he turned his attention to her clit.

Rubbing, circling, massaging, anointing her with her own juices to slick his touch. Agitated, she started to move, but he held her hip with his free hand, keeping her clamped right down on him, her pelvis immobilised while he tormented her with pleasure. Even when she climaxed, with a little scream, he held her still.

'Please let me move,' she begged him, realising the balance of power had tipped again and he controlled her completely, even though she was the one riding atop him.

'Hush,' he said. 'Keep still, baby,' as he rolled her clit between his slippery finger and thumb.

She came again, the pleasure excruciating, her head tossing even if her body was paralysed by his will. Her hard wrenching spasms embraced his cock and she saw him bare his strong white teeth as he endured the rippling caress and fought to torment her even further with yet more pleasure.

Floating somewhere near the ceiling, Sandy looked down on him and a clear lucid part of her met his eyes, held them, and she smiled.

'Enough already!' she said, dashing his hand away from her crotch. Replacing it with her own, she set her other hand on his broad scarred chest and began to lift and settle, lift and settle, lift and settle until she was bouncing up and down on his cock and doing her utmost, her very utmost, to wring an orgasm out of it.

Jay laughed and groaned and snarled at her. She did the same to him. And within a couple of minutes, they both surrendered to one another. Their incoherent cries were a song of joy that rang in the room.

On waking, Sandy patted the bed at her side, and even half asleep she recognised the action as a cliché from the movies or the telly.

Girl has fabulous shag with amazing man. Falls asleep. Wakes up, he's gone.

Cold and dread and sadness and bubbling anger gripped her all in the course of a few split-seconds – until she cracked her eyes open and saw Jay's black shirt draped over the back of a chair, and his shoes lying on their sides underneath it.

Amazing man who shagged fabulously had *not* gone. Well, not too far, without his shoes and some of his clothing.

Sandy scrabbled into her robe, and padded barefoot onto the landing. She was aware of various tender areas as she walked. Not so much in her spanked bottom or her briefly clamped nipples, but more a general sensitivity and awareness that she'd been fucked, and fucked very soundly, by a big strong energetic man.

But where the hell was he? Not in the bathroom or the kitchen or the sitting room that was for sure, although he'd certainly been in the bathroom. A towel was slightly damp, although spread out carefully on the rail to dry rather than in a heap on the floor.

And to her astonishment, he seemed to have washed the gag he'd used and the love-egg that had been inside her.

A neatness freak? Or maybe obsessive-compulsive about cleanliness?

Either way, it was refreshing after her husband and the few boyfriends she'd had, who were all of the towels-on-the-floor and piddle-all-over-the-seat persuasion.

So, he must be in the café. There was nowhere else.

She pushed open the door and entered her workplace.

He was standing at the window in the dark. Light from the window on the other side of the room bathed his broad bare back, making his scars look like the tribal wounds of some battle-tested warrior. His feet were bare and she found the vulnerability of his naked toes strangely touching.

She could tell he was aware of her, but he didn't turn or speak. He simply stared out into the precinct in the direction of the problematical site of the old supermarket.

Sandy brushed the nagging thoughts on that score away. She didn't want to think about it now. She just wanted to know what was up with Jay, because something certainly was. His marked but beautiful back was rigid with tension.

You're a stranger. I've known you less than a week. And yet I feel closer to you than I've ever felt to anybody.

The tension was unbearable. The question that lurked below the surface all the time surfaced again.

'Who are you?'

'I don't think you really want to know.'

Sandy jumped, clutching her robe tighter. She'd spoken aloud without realising it.

'I think I do.'

His gleaming shoulders sagged, as if weighed down.

'Yes, you probably do, but you won't like the answer, so I don't want to tell you. Even though I know I ought to.'

'What are you going on about?' The plain-speaking woman from a small town got the better of her. He was an incredible man, a wonderful strange man, but goodness, he could be obtuse when he wanted to.

She walked across to him, and saw his mouth in the moonlight, tight and tense and compressed.

'Who are you?' she repeated, low and firm. Firmer than she felt because a sudden great clamour of fear arose inside her. She had a feeling that the last vestiges of her fairytale dream about him were about to be shattered, and it was a horrible premonition.

He stared out, eyes focused on the far side of the precinct and the empty shell of the supermarket. Then he straightened up, his spine locked, and he looked like a fatalistic boxer inviting the knockout punch.

'My name is Jason Bentley Forbes.'

Sandy frowned. What was the problem? He'd given her more or less his real name.

Wait a minute. Forbes. Forbes? Bloody hell ... *Forbes*?

For a split-second her knees felt a bit strange, then riding a tide of cold anger she braced them. Her fists clenched and she forced them to remain at her side, even though she was rocked by the wildest urge to pummel and punch him and shout and stomp.

Forbes. He was Forbes. Forbes Enterprises. The bloody goddamn property developer who was going to build a fun pub across the precinct and put her out of business!

Not intentionally, the voice of sweet reason reminded her. How was he to know? He'd probably bought the site and had the plans drawn up before he even knew the Teapot existed.

True, but when she'd asked, half-asleep after sex, how he'd found her, he'd mentioned the Fresh Food award article he'd seen in a local magazine when he'd been doing some background reading on Kissley. He'd started kissing her again before she'd been able to ask *why* he was doing background reading, but it was obvious now that he must have known about her café for a while at least. The Fresh Food award was ages ago. And yet the bastard had still pursued her sexually, and seduced her. *And* made her love him.

That did buckle her knees, and she sat down, her head whirling.

Jay was on his feet beside her, tall and towering. He looked strong and rocklike and watchful as he looked down at her, his expression complex. She saw neither apology nor defensiveness, just a heavy look of tiredness.

'Why didn't you tell me *before* you fucked me?'

She wanted to shoot venom at him, but somehow she just felt tired too, and weighed down by wearisome inevitability.

Prince Charming had been too good to be true. He'd turned into the Evil Robber Baron already.

Guilt came in his eyes then. Angry guilt.

'I wanted you. I still want you. I'd dreamed of you so long.' He sighed out a long breath. 'And I knew I wouldn't get so much as the time of day if you knew who I was. When you talked about the supermarket development at the cocktail party, and confirmed what I'd feared about its potential effects on your business, I knew it would be all over for us before it even started if I told you I was a Forbes.'

'What do you mean *a* Forbes? How many of you bloodsuckers are there?'

She was being ridiculous and she knew it. It was business. Just business. That was all it was.

'The company, or should I say the companies, they all belong to my father, William Forbes.' A sudden look of anguish swept across his scarred face. Deep worry. 'And I have an older brother who's very much involved in the day-to-day running of the various divisions, especially overseas. You could say I'm just the worthless playboy son. Or I was until I ruined my dazzling looks in a smashed-up supercar and decided I wasn't the darling of the ladies and the media any more. So I decided to finally give in and work with my old dad.'

'God, if they made a movie or a telly series about this it'd get panned for being too unlikely and full of coincidences.'

She scowled at him, as angry with herself as she was with him.

He'd fucked her senseless and played her body like a finely tuned instrument whenever it suited him. And she'd let him, without having the gumption to get to know him even the slightest bit first. Even now, she could feel his mouth and tongue on her, working between her thighs that first night in the garden. The memory was so vivid her clit jumped, quickening just at the thought of it.

'I can't get over the fact that you knew who *I* was, and how I'd be affected by your father's business plans, and you still – you still –' She couldn't get the words out, even if her body was replaying the effects of the action.

'Put my face between your legs and made you come?'

'I should have slapped you and told you to fuck off! I must have been insane to let you anywhere near me, whoever the hell you were . . . are.'

But that was wrong. Even now, she knew she couldn't refuse him. Maybe wouldn't have done then, knowing what she knew now. It was hard to believe but she suspected it was true. He'd put a spell on her right from the start.

'You don't mean that.'

Jay seemed angrier now, less tired. Maybe he was furious with himself, or her, it was hard to tell. There was a look in his eyes, something indefinable. Confused, like fury but somehow almost gentle, almost heartbreaking. Almost heartbroken. It was quite astonishing and she'd never seen anything like it.

'I think you still want me,' he said. 'I think that you don't regret anything, because you're too strong a woman for that. I think you still desire me, even now that you know I'm a Forbes.'

'So what if I do?' she flung at him. 'I don't have to do anything about it, do I?' She was playing with fire, yet she couldn't seem to turn away from it. 'I'm not a slave to my own sex drive. I can just ignore it. And *you*, for that matter.'

His eyes flashed like polished steel, as sharp as a blade, and within a single breath he was in front of her, looming like a bird of prey, staring down at her. Panicked, she started to push her chair back, afraid of what she'd started, but, before she could, he sank down onto his knees, with a visible grimace of pain, and pushed the wings of her robe apart, baring her.

Gripping her thighs hard, he parted them, drew in a great breath then laughed, low and bitter.

'Can you *really* ignore this?' he asked, closing his eyes for a second and rolling his head slightly like a gourmet or a wine connoisseur. 'You smell beautiful. You need sex. You need me to satisfy you.'

'What I need – what I want – is an orgasm. Not you. Any willing pair of hands, or mouth, would do.'

But they wouldn't, of course. Probably never would again. The last man on earth she should have allowed to get to her had ruined her for all other men.

'Fair enough,' snapped Jay. His voice was taut and combative, but in his eyes there was more, desperation and remorse.

He released her thighs and plunged in with his fingers, delicately working his way through her pubic hair and peeling apart her sticky labia. With what sounded like a sigh, or a gasp of regret, he dove in, finding her clit instantly with his tongue, and began to lick and work at her in fast angry strokes. When he'd settled into his rhythm, he reached beneath her, holding her buttocks, lifting her and feasting on her, punishing her with lashing relentless stimulation.

Sandy grabbed for him, wishing his hair was as long as it'd once been so she could dig her hands into it, grip it in hunks and pull it to punish him. As it was she could only claw at his shoulders, making tiny red marks amongst the bigger ones of his scars. She threw her own head back, no longer able to look at him, and started to growl and grunt as the sensations spiralled, not caring if she sounded like a she-beast in heat.

She didn't care what he thought of her. She didn't care about him. All she wanted was his skilled and hungry mouth, giving her pleasure.

And pleasure it did give, fast and rough and unremitting. Battering her with his tongue, he forced her at breakneck speed towards an orgasm that seemed to tear her into little pieces. It had come too soon, and was so violent that it was difficult to differentiate it from pain.

Climaxing, she cried out, clutched at him, forced her crotch against his mouth, demanding more. And when he gave more, she wanted even more than that. She wanted him in her.

Shoving him away, she slithered down onto the floor, threw apart her legs and reached for him. His eyes were on fire, and the bulge at the crotch of his elegant trousers was enormous. He wanted her, but in his moment of hesitation she realised he probably didn't have a condom. For once she didn't care, but he did, and he was about to say something, his face still full of wrath, when a tinkling trill of bell-like sound broke the spell.

Sandy sat up and looked around. It was the same 'Brocade' ringtone that she had, but her phone was in the bedroom, on the sideboard.

Jay refastened the zip he'd begun to tug down and rose to his feet. As he headed for the table by the window, Sandy noticed a mobile phone there that she hadn't seen before. He must have brought it with him. Was he expecting a call this late? Or early? It must be close to dawn.

Despite her anger and her pleasure-fuddled state, she got up and moved to the other end of the room, respecting his privacy. She slid behind the counter and pulled out the bottle of whisky she kept there for the occasional and totally unlicensed alcoholic coffee for favourite customers. After pouring some into the nearest glass, a tumbler, she knocked back a belt of the fiery spirit. She didn't normally drink like this but, hell, what more extenuating circumstances than these could there be?

Slowly sipping a second small measure, she returned her attention to Jay, and got a shock. He was talking in low tense tones. His back was to her but she could see it was rigid with some kind of powerful emotion. It was a little as he'd appeared earlier, when she'd first happened upon him at the window, but different, so different, as night from day.

'All right,' he said, hard, flat, but not emotionless, 'I'll be with you in a couple of hours.' There was some kind of retort from the caller, and Jay almost rocked back. 'All right then, three or four hours. Of course I don't want to fucking well total another Aston. I can drive fast and still be safe. I'm not a complete bloody idiot!'

He snapped shut the phone and just stood there for a moment, looking shell-shocked as if he were processing information that had come to him from another planet. As tall and strong as ever, he looked oddly deflated, as if he had literally had the stuffing knocked out of him. But then, the moment was gone and he stalked across the room towards her. For a second he glanced at the whisky bottle, then he scowled, shoving his phone in his pocket.

'Look, I don't want to go like this. But I have to.' His beautiful mouth worked for a moment, as if that inability to compute still remained. 'My father has had a heart attack and I must go to him. I knew he wasn't well. I should have stayed. But he made me so bloody angry and ... and I had to see you again as soon as I could.' He grabbed her by the shoulder, his expression fierce and conflicted. 'Look, I'm sorry ... about everything. But I must get on the road as soon as possible.'

'Of course. And, um, I'm sorry too.' She wasn't quite sure what for, but somehow she felt guilty. She'd raged at him, and not really given him the chance to explain. Now she probably never would get that chance. 'Is there anything I can do?'

By unspoken agreement, they were already returning to the bedroom where the rest of Jay's clothes were, and his car key, the Aston's fancifully named Emotional Control Device.

'Yes,' he said, turning as he entered the room. 'Just don't hate me too much.' He reached for his jacket, shrugged into it. 'I never meant to be the enemy, and I never wanted to lie to you. I just, well, I just had to have you and there was no other way. I wish there had been.' He was shoving his feet into his socks and loafers as he spoke, and when he straightened up, he stood staring down at her for a second.

But just a second. Sandy could feel them all ticking by just as Jay no doubt could. He had to go, and go now. Who knew how serious the older man's condition was. He might have to drive at breakneck speed again to reach his father's side before he died.

He took her mouth again in a swift brutal kiss. It was as hungry and desperate as it was fleeting.

Kiss it better, thought Sandy as he put her from him and strode away towards the door. She made to follow, but he shook his head, made a chopping gesture. He seemed unable to speak, but she understood him on a deep level she found it impossible to quantify.

Kiss it better, she thought again, standing exactly where he'd left her as the Aston's powerful engine roared into life in the yard below.

We could probably never kiss it better ever again.

A tear rolled down her cheek as the car-growl faded to nothing, leaving silence.

18

'Galleria? What Galleria?'

'I don't know. But at least it's not an all-day coffee fun pub. I suppose we should be grateful for that.'

Confused by what she was seeing, Sandy glanced at Kat. They were standing outside the rapidly transforming site of the old Bradbury's supermarket, staring at a billboard that had just gone up. A billboard that had finally confirmed once and for all that the new development wasn't a fun pub, but a mini mall-type shopping centre called The Galleria, with over a dozen distinct units, all fashioned within the existing shell of the large old store. The Chamber of Commerce jungle drums had hinted as much, but details had been sketchy, hush-hush.

Now it was all official.

'Well, why the fuck hasn't your boyfriend told you all about it?' demanded Kat. 'After all, it's his company that's building the thing.'

Sandy sighed, suddenly deflated. 'He's not my boyfriend. And when we've chatted on the phone, we ... well, we had an unspoken pact not to talk about developments and pubs and business or anything. Just casual stuff.'

She frowned, staring at the plan. The names of some businesses were already marked in with whatever they sold or did. But one prime location, right by the entrance where everyone would pass, was simply marked 'café'.

Great, you're just building another café instead *of a pub, you git.*

It was true, they'd spoken only of trivia. Of day-to-day minutiae. Television, movies, funny incidents. Details of Jay's father's health progress, which was good, because, even though Forbes Senior was an old bird, he was as tough and bloody stubborn as nails, just as his son was. Sandy didn't know Jay's dad and, since the news of the supermarket sale, she'd heaped many a curse on his name. But she was glad to hear he was recovered, if only for Jay's sake.

Yes, it had been a strange, almost mannered communication at best that had passed between them, especially after the raw intimacy they'd shared, but to her dismay, she still clung to it like a starving woman scrabbling after stale bread crusts that'd been thrown to the birds.

Pathetic. And this is the end of it. This is a dirty trick too far, you conniving bastard. Just business or no just business. Fuck you.

The trouble was, she didn't really feel that way at all, just a little sad, and confused.

But the next morning, the day after the billboard went up, a letter arrived that only added to her confusion. Sandy stared at it for a long while, as if she needed a Rosetta Stone to decipher it.

What the hell does it mean 'lease negotiable'? And why a Sunday afternoon of all times?

Tap. Tap. Tap. Tap. Shazam!

The key code worked and the gated entrance to the Galleria site sprang open. Sandy consulted the plan, still surprised she'd been supplied with access codes to what amounted to a building site. The letter had said that she could look around the proposed café, sticking only to that area for safety reasons, in order to assess the facilities. With a view to purchasing the lease.

I can't afford this. It'll cost a fortune. He's probably doing this as a courtesy, out of guilt or something.

Oh, but the café unit was fabulous though. Perfect accessibility. Perfect position. Perfect ergonomic design. It would be a pleasure to work here. And the 'soul' of the Little Teapot could happily dwell and thrive in a new home like this. Sandy did a rapid review of all the possible sources of finance she had access to, and wondered and wondered if there was any way at all she could swing it.

The kitchen to the rear of the serving area was gorgeous too. Small, but efficiently laid out, with a professional range already installed and a big central unit for prep.

A short passage to the right led to a cloakroom. Bigger than the one in the Teapot, fully fitted out for accessibility. Everything perfect. She turned the tap. The water was already on.

The mirror above the sink made her shudder as memories rose up. Her own face in a mirror as Jay worked her from behind, his own face harsh, scarred, but still beautiful to her.

He hadn't meant to jeopardise her precious café. It was business, just business. Like *The Godfather*, but without the guns, the horse's heads and the cold-blooded murder. He'd been the wrong man at the right time. Or the right man at the wrong time. Or just the wrong man at the wrong time. She'd probably never see him again and the calls and texts would peter out sooner rather than later.

Her phone chimed announcing a text.

How do you like it? Good bathroom?

She pressed the key to reply, started tapping in a 'y', then an 'e' – then she stopped and cancelled the message. How the hell did he know she was in the bathroom?

Sandy stormed out of the loo and ducked back into the kitchen.

Jay was leaning on the main prep counter, waiting and watchful like some dark predatory beast. He gave her a quirk of a smile, but didn't speak straight away, almost as if he wasn't sure what to say – which well he might not be, given this latest stunt: luring her to a deserted half-finished mini mall on a Sunday afternoon.

In the few seconds before she found her own words, Sandy drank in the sight of him, devoured it, feasted upon it.

Hell, he looked good!

Black suited him, and he wore it now, head to foot. Boots, jeans, shirt, one of his very, very good jackets. He appeared just as she'd last seen him, but somehow very different. His hair, for one thing. The semi-shaven crop had grown out, and his hair was thick and very dark and brushed straight back from his face in a hawkish sort of way that really suited him. He was still clean-shaven, which she realised she liked better than the beard, but he had a bit of a down and dirty stubble thing going on which made her blood race. Or race even more than it already was. Even his scars looked a little faded, a little mellowed. She wondered momentarily how he was doing with the pain.

'So, I suppose it's no coincidence you're here,' she said cautiously. There was no point raging at him. What would she be raging about? He'd made no promises when he'd left, and their communications had been non-committal. Seeing him today was a bonus, and she supposed she should view it that way.

'No, it's no coincidence. I wanted to meet you here. I set it up.' He had the grace to look uncomfortable.

'Then why hide behind the signature of one of your flunkies?'

Jay shrugged and made an elegant gesture of befuddlement with his long scarred hands.

'God knows. I can't seem to think straight when it's anything to do with you,' he said, straightening up. 'I suppose that's why I had to stay strictly away these last few months. There was some serious stuff that needed to be sorted out for, and with, my father, and I knew if I allowed myself the luxury of visiting you, and trying to explain myself, I wouldn't want to go back.'

'I'm touched.' It came out sarcastically, but that was because she was the befuddled one now. Contrived as they sounded, his words did make sense to her. And it was a sense that thrilled and excited her and made all the silly insane dreams that she'd unequivocally squashed down, or *thought* she'd squashed down, flare up again like a wildfire. 'But why here? Why the cloak and dagger?'

Jay laughed, a delicious sound. It made the hairs on the back of her neck stand up and a slow honeyed surge roll low in her pelvis. She hadn't stopped wanting him one second during all the time he'd been away, regardless of what had happened, and she'd made much use of some of his sexy gifts in his absence. A blush rose to her face at the thought of some of those sessions. Crying out his name as she'd climaxed, and then feeling cross with herself for clinging on and not letting go of his influence upon her.

'I said, I don't know. I wanted to make a dramatic entrance or something, a bit of theatre.' He walked towards her, and a delicate wave of his spicy cologne met her before he did, overwhelming the vaguely plastery odour of the still unfinished walls. 'We first met in dramatic circumstances. And we got together again in dramatic circumstances ... sort of.' A little touch of blush flowed into his face now, high on his perfectly reconstructed cheekbones. She knew he was thinking of the garden at the Waverley. She certainly was. 'And I wanted our reunion to match it.'

'Reunion?'

'Well, yes. With my dad pretty much back on top form again now, he doesn't need me at his side all the time, and he bloody well doesn't want me there either.' He was in front of her now, looking down, his grey eyes steady and dark. 'So I'm free to pursue my own projects. We've got a lot going on in this region now the credit crunch is easing and business is bouncing back again. I thought I'd relocate up here, to be on hand. And pursue other things too.'

Sandy could feel herself trembling. It was him, his presence, his body and his fragrance and his eyes and his low rough voice. She knew she should quiz him about the café and the lease and all that practical stuff. But she couldn't. All she wanted was to touch him. Be with him. Come to know him in the real world as well as she'd known – and loved – him in her dreams for fifteen long years.

They stared at each other, just inches apart. Who would be the first to succumb?

Sandy gave in. She reached up and touched Jay's face, drawing her fingers over his ever so slightly stubbled cheeks, loving the rough texture. It was like him, a bit rough, a bit edgy, but irresistibly attractive and wonderful. Jay turned his face into the caress and kissed her palm.

Rational sense tried to reassert itself. 'Why should I just let you back into my life like this?' she demanded, even while she was finding it difficult to breathe. His lips were soft yet demanding, still exploring her palm, and his tongue darted out, reminding her of other dartings in other more intimate places. Oh God, he was so good at that and she'd missed it like the very devil.

'Because we've known each other fifteen years. We should

be together,' he insisted, the breath of the words a caress in itself. She felt his hand close over hers, and his other hand settle lightly against her waist. It felt hot through the black camisole she was wearing beneath her cardigan. The very one, she realised, that he'd given her in one of his boxes of exquisite goodies.

How had she known to wear that today? How could she have *not* worn it? Accepting fate, and embracing it, loving it . . .

'Jay,' she gasped, feeling the fight for control and resistance dissipating, dissolving, burnt off by the heat in his eyes and in his skin, 'we've barely actually spent more than fifteen *hours* together all told. What kind of basis is that for being together?'

'It's a good start,' he said, more crisply now. She could tell that, as always, he'd decided what he wanted and was determined to get it. A voice inside that should have had her telling him to hold his horses and not get ahead of himself was in fact making her melt, urging her to rub herself crazily against him, prior to demanding that he fuck her. 'And all the more reason why we should do everything we can to make up for lost time,' he finished triumphantly, not pausing for her reply but just sliding his hand around the back of her head and propelling her face towards his, for a kiss at last.

How could it be that everything in the world could be right, just because one pair of lips met another? It wasn't sensible. It wasn't logical. But it was true.

Jay's touch had felt right, in innocence, fifteen years ago. And it felt just as right now, informed by a wealth of shared sensual desire and exploration. The innocent connection was still there, but so was sex, wild and immediate and impossible to resist.

They were in the middle of an instant conflagration. No slow sweeping of arms around each other, just hungry, almost angry grabbing and searching and touching and owning. Jay's tongue was in her mouth, and she didn't care about anything to do with cafés and business and owing or being owed or whatever. She just wanted him.

Her hands were beneath his coat, pulling at his shirt, searching for bare contact with his hot skin and his muscles and his scars. His hands were on her, pushing up the camisole, sliding over her back and her ribcage, one coming around the front to cup her breast and strum her nipple in a rough stroke of possession. The black silky top was shaped, and she didn't need a bra with it. More fate, she supposed, dressing for sex because some sixth sense had told her that she'd get some.

She laughed into his mouth, and he pulled away, pressing his lips to her ear, demanding, 'What?' while his fingers still worked on her teat.

'I don't know. Really, I don't know. It doesn't make sense.'

'Whatever,' he observed pithily, angling her head with his hand so he could kiss her again, hard, and with total authority.

Sandy's hips started moving of their own accord, circling and pressing her belly against his crotch. He was rock-hard and he growled, grinding back at her, while she dropped her hands to his buttocks and grabbed them, two hard muscular rounds, and squeezed hard.

God, you have such a fabulous arse, Mr Forbes! I could forgive you just about anything for this!

Jay's mouth roved over her face in little nibbling tasting kisses that somehow managed to be totally possessive and aggressive at the same time. He abandoned her breast and paused to fling his beautiful jacket away across the dusty floor. Then he applied himself to her jeans, unfastening the button, sliding down the zip, and working them down to her hips so he could wiggle one hand down into the front of her knickers, and one down the back, beneath the elastic.

'Oh God!' Sandy gasped, as he started to finger her, fore and aft, roughly yet artfully.

It was no time to grope his bottom now. She had to throw her arms around his neck and cling on for dear life. Her own hungry body was betraying her, wriggling and jerking as she rubbed herself against his fingers, just as they rubbed themselves against her.

'You like that, don't you, Princess?' he murmured in the most disgustingly smug macho voice.

Sandy could have smacked him if she hadn't been too thoroughly otherwise occupied. But it made her laugh too, in the small part of her mind that wasn't completely blown by the way he was circling and slicking around her clit and probing at her bottom, all wicked and rude.

'Admit it!' he growled, redoubling his efforts. The sweet mock ferocity in his voice made her sex pulsate, and the low sound of approval he made told her he'd felt it.

She bit her lip, even if she couldn't stop her body gyrating like a houri in blatant lust.

'Stubborn little bitch! I'll make you come for that. I'll make you speak!'

Still probing and rubbing in the groove of her bottom, he pinched her clitoris between finger and thumb, tugging delicately.

Sandy yelled, her orgasm soaring like a skyrocket. She was helpless against his moves, his knowing, knowing touch. Kicking and shaking she hung onto him like a limpet, locking her hands at the back of his neck instinctively. If she hadn't she would have bucked and wriggled her way clean out of his grip, and ended up in a moaning spasming heap at his booted feet.

'Oh my Princess, my Princess,' he crowed more gently, still working her as she arched and gasped and clung to him, 'I love to feel you come like that. I can't get enough of it.'

Sandy slumped, played out completely for the moment as he gently released her. She was so overheated and sated that she imagined she could actually hear her pussy sizzling. Gulping in air, she tried to remember when she'd last taken a proper breath, and she could feel sweat trickling down between her breasts, her camisole sticking to her.

With her head against his shoulder and her body draped against him, she could feel Jay's heart pounding in time to hers, and his deep chest lifting and falling. He was breathing hard and, when she moved uneasily against his pelvis, his cock seemed to jump inside his jeans. And she wanted some of that! Oh how she wanted it!

Energised by his hardness, his unhidden desire for her, she came back to life again. Finding her feet, she cupped his cock in her fingers and squeezed. Not hard or roughly, but assertively, looking up into his eyes, challenging him now. The grey depths glinted like brilliant sunshine bouncing off the polished surface of the Aston, and he smiled his fierce tough smile, accepting the challenge. Sandy reached up and brushed fingers through his hair. It was thick and soft and smelled really good.

'I like this,' she said, tugging a little hank of it between her finger and thumb. 'Makes you look like less of a thug.'

'I thought you liked my thuggish behaviour,' he purred, sliding his hand between her legs again, gripping her. She didn't melt into a pool of lust this time, even though it felt so good. She just stared back at him, her head up, her eyes narrowed and defiant.

'When it suits me.' She rode his hand, taking what she wanted, and then, when she could tell he thought he'd got her again, she grabbed at his black shirt and ripped it open by main force, sending buttons flying everywhere.

'Jesus, Sandy, that shirt cost two hundred quid!' But he was laughing, just as she was. And a breath later, he was ripping at the thing himself, wrenching at the cuffs to free himself.

While it still hung half on him, half off, she ran her hands over his warm skin, feeling the pop of fine perspiration rise on the smooth areas and the ones ridged by scarring and pain. She saw nothing ugly about the marks, just a pagan beauty, as harsh and uncompromising as he was. Leaning down, she kissed the ones she could reach, licking and nibbling too.

Then she unzipped him and drew out his big hot cock.

Sinking to her knees, jeans still bunched around her hips, she mouthed him for a little while, laughing around his flesh as she wrung groans from him with her enthusiasm if not her polished artistry.

'Jesus, Sandy,' he complained again, his voice more broken than ever by his gasps, 'do you want me to come in your mouth? Because you're heading that way.' She plunged her tongue at a tender spot beneath his glans and he yelped, his hips working of their own accord. 'I don't really mind,' he panted, 'but I'd rather like to get in you if I could.'

'Fair enough,' she said in a muffled voice, her mouth still enclosing him. They both laughed like maniacs as she let him slip out.

Reaching down, he grabbed her under her arms and hauled her to her feet. Then he backed her up, kicked the door to the kitchen closed and then pressed her against it. Sandy realised there were no locks, and the combined weight of their bodies was a form of security. Not that thoughts of being discovered had even come within a mile of her mind while he'd been touching her and caressing her, and she'd been on her knees, giving him head.

Against the door, he kissed her hard, fondling her breasts through her camisole, and flicking at her nipples. Roused all over again, Sandy squirmed against him, pushing with her hips, while he pushed back against her, the heat of his exposed cock searing her. With their mouths still fused and their tongues still duelling, he peeled her cardigan off her and flung it behind him, over his shoulder, then he went for her jeans, grabbing them and tugging them down her legs. Sandy kicked away her shoes, helping him to strip the jeans right off her, and her panties too. She was vaguely aware that she still had on her cute and rather silly white ankle socks trimmed with pictures of Winnie the Pooh and Tigger.

She didn't think Jay had noticed them, but when he whispered, 'Love the socks,' in her ear, she blushed even more than when he'd been masturbating her.

Naked from the waist down, she reached up, ripping at his shirt again, and though Jay gave her a fierce look, he allowed her to drag it off him.

'That's it, no more shilly-shallying around,' he gasped as she stroked his back and his ribcage, and kissed the scars on his shoulders and his neck. 'I've got to fuck you now whether you like it or not!'

Oh, I'll like it! I'll like it!

She didn't speak though, because she couldn't. As a precursor to his cock, he slid two hard curved fingers straight into her sex, and then went deep because she was dripping wet. For a few moments he caressed the tender spot on the front wall of her vagina until she mewled and wailed and shimmied around. But when he made her come again, sharp and hard, and she bit his neck in the process, he dragged out the digits with a low grunt of pain.

'You little she-devil,' he gasped, 'I'll get you for that.' And as her sex steamed and throbbed, waiting for him, he fished a condom out of his pocket. After shoving his jeans and shorts down his thighs, he ripped the contraceptive from its wrapper and rolled it on. No more niceties. No more foreplay. No more going around the houses. Grabbing her hip with one hand, and his cock with the other, he positioned himself, hefted his hips and shoved in hard.

'Oh God,' gasped Sandy as he thrust in, home and deep.

Then she wrapped her arms around his shoulders again and clung on, while he lifted and moved her with his hand under her buttocks and her back banging against the door.

'Touch yourself!' he ordered, his voice harsh and rasping.

'I'll fall.'

'No you won't. I've got you. I'll always have you. I'll never let you fall.'

Grabbing on with one arm and hand, her nails digging into the mass of muscle at the juncture of his shoulder and neck, she reached down blindly between the heat of their two perspiring bodies and searched clumsily for her clit, hampered by the wild rocking motion of the fuck.

When she found it, she moaned. Silvery sensations bloomed there, she was so on fire, so deeply stirred on every level by Jay and his body and his presence. Her legs locked around him and she arched, pushing her pelvis against his, almost crushing her hand where she was touching herself. The manual stimulation was barely necessary, she was so close, so hot, so totally besotted body and soul with him, but the fact that he wanted to be sure that she came was the thing that tipped her over.

She howled, her body clenching around him, her heels beating against his bare buttocks. Her nails dug harder into his musculature, creating new scars, no doubt, to add to his old ones. But he didn't seem to care, he just fucked harder, lifting her higher, making her soar.

'Princess! Princess!' he snarled, his mouth at her neck, then pressed into her hair, which was loose and flying around them. Like a jackhammer, his hips pounded, driving him deep, deeper, deepest, until he shouted a profanity and gripped her buttocks with all the force she was gripping him.

Deep inside her, Sandy felt the repeated pulse of his ejaculation, his semen filling the condom, and in a tiny mad part of her mind she wished he wasn't wearing one.

Then that thought was gone, along with most of her consciousness, as she came again.

Afterwards they slumped in an exhausted heap against the door, bare-arsed on the dusty concrete surface of the floor.

But despite their makeshift surroundings, Sandy had never felt more comfortable, more safe and secure, in her entire life. Being next to Jay felt right, like being home somehow, regardless of whatever complications there were between them in the past, the present or the future. Whatever confronted them, she knew in her bones that they could work it out.

'So, this place,' said Jay suddenly, and in an almost laughably conversational tone, considering his jeans were still at half-mast and his sticky sated cock was lying bare and heavy against his thigh, 'do you think that the "soul" or whatever it is of the Little Teapot could reside here?' He touched his lips to her neck. 'Do the facilities meet with your approval?'

Sandy giggled when she saw him nod towards his crotch.

'Yep, the facilities are first class.' She trailed the back of her hand across the head of his penis, and enjoyed the way he bared his teeth and his head went back, his neck arched. 'But what about this negotiable lease? Will I be able to afford it?'

Jay's grey eyes glittered and he glanced down at her crotch in return.

'Oh, I've no doubt about that.'

As an independent woman and someone who'd always paid

her way, she supposed she should contest the fact that he was obviously as good as giving her a valuable piece of property. It was ridiculous really, but she felt too mellow and too sensualised to worry about anything at the moment, least of all that.

But when she looked into Jay's eyes, she could see he was thinking about it.

'I love you, Sandy,' he said, his voice simple and soft, almost mellifluous for him. 'I want you to have *this*.' He made an elegant expansive gesture, taking in the room, its facilities. 'No strings. It'd just make me happy to see you here, and see your business thrive and make other people happy too. And I want to be here to see it *every single day*.'

His grey eyes were intent, luminous. She knew what he was saying.

It'd make me happy as well, she thought. *Every single day*.

With her heart feeling shaky and strange and thudding fit to burst at the thought of 'every day', it was as if the weight of complications just seemed to slide away from them, like mist that dissipated as it went, leaving the future clear. *Their* future.

And I love you too.

'OK,' she said, sliding her legs beneath her, and coming up on her knees. 'But only after more negotiation. A lot more negotiation. I think we should engage in some long, hard and very strenuous discussions on the matter.'

And then Prince Charming smiled, his scarred face beautiful and laughing as she pushed him onto his back and climbed astride him.

Leaning down, she found his lips, and kissed everything better.

Visit the Black Lace website at
www.blacklace.co.uk

FIND OUT THE LATEST INFORMATION AND TAKE ADVANTAGE OF OUR FANTASTIC FREE BOOK OFFER! ALSO VISIT THE SITE FOR . . .

- All Black Lace titles currently available
  and how to order online
- Great new offers
- Writers' guidelines
- Author interviews
- An erotica newsletter
- Features
- Cool links

BLACK LACE – THE LEADING IMPRINT OF WOMEN'S SEXY FICTION

TAKING YOUR EROTIC READING PLEASURE TO NEW HORIZONS

LOOK OUT FOR THE ALL-NEW BLACK LACE BOOKS – AVAILABLE NOW!

All books priced £7.99 in the UK. Please note publication dates apply to the UK only. For other territories, please contact your retailer.

To be published in June 2009

DOCTOR'S ORDERS
Deanna Ashford
ISBN 978 0 352 33453 4

Helen Dawson is a dedicated doctor who has taken a short-term assignment at an exclusive private hospital that caters for every need of its rich and famous clients. The matron, Sandra Pope, ensures this includes their most curious sexual fantasies. When Helen forms a risky affair with a famous actor, she is drawn deeper into the hedonistic lifestyle of the clinic. But will she risk her own privileges when she uncovers the dubious activities of Sandra and her team?

DARK OBSESSION
Fredrica Alleyn
ISBN 978 0 352 34524 0

Ambitious young interior designer Annabel Moss is delighted when a new assignment takes her to Leyton Hall – home of the very wealthy Lord and Lady Corbett-Wynne. But the grandeur of the house and the impeccable family credentials are a façade for some shockingly salacious practices. Lord James is spending an unusual amount of time in the stables while his idle son shows little interest in anything save his step-sister, Tania. Meanwhile, Lady Marina is harbouring dark secrets of her own. Annabel is drawn into a world of decadence where anything is allowed as long as a respectable appearance prevails. In an atmosphere of intensity and sexual secrecy, she becomes involved in a variety of interesting situations.

To be published in July 2009

SARAH'S EDUCATION
Madeline Moore
ISBN 978 0 352 34539 4

Nineteen-year-old Sarah is an ordinary but beautiful girl engaged to a wealthy fiancé, and soon to be the recipient of all the privileges and opportunities marriage into the upper class can bring. She is also a virgin but, at an exclusive party at a hotel, loses her virginity to a man who is not her fiancé. In the morning she wakes to find an envelope containing $2,500 on the bedside table; Sarah has been mistaken for a high-class call-girl. Soon, she is leading a secret life in top hotels with strange and exciting men, until one of her clients turns out to be her professor from university and a man she has long had a crush on. Their nights of passion and journeys into erotic role-playing become an expensive obsession for each of them. The biggest decision of all for their future has to be made when they are both threatened with exposure. What will Sarah sacrifice for the passion of a lifetime?

GOING TOO FAR
Laura Hamilton
ISBN 978 0 352 33657 6

Spirited adventurer Bliss Van Bon sets off on a three-month tour of South America. Along the way there's no shortage of company. From flirting on the plane to being tied up in Peru; from sex on snowy mountain peaks to finding herself out of her depth with local crooks, Bliss hardly has time to draw breath. And when brawny Australians Red and Robbie are happy to share their tent and their gorgeous bodies with her, she's spoilt for choice. But Bliss soon finds herself caught between her lovers' agendas. Will she help Red and Robbie save the planet, or will she stick with Carlos, whose wealthy lifestyle has dubious origins?

THE SEVEN-YEAR LIST
Zoe Le Verdier
ISBN 978 0 352 33254 7

Newspaper photographer Julia Sargent should be happy and fulfilled. But flattering minor celebrities is not her idea of a challenge, and she's also having doubts about her impending marriage to heart-throb actor David Tindall. In the midst of her uncertainty comes an invitation to a school reunion. When the group meet up, adolescent passions are rekindled – and so are bitter rivalries – as Julia flirts with old flames Nick and Steve. Julia cannot resist one last fling with Steve, but he will not let her go – not until he has achieved the final goal on his seven-year list.

To be published in August 2009

SEXY LITTLE NUMBERS
Various
ISBN 978 0 352 34538 7

Sexy Little Numbers is a choice cut of all new and original erotic stories and the latest addition to Black Lace's immensely popular series of erotica collections. This longer collection will contain even more variety and a greater range of female sexual desire than ever before. It will be the first of an annual collection of the best erotica stories written by women. Fun, irreverent and deliciously decadent, *Sexy Little Numbers* will combine humour and attitude with wildly imaginative writing from all over the world.

UP TO NO GOOD
Karen S Smith
ISBN 978 0 352 34528 8

Emma is resigned to attending her cousin's wedding, expecting the usual excruciating round of polite conversation and bad dancing. Instead it's the scene of a horny encounter which encourages her to behave even more scandalously than usual. When she meets motorbike fanatic Kit, it's lust at first sight, and they waste no time in getting each other off behind the marquee. They don't get the chance to say goodbye, however, and Emma resigns herself to the fact that she'll never see her spontaneous lover again. Then fate intervenes as Emma and Kit are reunited at another wedding – and so begins a year of outrageous sex, wild behaviour and lots of getting up to no good.

THE CAPTIVE FLESH
Cleo Cordell
ISBN 978 0352 34529 5

A tale of decadent orgies amidst the sumptuous splendour of a North African mansion. 19th-century French convent girls Marietta and Claudine learn their invitation to stay in the exotic palace of their handsome host requires something in return – the ecstasy of pleasure in pain.

ALSO LOOK OUT FOR

THE BLACK LACE BOOK OF WOMEN'S SEXUAL FANTASIES
Kerri Sharp
ISBN 978 0 352 33793 1

The Black Lace Book of Women's Sexual Fantasies reveals the most private thoughts
of hundreds of women. Here are sexual fantasies which on first sight appear
shocking or bizarre – such as the bank clerk who wants to be a vampire and the
nanny with a passion for Darth Vader. Kerri Sharp investigates the recurrent themes
in female fantasies and the cultural influences that have determined them: from
fairy stories to cult TV; from fetish fashion to historical novels. Sharp argues that
sexual archetypes – such as the 'dark man of the psyche' – play an important role
in arousal, allowing us to find gratification safely through personal narratives of
adventure and sexual abandon.

THE NEW BLACK LACE BOOK OF WOMEN'S SEXUAL FANTASIES
Edited and compiled by Mitzi Szereto
ISBN 978 0 352 34172 3

The second anthology of detailed sexual fantasies contributed by women from
all over the world. The book is a result of a year's research by an expert on erotic
writing and gives a fascinating insight into the rich diversity of the female sexual
imagination.

Black Lace Booklist

Information is correct at time of printing. To avoid disappointment, check availability before ordering. Go to www.blacklace.co.uk
All books are priced £7.99 unless another price is given.

BLACK LACE BOOKS WITH A CONTEMPORARY SETTING

☐ AMANDA'S YOUNG MEN Madeline Moore — ISBN 978 0 352 34191 4
☐ THE ANGELS' SHARE Maya Hess — ISBN 978 0 352 34043 6
☐ THE APPRENTICE Carrie Williams — ISBN 978 0 352 34514 1
☐ ASKING FOR TROUBLE Kristina Lloyd — ISBN 978 0 352 33362 9
☐ BLACK ORCHID Roxanne Carr — ISBN 978 0 352 34188 4
☐ THE BLUE GUIDE Carrie Williams — ISBN 978 0 352 34132 7
☐ THE BOSS Monica Belle — ISBN 978 0 352 34088 7
☐ BOUND IN BLUE Monica Belle — ISBN 978 0 352 34012 2
☐ CAMPAIGN HEAT Gabrielle Marcola — ISBN 978 0 352 33941 6
☐ CASSANDRA'S CONFLICT Fredrica Alleyn — ISBN 978 0 352 34186 0
☐ CASSANDRA'S CHATEAU Fredrica Alleyn — ISBN 978 0 352 34523 3
☐ CAT SCRATCH FEVER Sophie Mouette — ISBN 978 0 352 34021 4
☐ CHILLI HEAT Carrie Williams — ISBN 978 0 352 34178 5
☐ THE CHOICE Monica Belle — ISBN 978 0 352 34512 7
☐ CIRCUS EXCITE Nikki Magennis — ISBN 978 0 352 34033 7
☐ CLUB CRÈME Primula Bond — ISBN 978 0 352 33907 2   £6.99
☐ CONTINUUM Portia Da Costa — ISBN 978 0 352 33120 5
☐ COOKING UP A STORM Emma Holly — ISBN 978 0 352 34114 3
☐ DANGEROUS CONSEQUENCES Pamela Rochford — ISBN 978 0 352 33185 4
☐ DARK DESIGNS Madelynne Ellis — ISBN 978 0 352 34075 7
☐ DARK OBSESSIONS Fredrica Alleyn — ISBN 978 0 352 34524 0
☐ THE DEVIL AND THE DEEP BLUE SEA Cheryl Mildenhall — ISBN 978 0 352 34200 3
☐ EDEN'S FLESH Robyn Russell — ISBN 978 0 352 32923 3
☐ EQUAL OPPORTUNITIES Mathilde Madden — ISBN 978 0 352 34070 2
☐ FIRE AND ICE Laura Hamilton — ISBN 978 0 352 33486 2
☐ FORBIDDEN FRUIT Susie Raymond — ISBN 978 0 352 34189 1
☐ GEMINI HEAT Portia Da Costa — ISBN 978 0 352 34187 7
☐ THE GIFT OF SHAME Sarah Hope-Walker — ISBN 978 0 352 34202 7
☐ GONE WILD Maria Eppie — ISBN 978 0 352 33670 5
☐ HOTBED Portia Da Costa — ISBN 978 0 352 33614 9

BLACK LACE BOOKS WITH AN HISTORICAL SETTING

☐ A GENTLEMAN'S WAGER Madelynne Ellis   ISBN 978 0 352 34173 0
☐ THE BARBARIAN GEISHA Charlotte Royal   ISBN 978 0 352 33267 7
☐ BARBARIAN PRIZE Deanna Ashford   ISBN 978 0 352 34017 7
☐ THE CAPTIVATION Natasha Rostova   ISBN 978 0 352 33234 9
☐ DARKER THAN LOVE Kristina Lloyd   ISBN 978 0 352 33279 0
☐ WILD KINGDOM Deanna Ashford   ISBN 978 0 352 33549 4
☐ DIVINE TORMENT Janine Ashbless   ISBN 978 0 352 33719 1
☐ FRENCH MANNERS Olivia Christie   ISBN 978 0 352 33214 1
☐ NICOLE'S REVENGE Lisette Allen   ISBN 978 0 352 32984 4
☐ THE SENSES BEJEWELLED Cleo Cordell   ISBN 978 0 352 32904 2   £6.99
☐ THE SOCIETY OF SIN Sian Lacey Taylder   ISBN 978 0 352 34080 1
☐ TEMPLAR PRIZE Deanna Ashford   ISBN 978 0 352 34137 2

BLACK LACE BOOKS WITH A PARANORMAL THEME

☐ BRIGHT FIRE Maya Hess   ISBN 978 0 352 34104 4
☐ BURNING BRIGHT Janine Ashbless   ISBN 978 0 352 34085 6
☐ CRUEL ENCHANTMENT Janine Ashbless   ISBN 978 0 352 33483 1
☐ DARK ENCHANTMENT Janine Ashbless   ISBN 978 0 352 34513 4
☐ ENCHANTED Various   ISBN 978 0 352 34195 2
☐ FLOOD Anna Clare   ISBN 978 0 352 34094 8
☐ GOTHIC BLUE Portia Da Costa   ISBN 978 0 352 33075 8
☐ GOTHIC HEAT   ISBN 978 0 352 34170 9
☐ THE PASSION OF ISIS Madelynne Ellis   ISBN 978 0 352 33993 4
☐ PHANTASMAGORIA Madelynne Ellis   ISBN 978 0 352 34168 6
☐ THE PRIDE Edie Bingham   ISBN 978 0 352 33997 3
☐ THE SILVER CAGE Mathilde Madden   ISBN 978 0 352 34164 8
☐ THE SILVER COLLAR Mathilde Madden   ISBN 978 0 352 34141 9
☐ THE SILVER CROWN Mathilde Madden   ISBN 978 0 352 34157 0
☐ SOUTHERN SPIRITS Edie Bingham   ISBN 978 0 352 34180 8
☐ THE TEN VISIONS Olivia Knight   ISBN 978 0 352 34119 8
☐ WILD KINGDOM Deana Ashford   ISBN 978 0 352 34152 5
☐ WILDWOOD Janine Ashbless   ISBN 978 0 352 34194 5

BLACK LACE ANTHOLOGIES

☐ BLACK LACE QUICKIES 1 Various   ISBN 978 0 352 34126 6   £2.99
☐ BLACK LACE QUICKIES 2 Various   ISBN 978 0 352 34127 3   £2.99

To find out the latest information about Black Lace titles, check out the website: www.blacklace.co.uk or send for a booklist with complete synopses by writing to:

Black Lace Booklist, Virgin Books Ltd
Random House
20 Vauxhall Bridge Road
London SW1V 2SA

Please include an SAE of decent size. Please note only British stamps are valid.

Our privacy policy
We will not disclose information you supply us to any other parties. We will not disclose any information which identifies you personally to any person without your express consent.

From time to time we may send out information about Black Lace books and special offers. Please tick here if you do not wish to receive Black Lace information. ❏

Please send me the books I have ticked above.

Name ....

Address ....

....

....

....

Post Code ....

Send to: Virgin Books Cash Sales, Black Lace,
Random House, 20 Vauxhall Bridge Road, London SW1V 2SA.

US customers: for prices and details of how to order
books for delivery by mail, call 888-330-8477.

Please enclose a cheque or postal order, made payable
to Virgin Books Ltd, to the value of the books you have
ordered plus postage and packing costs as follows:

UK and BFPO – £1.00 for the first book, 50p for each
subsequent book.

Overseas (including Republic of Ireland) – £2.00 for
the first book, £1.00 for each subsequent book.

If you would prefer to pay by VISA, ACCESS/MASTERCARD,
DINERS CLUB, AMEX or MAESTRO, please write your card
number and expiry date here: ....

....

Signature ....

Please allow up to 28 days for delivery.